THE VANQUISHED

Also by David Putnam

The Squandered

The Replacements

The Disposables

THE VANQUISHED

A BRUNO JOHNSON NOVEL

DAVID PUTNAM

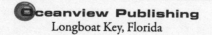

Oceanview Publishing
Longboat Key, Florida

ISBN 978-1-60809-216-1

Published in the United States of America by Oceanview Publishing

Longboat Key, Florida

www.oceanviewpub.com

10 9 8 7 6 5 4 3 2 1

To Jo Ann June, the greatest woman in the world: our mom. A woman who nurtured my voracious need to read everything in fiction. Without her, I would not be an author today. She passed away during the writing of this novel.

THE VANQUISHED

PART ONE

CHAPTER ONE

LYNWOOD SHERIFF'S STATION
1988

TWENTY MINUTES BEFORE I met Maury Abrams and realized his life would be marked for a cruel and inevitable death, I walked down the long hall that led to the watch commander's office.

I stopped at his door and looked back for Sonja. It would be just like her to follow along and stand tall in front of the WC and take the lumps we had coming. Do it together. But I was the training officer, her TO. This landed square on my shoulders. I should never have let this happen. I knocked and waited.

Lieutenant Carr yelled, "Come."

I opened the door and stepped into his office. I wished this hadn't come down to Carr, the one lieutenant at the station who knew about the street, what it was like to chase calls, to deal with the abrupt violence that tended to catch you unaware. I respected the man too much, and with that respect came the shame for my stupidity.

Carr sat behind his desk, the one he shared with the other lieutenants on different shifts. His gray eyes followed me. I stood in front of his desk, my hands folded at my Sam Brown buckle. My leather creaked when I moved, even though I had two full years working the streets.

"Sit."

"I think I'd rather stand, sir."

"What kinda stick you got up your butt, Bruno? Relax, would ya? I didn't call you here to chew your ass. Wait—you do something that warrants an ass chewin'?"

"What? Ah, no, no not at all, sorry. I think I got a bad taco at Lucy's." I held my stomach and grimaced.

I'd almost blown it. And still, I fought the urge to spill it, to come clean with him. He looked at me a moment longer.

"I called you in to tell you that, at the end of the month, we're going to rotate the trainees. We have a new group of five comin' in, and you're the best we got for Phase One. I don't have to tell you Phase One's the most important. It lays the foundation for these new guys and helps set their moral compass."

"Sure, right, no problem."

I didn't have time to dwell on the irony of his statement. A large trapdoor opened and my stomach went into a freefall. Sonja would be with another TO. Probably even on another shift. I didn't want her out of my car. I didn't want her out of my sight. I wanted her close enough to feel her breath. I wanted her with me all the time.

Right at that moment I realized I had not told her. I'd not told her how I felt about her. Sure, she had to know, if by nothing else than by our nonverbal communications, the hot passionate kisses, the gentle caresses—everything, sure, everything else, but not the spoken words. I'd been a coward and had not said those simple words. Twenty-four years old and I acted like a sixteen-year-old high school kid mooning after his first crush.

"From the look on your ugly mug, I think there might be a problem. Spill it, Bruno."

"Ah, it's just that Phase One is two months, and I've only had Sonj—I mean Kowalski—for little over one month."

Carr looked at me another long, agonizing moment. He'd promoted out of homicide and came with a reputation of being their best interrogator. Now I understood why. He looked down at the desk, shuffled a file folder, and picked up a trainee eval. "Says here your trainee's more than competent, 'above average' in fact. Twenty-six years old, mature for her age, with a degree in sociology." He looked over the top of the papers at me. "We discussed this at the TO meetings. No trainee was to get above 'competent' in Phase One in case we have to wash them out in Phase Two or Three. Later on it makes it too difficult to justify having above average marks and then having to shift to 'needs improvement.' So I assumed this trainee has to be some kind of blue-flamer, that is if Bruno Johnson's giving her the seal of approval. Am I wrong here, Bruno? Am I missing something?"

"No, not at all, sir. She's an excellent trainee. Who are you going to put her with?"

He picked up another paper on his desk. "We're a little jammed up right now with TOs. She's above average, according to you, so Sergeant Cole's put her with Good. He's our newest Training Officer."

My mouth sagged open. I recovered, closed it, then opened my mouth to protest vehemently against the choice, and realized that to advocate for Sonja would lead me down the wrong path, lead Carr right to the dirty little secret. Sonja would just have to live with this terrible choice the training staff had made. Good Johnson, of all people. Damn.

"Yes, sir, and who will I be getting?"

"That's part of what's at issue here. I'm putting you with a kid named Bobby Crews. Great kid, great evals from MCJ, he just needs to be brought down a notch or two. He's a little full of himself, and you and I both know overconfidence will get you killed out there. That's why I'm putting him with you."

"Yes, sir. Crews, no problem. Anything else?"

He hesitated a moment longer, his look burning a hole right through me. "No, that's all, Bruno."

I turned and headed for the door.

"Bruno?"

I stopped and turned.

"Everything all right with you? You seem distracted. You're not smiling. You're always smiling."

"Fine, sir. I'm just fighting off that bad taco, that's all." I put my hand to my stomach again and gave him a fake little burp.

"You take it easy, and if you need some sick time, you take it. I know how you are."

"Yes, sir. Thank you, sir."

"And knock that 'sir' shit off when it's just you and me."

"Yes, sir." I turned and headed out.

Now I had to face Sonja. Give her the word.

CHAPTER TWO

SONJA WAITED FOR me in the stairwell. I put my finger up to my lips and waved her to follow me. We went down the second flight of stairs, across the briefing room, and out to the landing that led to the rear parking lot.

"What happened?"

"It wasn't what we thought."

Her smile returned. I liked it when she smiled.

"Whew," she said, "that's great. What a relief. Hey, there was a four-hour overtime slot open for a Willowbrook car on graves."

She, too, felt it.

Working a two-person patrol car in the ghetto with her—someone I cared about—could be more intimate than making love. The need to rely so heavily on one another brought us together even closer. And once I'd tasted that level of intimacy, I never wanted to let it go.

She said, "I hope it's okay, I took the shift, I signed us both up for it. What? What's wrong?"

"The LT called me in to tell me that they're rotating TOs."

Her smile fled and shifted to a look of concern. "You're kidding. That's bullshit, we have one more month in Phase One, right?"

"I know. They want me to handle this new kid coming in. He's got a bad case of ghetto gunfighter, and he isn't even here yet."

She looked away as her mind absorbed this new information. "I guess that's not so bad. In fact, maybe it's for the best. We can still . . ." She looked around the parking lot to see if anyone stood close enough to hear. "We can still see each other after shift, right?"

I didn't answer her soon enough.

"What? What's wrong?" she asked. "You're not telling me something."

"It's your new TO."

"Who?"

I said nothing.

"Who, Bruno? Tell me."

"It's Good."

"The other Johnson? Good Johnson? I hate that asshole."

Hate was a heavy word. I didn't think *I* hated him. I felt sorry for him more than anything else. When I arrived at Lynwood station two years before, the station already had one Johnson, a white one. The other Johnson, a sadistic racist right from the start, called me "boy." The other deputies called us "the good" and "the bad" Johnsons. That's how I got stuck with "Bruno The Bad Boy Johnson." I made Training Officer before Good and it really chapped his ass. He had more time on and he was white.

"I know," I said, agreeing with her rather than arguing, "but you're just gonna have to bite the bullet through Phase Two. You'll get someone different for the final phase, Phase Three."

"Maybe I could get you back for Phase Three?"

"Sure, sure."

We both knew those were long odds.

"I have another month in Phase One," she said, "so that means I'll have that asshole Good for three months, the last half of Phase One and all of Two. I can't take three months with him, Bruno. I'm telling you right now. I won't be able to take one week with him. I'll end up capping his sorry ass."

She already talked like a seasoned veteran. Maybe she, too, had a touch of the ghetto gunfighter syndrome. Had I failed to see it because of my feelings for her? Had I done her that disservice?

I wanted to put my hands on her shoulders. I needed to touch her and couldn't. "I know it's going to be bad but you can—"

The outside PA blared, "Two-Fifty-Five to handle, Two-Fifty-Three to assist a two-eleven with a man down. Just occurred at 16637 White Avenue, Compton. Tag one-zero-one. Two-Five-Five handle Code-Three."

We ran for our cop car. We jumped into the Dodge Diplomat, and I started up and slammed it in gear. The tires screeched out of the station's rear parking lot. Normally a hot call would jack up my adrenaline. Normally with a trainee I'd go over what she needed to do once we arrived on scene. Not this time. This time my mind wouldn't move away from the idea, the cold emptiness that would come with being away from her. I didn't want that to happen.

Sonja flipped on the lights and siren. The noise snapped me out of my dangerous funk. I spoke over the loud whine. "What are we going to do when we get there?"

"Secure the scene, make it safe. Contact the witnesses and the victims, and put out a broadcast to other Lynwood units to be on the lookout for the suspects."

"What else?"

"If the suspects are still on scene, we take cover and contain, request backup."

"If it goes to guns?"

"Watch my backdrop and shoot for the largest part of the body."

I nodded, and for the first time since she got in my car as a trainee a few weeks prior, I realized I didn't want her going on a dangerous call. I wanted to protect her, to keep her out of harm's way.

How could that be?

How could that possibly work?

She wore the same uniform I did, the same badge. She carried the same gun. She had sworn an oath to protect and serve. But worse, far worse than those things, was that she, too, possessed the same drive I did to jump right in to the most dangerous situation, to live in the moment way out on that narrow ledge where safety no longer mattered.

What a screwed-up mess I'd made. What a God-awful mess.

I shook it off and tried to get my head back in the game. I stole a glance at her. With her left hand she held on to the upright shotgun in the rack. With the other she grasped the spotlight handle, her eyes front, alive with excitement, the adventure of responding to a robbery call, alive with the threat of the unknown.

The cool wind off the ghetto blew in through her open window, making her squint a little. She sensed my quick glance. She turned in time to catch me.

In that brief second I realized I didn't have to tell her that I loved her.

She already knew.

CHAPTER THREE

I WHIPPED THE car in a tight turn off Atlantic to westbound Rose-crans, then made a quick left onto White Avenue.

Large old houses sat quiet and dark, houses left over from a time when East Compton was all white and affluent. Now the houses came retrofitted with bars on the windows and doors, making them nocturnal caves to wait out the evil that walked the night.

Graffiti marked every available wall with gang monikers declaring territory not to be violated by rivals. Monikers like Spooky, Lil' Gun, Big Mac, Junior, and K-dog. The roll call went on and on, interspersed with "RIP" next to some to indicate the members who'd given the ultimate sacrifice for their hood. What an absolute senseless way of life.

I didn't have to tell Sonja. She picked up the mic and said, "Two-Fifty-Five is ten-ninety-seven, tag one-zero-one, Two-Five-Five."

We were about to go on-scene.

Dispatch came back with "Ten four, all Lynwood units limit your air traffic, Two-Fifty-Five is ninety-seven on a two-eleven with a man down."

I shoved it in park and got out. "Watch your back and don't forget to look up."

Out on dangerous scenes, cops are notorious for tunnel vision. They do a good job watching what comes right in front, but in the heat of the moment, they tend to forget their flank and hardly ever look up. It doesn't happen often, but it does happen. Crooks some-times double back. They come in from behind or climb a tree or lie low on a roof or overhang in a perfect position to ambush.

Sonja drew her service revolver and said, "Roger that."

We moved up the sidewalk toward the house. I whispered, "Don't turn your flashlight on until you have to, then hold it away from your body."

"Bruno, take it easy. I got this."

I nodded in the dark. She couldn't see me nod; her focus re-mained on what lay ahead, her eyes wider than normal, taking it all in.

The old three-foot chain-link gate hung open and crooked. Even in the moonless night the discoloration from all the rust stood out. Shrubs and trees grew out of control and obscured the windows and front door to 16637 White Avenue.

I took the lead and we passed through the fence. The black wrought-iron security gate at the front door also hung open. Behind the gate the thick door stood ajar. A subdued yellow light sliced into the darkness angled away from us. Splotches of fresh blood marred the waxed tile porch. I pointed to it. Sonja nodded.

I stopped at the entrance, peered in, and yelled, "Sheriff's department."

No answer.

"Los Angeles County Sheriff's Department. We're comin' in." I moved up closer and eased the front door open the rest of the way. In the living room, a frail, elderly gentleman sat on an ottoman covered in an antimacassar from the divan. He held a bunch of wadded-up paper towels to his head. They'd turned red, saturated with blood.

"Where are they? How many were there?" Sonja asked as she moved past the old man, following her extended gun to check out the rest of the house.

"They're gone. They ran out that way." His voice was feeble. He took his bloodied hand with the towels from his head and pointed to the front door.

Sonja checked anyway. She turned on her flashlight and disappeared down the hallway, her shadow tall and dancing.

I put my hand on the old man's leg, which was covered in thick cotton pajamas. "What happened?"

"I'm a fool, a doddering old fool. That's what happened, Deputy."

I said nothing and waited for him.

"I knew better, I did," he said.

"In here. Bruno, there's an old woman in here. She's okay."

Low murmurs came from the bedroom as Sonja spoke with the old woman.

The old man got up, his legs shaking, and headed toward Sonja's voice. "That's my wife. We've been married for fifty-five years," he said over his shoulder as I followed him.

"Wait, you shouldn't move around. Paramedics are on the way." I caught up, took him by the arm, and fought down my reaction. His arm had hardly any muscle at all, just bone.

"I've always protected her. Always. Until tonight. Tonight I let her down. I let those ugly people into our house. And I let my wife down. I jeopardized her safety."

The man looked to be in his mid- to late-eighties and was decrepit with age. His hair was snow-white, now matted with wet red. With his slumped shoulders and no ass, I don't know how his pajamas stayed up. He couldn't defend his wife against any kind of threat. Maybe if he had a cast-iron frying pan he could defend against a charging mouse. But then he wouldn't have the strength to lift the frying pan and wield it with any effectiveness.

The carpet under our feet looked Asian, a long runner over a polished hardwood floor. At one time this old white man and woman lived an affluent life in an all-white Compton that had turned bad on them. Their problem: they'd lived too long. They outlived their savings and had been forced to stay in the same house in the same neighborhood as it deteriorated all around them. The criminal element moved in, the gangs. I'd seen it far too often.

In the bedroom Sonja stood over by the nightstand, the phone to her ear. "Have paramedics roll in, it's Code-Four here, suspects fled the scene. More to follow on the broadcast."

On the street out front, the patrol unit's PA blared out into the neighborhood and repeated some of her disposition of the call. "Two-Fifty-Three, Two-Five-Five is Code-Four, shut down your Code-Three and continue for an area check. Broadcast of suspects to follow."

The man's wife lay in bed with the covers pulled up to her nose, her eyes clouded with cataracts. Her overly wrinkled skin made her face sag, hound-dog style, her wispy white hair in disarray. "Maury," she said, "it's not your fault. Quit talkin' like it's your fault."

This man and woman had no business living alone in the ghetto. They needed to be in an assisted-care home. I eased him down to a sitting position at the foot of the bed. Something out of the ordinary caught my attention. I raised my head and sniffed the air. The house smelled of old age, that hint of sour and dust combined with musty clothes and mothballs. But something else layered in with it that I couldn't quite place, and it niggled at my brain.

The old man patted the bed. "Sit. Sit."

I got down on one knee. "Please tell me what happened. What did they look like? Which way did they run? What were they armed with?"

We'd been in the house for about three minutes and needed to get out the broadcast update.

"Sit, sit." He patted the bed again.

I sat down next to him. I got a closer look at his injury when he took his hand away. He'd been whacked with a long and slim and heavy weapon that had torn his paper-thin skin. The wound sagged open with an ugly goose egg underneath. When he'd pulled away the wad of paper towels, a rivulet of blood ran down next to his eye, filling the wrinkles and branching out like a river delta to meet up again and roll down to his chin, where it dripped in fat droplets on his pajama leg.

The unit PA outside blared again. "Two-Fifty-Five, shots fired, man down, 14367 Rose Avenue cross of White, tag one-zero-two, handle Code-Three."

Sonja started to move on past us and hesitated, not knowing what to do, conflicted with going to the call or staying to help the old couple. She chose correctly to respond to the call. She picked up the old man's hand and said, "Listen, we have to go, but we'll be right back, I promise you we'll be back. The paramedics will be here in just a minute."

"No, please, don't go. Please."

She looked at me, expecting me to say it was okay, we could stay. I shook my head.

She said to the old man, "Sorry, we have to go."

CHAPTER FOUR

WE RAN OUT to the car and got in. "I hate like hell to leave them like this," she said.

I started up, slammed the car in gear, and stuck my foot on the accelerator. The car leapt forward. "I know, but that's the job. This call's only three blocks away. We'll secure the scene, let Two-Fifty-Three handle it, and we'll come back."

"It's our tag. We can't let them handle our call."

"Johnny's in Two-Fifty-Three, he owes me, he'll do it this time and not squawk about it. Now look sharp, here we go."

She put the mic up close to her mouth. "Two-Five-Five is going ninety-seven on tag one-zero-two. Two-Five-Five."

A small crowd of neighbors, all black, stood in front of the house and waved to us to hurry as we pulled up. I got out and said, "What's going on?"

"Out back," a man in a maroon robe said. "Go around to the rear. There's some poor child gunshot. It's horrible. Horrible, I tell you."

The cedar-plank gate stood open. Around back, the owner had put on the patio floodlights, which lit up the grass area with an intense white. A black kid writhed on the ground and tried with his hand to get to the wound in his upper back. Sonja shoved the lookie-loos aside and went down to her knees next to him just as he went completely still.

Except for his chest. His breath came shallow.

The kid, who was seventeen or so, started to convulse. Thick red chunks came out of his mouth and made a small pyramid on the grass. Lung shot. His odds weren't good, no better than ten-to-one against.

I turned to a black man who held a ball bat and took it from him. "What happened here?"

"Whoa, hold on there, pal. I didn't hit him. Someone shot him. You can see that. I didn't hit him."

"What happened?"

"I was asleep and heard something out here in the backyard at my gate." He pointed to his cedar-plank gate. "I turned on the lights and grabbed my bat. You know what kind of neighborhood this is. I wasn't gonna come out here with nothing in my hand. And I found this kid just like this."

"Kowalski, put out a Code-Four, no description at this time."

"Roger that, boss." She got up and ran for the car.

She passed Two-Fifty-Three, Johnny Cane coming through the gate with his trainee. "What's up, Bruno?"

"The kid here took one in the back somewhere on the street and . . . ah shit."

"What?" Johnny asked. He stood two inches shorter than my six-three and wore his sandy blond hair down across his forehead like a kid.

"Ah, man," I said. "I missed something. I missed something real important, because I was distracted. We gotta go back to that last call. Can you handle this one for me? Just take a face page and my trainee will follow up at the hospital."

"Not a problem, and don't worry about the follow-up, we'll handle it."

"Thanks, Johnny, I owe you." I headed toward the gate. Johnny said, "Bruno?"

I turned back to look. "You're the man." He winked.

"Ah, shit." I turned and hurried to the car and met Sonja halfway, coming back.

"What's the matter?" she asked.

I kept hustling to the car. She came along, skipping in her step to keep up.

"Looks like the cat's outta the bag," I said.

She grabbed my arm. I stopped.

"They know about us?" Her words harsh, angry.

"Yeah, they know."

"Shit."

"Yeah, come on, let's go." I moved around to the driver's side and opened the door.

She opened the passenger door. "You sure?"

"I'm sure."

"Shit."

We got in. I started up and headed back to the White Street address. She looked straight ahead, pondering this new information, what it would mean, how it would impact us. I didn't have that luxury. I had to get my mind back in the game. I'd missed something too important, and that only further confirmed that we needed to split up.

Out in front of 16637 White Street, paramedics worked at loading their truck with gear from the medical aid run for the old man's lacerated head.

"How is he?"

The paramedic closed the exterior door to the red county fire truck. "He needs some serious sutures and an X-ray, but he won't take the ride in the ambulance."

Sonja came up next to me and said, "He won't leave his wife."

The paramedic nodded. "That's my guess. We'll leave you to it." They got in their truck and drove off. The front door stood open.

We found the old man sitting on the bed with a Ruger .357 in his feeble hands, tears running down his wrinkled cheeks. The paramedics had patched up his head, the gauze already splotched red with seep-through.

Sonja saw the gun and said, "Ah, shit." She'd figured out what I already knew, what had dawned on me while looking down at the gunshot kid in the backyard, where that thing that niggled at my brain locked in solid. I'd smelled burnt cordite, gun smoke, when I'd first entered the house on White, but the acrid odor had been mixed with the old-person smell, the musty and mold and little bit of sour. So I wanted to believe it that way, but I knew different.

Had I not been thinking about Sonja, would I have still missed it?

CHAPTER FIVE

I SAT DOWN on the bed next to the old man and gently took the gun from his shaky hands. I handed it to Sonja. She broke open the cylinder. "Two fired."

I sat there and waited for him, to let him tell the story in his own way. I said, "I'm sorry, my fault, I should've slowed down, took a minute with you when we were here last time. You *were* trying to tell me. I know that now. I'm sorry."

He nodded. I gave him another long minute. He said, "The kid knocked on my door . . . said his friend was out on the sidewalk, gut-shot. I could see his friend out there, lying on the sidewalk writhing in pain. The kid at the door on the other side of the bars, said he needed some towels . . . or . . . or his best friend would bleed to death . . . said that there wasn't time for the paramedics to get here." The old man turned and looked at me, his eyes wet with tears. "He looked like just a kid, Deputy, just some young kid who needed help."

Sonja stood close and muttered, almost too low to hear, "Those little sons of bitches."

The old man looked from me to her. He spoke to her. "I opened the door to hand him a roll of paper towels. He hit me over the head with my own hedge pruners I'd left out in the yard. Why did I leave those things out in the yard?" He moved a shaky hand up to his head and gently probed the bandages. "They both came in.

They shoved me down as I tried to get up. They danced and yelled and ran in and out of all the rooms like . . . like banshees, like this was some sort of game. Scared the hell out of my dear Rose. My dear, frightened Rose."

"I'm okay, Maury."

He waved his hand over his head to her on the bed behind him. "They said they were going to kill us both . . . they said it would be easy. They said we were already so old we were almost dead anyway."

Sonja, next to me, clenched her fists.

I held my hand up to silence her and said to him, "Then what happened?"

He looked back to me. "They wanted the keys to my *hoopty*. I could only guess they meant my car. They said, 'Tell us, old man, or we're going to cut off your wife's fingers.' He snapped those shears and cackled like he was insane. I had no doubt he intended to do it whether I gave him the keys or not. That's what I believed, Deputy. Then they ran into the bedroom.

"I was dizzy, too dizzy to stand. He'd whacked me good, knocked the sense right out of me. I'm not making excuses, you understand, I'm not."

"It's okay, Maury, it's okay," his wife said from the bed.

The old man continued, "In the living room, I crawled over to the cabinet by the door. I didn't want them cutting off my Rose's fingers. No, I didn't. I got my gun and stood up. When I came into the bedroom, one of them was jumping on the bed, bouncing my poor Rose in the air. The other was in my closet right there, rooting around. They didn't even see me, didn't even care.

"Until I shot the first one, the one jumping on the bed, the one with the garden shears in his hands. The one who was going to cut off Rose's fingers."

He had his back to me.

"I just pulled the hammer back and shot that poor young man right in the back. I'm not a bad man, Deputy. I'm not."

"You did what you had to do, Maury, don't you dare feel bad about it."

"Those sons of bitches," Sonja whispered.

I put my arm around him. His frailty caused a small knot in my stomach. He continued, "That gun kicked like a mule and fell out of my hands. They ran out, one helping the other. I guess they were friends. A horrible thing, I'd shot him. I never in all my life thought I'd have to shoot someone in my own house." He shook his head in despair. "They ran out, but stopped in the living room. The second one . . . the second left his wounded friend and came back. He came back down the hall with the fireplace poker in his hand.

"Why would he do that if he knew I had a gun. Crazy. They both had to be crazy."

"They were crazy, Maury."

"I picked up the gun and shot the second one. He fell back. Got up like it was nothing at all, grabbed his friend, and left."

He nodded his head again and again. "I got them both, Deputy. Are you going to take me to jail now? Who's going to take care of my Rose? Who? There isn't anyone."

Sonja said, "You're not going to jail. You didn't do anything wrong here, Mr. Abrams. But we do need to get you to the hospital."

Sonja stepped over to the phone and called for an ambulance. When it arrived, we helped them both out of the house on gurneys. We watched the ambulance drive away. On the unit, PA dispatch said, "Two-Fifty-Five go to Charlie for Two-Fifty-Three."

I turned to go to the radio. My flashlight picked up fresh paint on the sidewalk.

Trey-Five-Seven.

And underneath that gang moniker in fresh and runny script, that same gang member had written, *187*. The penal code section for murder. They'd marked the house for death.

Sonja saw it, too. "Not this time, Bruno. I'm not going to let them get away with this."

I'd never seen her so angry. She looked pale and her body vibrated with pent-up anger. She suddenly went over to the chain-link fence and threw up. The emotions of the situation hit her hard. The violence in the ghetto could do that to a person not yet familiar with it. I patted her back.

Dispatch spoke again. "Two-Five-Five, did you copy? Go to Charlie for Two-Five-Three."

"You okay?"

Sonja waved me off. "Go, get it. I'm good. I think it was that cat taco from Lucy's."

"Sure, sure, you're probably right."

I went to the patrol car and switched the channel down to the talk-around frequency, channel three, called Charlie. "You there, Johnny?"

"Bruno, this guy is Nine-Twenty-Seven-D. I'm callin' in homicide."

He was telling me that the kid shot in the back, the kid Maury Abrams shot, had just been declared dead.

I let the radio mic sag to my lap.

"You copy, Bruno, Nine-Twenty-Seven-D, as in David."

"Affirm, I copy. It's related to my tag, one-zero-one, but it's a straight-up One-Ninety-Six." Justifiable homicide. "Advise homicide the shooter is my two-eleven victim who's now en route to St. Francis with a head wound."

When I let off the mic, dispatch said, "Dispatch copies, we'll make the notifications."

"Put this location down for heavy extra patrol," I said to dispatch. "The Trey-Five-Sevens have already marked the victim's house."

"Ten-four."

Sonja got in on the passenger side. "What are we going to do? These old people don't have a chance in hell of defending themselves. Not against the Trey-Five-Sevens."

We sat in the car and waited for homicide to arrive to take over the scene. "All we can do is turn it over to OSS." Operation Safe Streets was the department's gang detail.

"What are they gonna do? What can they do? They can't sit on this house twenty-four-seven."

She shook her head in frustration. "Those people can't come back to this house, they can't. We can't allow it. The little bastards snuck up and tagged the sidewalk with our patrol unit parked right out front. They did it while we were inside, for crying out loud. No, no, no, we need to hunt every one of these punks down and—"

"And what? There's nothing we can do, not under the law. They're protected until they commit a crime."

"That's not fair, Bruno. That's just not fair."

"No, it's not."

CHAPTER SIX

TWO HOURS LATER, I turned the patrol car down Bullis Road from Century, and half a block after that, turned into the Lynwood Station entrance. Neither of us spoke on the drive back. All the emotions of the evening had caught up to us and smothered any conscious thought that didn't deal with injustice on the street and the soon-to-be loss of our heated love affair. I steered around back and parked in the unit's slot.

We grabbed all of our gear. Sometimes the watch commander making out the watch list kept the overtime crew in the same car, but more often than not, they wouldn't notice that the same crew was staying over, so then we'd have to change units. I didn't mind. Hopefully, we'd get assigned a newer car, like a Chevy Malibu, which, unlike the big Dodge Diplomats, didn't stall out when you made a sharp left turn at high speed.

We carried our war bags down the stairs into the basement briefing room, where the graveyard shift had started to trickle in from the locker room.

Good Johnson sat at the briefing table and smiled that shit-eating grin of his when he saw Sonja come in. "Hey, there she is, Lynwood's newest chrome-plated mama. What's it like ta burn a little coal?"

Sonja dropped her war bag, her eyes going large, her mouth sagging open.

Too much had happened in the last three hours that had stretched my emotions beyond their tensile strength. And now he'd just insulted the woman I loved. I dropped my bag, my hands turning to fists. I took short deliberate steps around the table and headed toward Good.

The other deputies jumped up from the table and stood back, some murmuring, "Oh, shit," and "Good, you done fucked the pooch this time."

Good still grinned but with less confidence. He stood, knocking his chair back, and said, "Don't worry, boys, this smoke doesn't have the balls to go head to head with ol' Black Bart Johnson."

I didn't slow and kept moving right at him. He lost his grin, backed up to the wall, and let his hand drop to the handle of his service revolver in his holster. I stopped, my chest six inches from his, my face looking down at him, his breath sweet with Red Man chewing tobacco, his eyes a little wider with fear. I hesitated, scared of my feelings or the lack of restraint present. I double-checked my "give-a-shit" meter and found nothing left. He mistook my hesitation for fear, a big mistake.

Good's grim expression slowly turned back to his white-trash smile. "Cole just told me I'm getting her at the end of the month. Don't worry, Kimosabe, I won't touch her. I'm not gonna dip into something contaminated by some nig—"

I snapped. My hand shot out and grabbed him by the throat. I lifted until his feet came off the ground. I moved my face to inches away from his. His face bloated with red, his eyes bulged. I didn't see it, but I sensed him going for his gun.

This dumbass thought he could get away with shooting a fellow deputy in the Sheriff's station. With my free hand, I grabbed at his and found another hand already there. Sonja had moved in close and had slammed her hand on top of Good's so he couldn't throw down on me. Her teeth clenched, she whispered, "Go ahead, Bruno, pinch this peckerwood's head off. Pinch the son of a bitch's head right off."

Good's eyes went wide with fear as he realized this was for real. He'd pushed too far.

I looked down at Sonja, her words getting through to my out-of-control violence center.

Just then Sergeant Cole walked into the briefing room carrying the briefing board. He took in the entire scene in a fraction of a second, and from his expression, he knew exactly what had transpired. "Bruno, quit fucking around and take your seat."

I let go of Good. He slid down almost to the floor before he caught his balance. He coughed and sputtered as he tried to get his breath back. "You see that?" He gulped for more air. "You all saw that, didn't you? I . . . I want him arrested. This . . . this deputy attacked me and I want his black ass back in that jail right fucking now."

Cole took his position at the head of the table. "Sit down, Good."

With one hand at his throat, Good slapped the table. "No, sir, I won't. You saw it. You saw how he assaulted me. I want satisfaction."

Cole stood up. "I didn't see a thing." He looked to the other deputies, who tried to cover their smiles. "Anybody else here see anything?"

Everyone shook their heads.

Cole pointed to the back door. "Bruno, outside now."

I moved to the back door with Sonja in tow. Cole came around the table to follow. He held up his hand to Sonja and said, "Not you."

She opened her mouth to protest. I shook my head at her. She stopped and watched us exit.

Outside in the stairwell that led up to the parking lot, Cole closed the door and lowered his voice. "Listen, I don't care if you're bangin' Kowalski, I don't. It's not the smartest idea, but I truly don't care. I think the fraternizing policy is illegal, and if someone takes it to task, they'll win hands down. But you and I both know how dangerous working the street is with a partner that you have a . . . ah . . . special relationship with. Especially at this station."

I wanted to deny it but thought too much of Cole to blow smoke. He held up his hand to silence me.

"The cycle change is in a week. I'm going to change you and Kowalski out then, no arguments."

That cut Sonja's time in my car a week shorter than what Carr had said.

"Bruno? You listening to me?"

"Yeah, Sarge," I said. "I'm sorry about what happened in there. I just sort of snapped."

Cole waved his hand. "Jesus, don't let that sorry sack of shit get the better of you. Now he's really going to be gunnin' for you. You know what I mean?"

I nodded. I didn't care about Good and what he represented. After I calmed down, I would care even less. Sonja returned to the foremost problem at hand. I didn't want to lose her.

Cole put his hand on the door. "Keep your thing with Kowalski on the down-low, you understand?"

I nodded.

"I don't think you do. Don't let him get any pictures. And you know what I mean."

"Yes, sir."

Cole often threw out a saying that, when it came to evidence, "*If you don't have pictures, you don't have shit.*" Meaning that there can be all the rumors and supposition in the world, but without evidence, it never happened.

"Stay out of Good's way; he'll ruin your career."

"Yes, sir."

We went back inside to start briefing.

I sat across from Good and glared at him until he looked away. He didn't make eye contact the rest of the briefing. Cole read the briefing board. His words went off to another place and never penetrated the funk that clouded all other thought. And the sad part, the dangerous part, was that I needed to listen to be prepared for what waited out there on the street.

I looked over at Sonja and my heart skipped several beats.

I couldn't work that way, not safely. And worse, much worse, was that she just didn't understand how bad the white on black would be, the pain she'd go through the rest of her life. We'd caught just a small glimpse of what the future would have in store with the likes of Good Johnson.

If we had children, the ridicule, the way they would be ostracized, would be heart-wrenching, and we'd only be able to stand by and watch. I thought of myself as a strong man, but I couldn't handle that. I'd end up hurting someone and going off to prison.

I'd have to break it off with Sonja. I didn't have a choice, not if I wanted to continue to be a deputy sheriff for the Los Angles County Sheriff's Department. Not if I wanted her to have a chance at a normal life.

I'd tell her tonight after shift.

PART TWO

CHAPTER SEVEN

Tamarindo Park—Tamarindo, a coastal village in
   Costa Rica
Current Day

"Okay, who's next?"

The kids screamed and jumped and raised their hands.

I stood among eight of our kids, breathing hard with a smile so huge it hurt. And at the same time loving life, a love generated from the pure joy on their young, innocent faces.

Rays of sun penetrated the jungle canopy with its tall Spanish Feeder trees at the top, and mango and banana closer to the ground. The vast park sat in the center of the village of Tamarindo, adjacent to the village's church.

My wife, Marie, stayed over by the picnic tables, close enough to watch us. The two oldest of our ten children sat next to Marie, doting on her. They rarely left her side since she announced she was three months pregnant.

I raised my hand to get the attention of the eight children bouncing all around and tried to quiet them down just a little. "Who wants the chance," I said, "to beat their Papi in a fair footrace? The prize is some melcochas for the winner." Melcochas are sugar candies popular in Costa Rica.

All of them jumped and screamed louder, waving their hands even more. Marie didn't often allow the kids to eat sugar, but this qualified as a special occasion. Eight-year-old Toby Bixler, for some unknown reason, had turned quiet two days earlier, and the trip to the park doubled as an excuse to exercise the children and to try and pull Toby out of his shell. Marie diagnosed it as post-traumatic stress from his past that had returned, and he just needed a little time to get over it.

Exercise the children, hell. These kids, with their endless energy, didn't need exercise, and now they were trying to run my tired old ass into the ground.

I pointed to Toby. "How 'bout you, Son, you want to take on your Papi? Take a chance at winning some melcochas?" The child didn't move or even smile. I froze; his eyes reminded me too much of the way he looked when Marie, my dad, and I grabbed all these children from abusive and toxic homes in South Central Los Angeles. We'd made our getaway down to Tamarindo, Costa Rica, where they'd been safe and thriving for the last year now. The ex-cop in me wanted to stop everything, take Toby aside, and quietly question him away from all other outside stimuli, do it by the book, work it out of him slow, build—no, rebuild—his confidence and get him to tell me what had happened to change things. Doubt no longer remained in my mind that *something* had happened. I no longer believed it to be an emotional relapse, as Marie had offered as a reason. I'd been away from the street too long and should've seen it a lot sooner. I looked up to catch Marie's eye, as if she, too, could've seen, from that far off, what I'd just seen. She was sitting on the picnic bench, weaving bright-colored potholders with the two girls.

My mind raced back to when and how Toby could've been exposed to any sort of danger. I couldn't come up with even one moment where jeopardy could weasel in and nip at his heels. We'd been that careful.

I worked full-time at the cabana bar at the El Margarite Hotel, and Marie volunteered at the local clinic as a physician's assistant. During our absence, Rosa, our live-in help, and my dad oversaw the safety of the children. I trusted them both implicitly. The kids could not be in better hands.

Alonzo, my grandson, stepped up close. "Pick me, Papi, pick me." He was five years old, with facial features that resembled my only natural daughter, Olivia. Olivia died of an overdose, leaving the twins, Alonzo and Albert, to live with their morally corrupt father, Derek Sams. Just the thought of that name caused the anger to rise up in my chest, looking for an outlet. Albert died at the hands of my son-in-law. I hunted Sams down and killed him after the justice system tried him and spit him out the other end, a free man. That same justice system tried me for my crime. I lost my job as a Los Angeles County Sheriff's detective on the Violent Crimes Team and did two years in the slam up in the Q. Marie had waited for me those two long years, caring for Alonzo.

I pointed to Alonzo and said, "Okay, you."

"Fix, the fix is in," Eddie Crane said. Eddie was one of our newest additions to the family.

"What do you mean *fix*?" I didn't have to ask.

The other children went quiet to see what would happen next.

Eddie shrugged, now a little sheepish. "You know exactly what I mean."

He didn't want to say it. Try as I might, I found it difficult not to favor my own grandson. I smiled at Eddie. I could beat him in a fair footrace as long as it was a short one, and he knew it, too. I got closer and whispered, "I think I liked it better when you couldn't talk."

He laughed, knowing I was only joking with him. He couldn't talk when we'd first rescued him. He'd been abused and then kidnapped by a sadistic and violent man named Jonas Mabry, who took him for no other reason than to get even with me for something that had happened twenty years earlier. Eddie had gradually come out of his shell, just as all the others had, and started talking and interacting like a normal child should as a full-fledged member of our pieced-together family.

"Okay, then, tough guy." I pointed at him. "I pick you."

He giggled at the description, *tough guy*.

"Don't laugh, my friend. You lose, you have to rake the leaves in the front yard for two weeks."

He lost his smile for a brief moment. "That wasn't part of the deal."

"Yeah, but if you don't have any skin in the game it won't be as exciting, will it?"

"Okay, then let's make it a fair race."

"Whatta ya have in mind, tough guy?"

"Aah . . . aah . . . okay, you have to carry him." He pointed at Alonzo.

Alonzo hopped up and down as if he had to pee, and clapped his hands. "Yes, yes, yes. Please carry me, Papi, please carry me, please."

The other kids took up his chant. "*Carry Alonzo. Carry Alonzo.*"

"Okay, but you have to give me a head start, at least as far as that bird of paradise off to the side there. This kid must weigh half a ton."

The kids all laughed. "Alonzo weighs a ton. Alonzo weighs a ton."

I held out my hand to Eddie Crane to shake. He didn't take it right away. "I'll give you a head start *if* you run through the playground in the sand and up and over the slides. I run on the outside of the playground, which is twice as far. Fair enough?"

"You're going to make a good lawyer one day." I again extended my hand.

He still didn't take it. "And if I win, it's not just melcochas for me. All the kids get some." Everyone cheered.

"Your mami's not gonna like that, I know that much for sure." I turned to Toby and said, "What do you think, little man, candy for everyone if Eddie Crane wins?"

Some of the kids close to him nudged him, saying, "Come on, speak, tell him yes."

He remained mum and gave those same eyes that threatened to rip my guts out.

I shook it off. I pointed to Eddie. "Count to three."

The kids cheered and chanted, "Go, Eddie, go. Go, Eddie, go."

Eddie said, "One."

When he said "two," I jumped the gun, scooped up Alonzo, and ran. The kids screamed with delight and took off after us. Eddie pulled ahead right away, but he had to go twice as far.

Out of breath, I said to my grandson, "No more tortillas for you, little man." He weighed more than I expected, and my breathing came hard right away.

We made it to the sandbox with the slides before Eddie hit the halfway mark for his leg of the race.

My feet dug into the sand and gravity grabbed hard at our combined weight. The platform had two ladders on opposite sides and two slides on the other sides of those. I slowed at the slide, not wanting to slip while I was holding Alonzo, took a couple of deep breaths to catch up, and moved up the slick surface. I held Alonzo with one hand, his legs high around my waist, his arms around my neck, and gripped the side rail with the other. I made it to the top and traversed across the platform to the opposite slide to go down. I looked back. The kids all stood close around the perimeter of the sandbox, cheering Eddie. Toby stood back where the race started. He hadn't moved an inch. He didn't watch our game. He stared in a different direction, at the parking lot and the street, waiting for an evil that wasn't there to saunter up and drag him back to a horrible place.

CHAPTER EIGHT

THAT SAME NIGHT after dinner and the kids all had their baths and went down for the night, I lay in bed next to my lovely Marie. The double French doors stood open, allowing in the humid summer night that helped keep our sweaty skin from drying too fast. The fan overhead went round and round, stirring air scented with hibiscus, fighting the humidity to cool down our heated bodies.

Marie rested her head on my shoulder, her naked thigh draped over mine. She bumped her chin up and down on my chest. A little out of breath herself, she said, "Now, all because of you, I'm going to have to take another shower."

"You complaining?"

"You know better than that." She rolled off me, sat on the edge of the bed, and slapped my damp thigh. "Come on, cowboy, come wash my back."

The kids had worn me to a frazzle at the park, and after the romp with her, I didn't have much left. Even so, I would never deny Marie anything. I followed her cute, little naked bottom into the bathroom.

Tile covered the floor, the walls, and even the ceiling. All of the tiles were lime-green with little colorful roosters in the middle. We'd leased the hacienda from an ex-pat who had decided he preferred to go back to the States and risk getting caught. Oddly, the man had missed the hustle and bustle of living amongst so many people, who all tried to get ahead of everyone else, as compared to the calm, quiet life in Costa Rica.

I turned on the light. "No," she said, "leave it off."

I did as instructed. "I told you," I said, "you're beautiful."

She stepped into the tiled shower, leaving the curtain open, and turned the water on to lukewarm. "I'm fat and it's all your fault." She put both hands down to cup her tummy. She'd only just started to show and now referred to our growing child inside as "The Bump." No way did she even remotely qualify as fat.

Her tone held a sharper edge than normal. As a physician's assistant, she knew what the pregnancy had in store for us more so than most mothers. She'd warned me several times that she'd, in all likelihood, be a victim of hormones, that I'd have to step easy around her when it happened, that it was nothing personal. And most important, not to ever forget, no matter what happened, that she still loved me dearly.

Her mood shifted yet again and she giggled.

"What?" I asked as I stepped in behind her.

She held up two fingers six inches apart. "What's this long, has nuts, and makes women fat?"

I played along. "I don't know, what?"

"A Baby Ruth candy bar."

I chuckled. She laughed harder than the joke needed.

In the shadowy light, she let the water sluice over her face and down between her breasts. I took up the bottled soap, squirted some in my hand, and went right to work washing her breasts.

"Bruno, those aren't as dirty as you're making them out to be."

"Oh, I don't know, you can never clean these—"

She grabbed my hands. I hesitated at my word choice. She didn't like me to refer to them as "knockers" —or worse, "fun-bags"—like our friend Drago called them. Not that I would. If nothing else, I was trainable.

I said, "Juicy, juicy mangoes."

She laughed. "Yes, that's much better, cowboy. Now get them clean." She reached around and slapped my ass. She arched her back a little. "They're not going to be juicy, juicy mangos much longer, more like coconuts or—"

"Casabas maybe?"

She giggled again. "You'd like that wouldn't you? Men!"

I spun her around, her back to me, and continued to soap up her breasts, my one hand wandering lower, past the bump. Lower still.

She reached back and took hold of my stiffness pressing against her lower back. "Just as I suspected. You said the kids tired you out, and here you go initiating the launch sequence all over again."

"It's not too late to stop this countdown."

She spun back around without letting go, went up on tiptoes, and kissed me full on the mouth, hot and wet. We broke, and, breathing hard, she whispered, "Houston, we are clear for liftoff."

A high-pitched scream caused us both to freeze.

Marie yelped, "The children!"

I rushed out of the shower, grabbed a towel, and then my robe, off the back of the bathroom door as I ran past. I swung open our bedroom door to enter the hall, my mind shifting automatically to defense. I needed a weapon. I needed a gun and didn't have one.

More kids screamed. My heart jumped into my throat. My feet wouldn't move fast enough as I struggled into the robe. I needed to be there right that instant, and my feet wouldn't cooperate, not with the speed I wanted.

I moved down the long hall to the source of the mayhem. I didn't need a weapon. I'd tear apart anyone who hurt our children, do it with my bare hands.

I turned into the kids' room and flipped on the light.

Toby stood on the top tier of the bunk bed, backed into a corner of the two connecting walls, his open hands up by his face, his eyes wide in terror, his open mouth emitting a horrifying screech that the other children mimicked. I looked around for the threat, my own heart up in my throat.

Ah, a nightmare.

His fear came from a nightmare. "It's okay, everyone, it's all over. You're safe. You're safe now. Get back into your beds." I moved slowly over to Toby. "Come on down, little man. Come on over here. I won't let anything happen to you, I promise." He still wore his clothes from two days ago. He wouldn't let us take them off him without a major fight. We chose to let him keep his clothes on in the hopes another day would see him through his rough patch and he'd start to return to normal.

Marie came in behind me and cooed to the children, instantly calming most of them.

I held my hand out to Toby. "Come on, take my hand, come sleep with us. It'll be much safer if you come sleep with us." He stopped the screaming but didn't move. I stepped up on the edge of the bottom bunk and leaned over, reaching for him. His eyes flitted from side to side; he was about to freak again. I stopped. "Toby, it's me, your Papi. I wouldn't ever hurt you. You know me, come on, take my hand. Let's go get us some warm chocolate milk, huh? What do you say to that, huh, champ?"

One of the children behind me said, "I want some chocolate milk."

Marie said, "Hush."

I wanted to climb up on the bed and lie down next to him, take my time, slowly coax him down from his fright, but I didn't think the bed would hold my weight.

Behind me, Marie said, "Bruno?"

Without looking, I said, "I got this." Then I said to Toby, "Okay, I guess you want me to leave. Do you want to stay here by yourself?"

He shook his head, his first reaction to me since I entered the room. "Come on, little man, take my hand, let's go get some warm chocolate milk."

He reached out a tentative hand that trembled. I let his hand come to me. I took it and gently pulled him toward me.

All of a sudden he leapt and just about knocked us both to the floor. He clung on with his legs around my waist, his arms around my neck in a stranglehold. He was much bigger than Alonzo. His head was buried in my neck. He gripped me like there was no to-morrow. And I had no doubt that, in his mind, there wasn't.

I rubbed his back and whispered to him as I walked us out of the room and into the hall. "It's all right now, little man, it was just a bad dream. It's over now."

No one followed. Marie kept them herded together, and in a calm, firm tone, she got them all back in their beds. As I made it farther down the hall, she started one of her fantastical stories the kids loved so much, one filled with children and forests with cas-tles and intelligent white horses that talked, black knights that were good, and white knights that were bad.

I carried Toby into the kitchen and knew better than to try to set him down. One-handed, I pulled the milk out of the refriger-ator and took a pan out of the cupboard. Rosie, our housekeeper, came out of her room off the kitchen, her long black hair in disarray, holding her robe together with both hands. I waved her off. "It's okay, it was just a nightmare. Go on back to bed."

She hesitated a long moment and then said, "Something is wrong, Mister Bruno." She shook her head. I put a free finger up to my lips to silence her and nodded in agreement. She turned and disappeared back into the darkness.

I put the milk and then the powdered chocolate in the pot and turned on the stove burner, all with one hand while holding Toby with the other. He started to get heavy. I turned around and let his bottom ease down to rest on the center kitchen island while I let the milk do a slow simmer. He hadn't let go of his death grip around my neck, and I didn't want him to. It gave me a little comfort that he trusted me, and as narcissistic as it might sound, it was also something I needed. I had no faith in my fathering capabilities, not with my past failure with my daughter Olivia, and I knew that, like with Olivia, I'd somehow failed Toby as well.

I gently rubbed his back. "It's okay, little man."

Marie came in and stopped at the kitchen entrance. Her hand flew to her open mouth and her eyes went wide with shock. "Oh my God, Bruno."

"What? What?"

"Look at his back."

CHAPTER NINE

TOBY HEARD HER. He freaked out, jumped and kicked and scratched, trying to get away from me. He didn't want anyone looking at his back. I picked him up and carried him still kicking and scratching into the large living room and sat with him on the leather couch. I ducked my head and held on. He eventually calmed. I held him close and gently stroked his sandy brown hair, saying over and over, "You're all right. You're all right. I'm not going to let anything happen to you, I promise." But I had let something happen to him, and that was the problem. He and I both knew I'd failed him, so how could I ever be trusted again?

After a time, all the energy left his body, and he relaxed. A minute later, his breathing evened out as he fell asleep, all the stress having worn him to a frazzle.

Marie came in carrying two mugs of hot cocoa.

I took a long slug from the one she handed me. The warm liquid calmed me down, and the sugar rush gave me energy to help my quaking nerves. "Could you please get me that afghan and cover us up?"

Marie covered us and whispered, "You're not going to sleep sitting there like that all night?"

"Damn straight. He needs to rest, and I'm not going to risk waking him up again. He'll feel much better in the morning with a good night's rest."

"You know your back's going to be a mess."

She got another afghan, wrapped herself up in it, and sat next to us. She rested her head on my shoulder.

A large lump rose in my throat when I tried to find the words to ask her what she'd seen in the kitchen. Eddie Crane had acted similarly when we recovered him back in the States, where a truly evil person—the man to whom the county had entrusted Eddie—had taken an extension cord to his back and whipped some of the flesh right off. Eddie still carried the scars, emotional and physical, and they'd probably be there the rest of his life. To us it came as a reminder that children were never really safe, not entirely, no matter how hard we tried to protect them.

And that's what I envisioned in that moment when I saw Marie's expression: those railroad-track scars across his back. We'd somehow let our guard down and allowed jeopardy to take hold of our Toby in the form of violence upon his little person.

I didn't want to wake him. I gently bumped Marie's head with mine. She looked up at me. I mouthed the words, "What did you see?"

She moved up close and whispered in my ear. I cringed, waiting for the worst kind of description.

"Numbers," she said.

I leaned back. "What?"

"Shush. Numbers. I saw a couple of large numbers written in black felt tip on his back."

"Numbers?" I found this hard to comprehend, especially after I'd conjured up the worst kinds of injuries.

"Yes," she said, "a nine and a six. I saw a part of another one, too. I bet there are more. I couldn't see the rest—his shirt and your hand covered them."

I relaxed a little. "One of the other children, probably playing a mean game, wrote on him with a marker, and he's afraid we're going to be mad."

She shook her head. "I don't think so, Bruno."

I didn't either, not with his over-the-top reaction.

"He's out cold," I said. "Take a peek."

She didn't argue. I held onto him and eased the afghan down. I couldn't see and could again only watch her expression as she raised the back of Toby's shirt. Her mouth dropped open in shock. Her eyes turned hard with anger. Then fear. Then grief.

"What?" I said. "Tell me."

"Oh my God, Bruno."

"What? What is it?" I fought the urge to spin Toby around and look for myself.

Tears filled her eyes.

"Marie, honey, tell me." My voice got louder, causing Toby to stir. She turned and sat down hard on the couch.

I leaned over and put my mouth close to her ear. "Babe, please tell me."

"You're going back to the States," she said, her voice a drone, "and there won't be anything I can do to stop you." Her eyes stared off into nowhere.

"What are you talking about? Go back to the States? Why? Over some silly numbers? Tell me."

She slowly turned to face me. Tears streaked down her cheeks. "And in a real sick way," she said, "I don't think I'd want to stop you. Even with the baby on the way, I don't think I'd want to stop you. I think you're going to have to crush them, Bruno. You're going to have to grind them into the dirt. It's the only thing those animals understand. Why does it have to be this way, Bruno? Why can't they just leave us alone?"

"Marie!"

Toby jumped a little and grabbed on, but didn't wake up.

She slowly moved around again and put her lips to my ear as if to speak some sort of deadly poison that, if overheard, would whither and kill the vulnerable child in my arms. "It's a phone number to Southern California with a San Bernardino prefix 909."

I still didn't get it. Maybe the fatigue masked my thought process.

My voice croaked this time as I whispered, "Tell me the rest."

She sobbed a little and got herself under control. "Right beside the number are two letters."

"Just two."

She nodded. "Double S's, written like thunderbolts, the German Nazis' S's."

My mind took a long moment to lock in, and when it did, I went into a slow burn. I wanted to jump up off the couch and hurt some people, smash something, break up the house, anything to quell this sudden, horrific need for revenge. I had been the cause of this, of Toby's fear and terrible emotional distress. My past actions, my choices, had brought this unimaginable pain on this young child. My past life had chased me down, and the evil in it now chose to make a statement through the pain of a small child in my care.

And for no other reason than to get at me.

I whispered through gritted teeth, "I'll make 'em pay. I promise you that I'll make every last damn one of 'em pay for this."

Marie stroked my arm as she sobbed and nodded. "Bruno, what are we going to do? You can't go. That's exactly what they want. They'll be waiting for you. There are too many of them for you to do anything about it. We have to run. We have to pack up right now and run to Panama. It's Rosebud, Bruno. We have to activate Rosebud."

We had an escape plan in place, not for something like this, but in case the feds came sniffing around. In 1994, Costa Rica signed an extradition treaty with the U.S., and even though thousands of Americans hid out in Costa Rica, most didn't have to worry. They were small fish compared to someone who'd taken ten children and fled. Rosebud was our code word to hit the eject button and move our family over to Panama.

Every nerve in my body vibrated with a rage more violent than I had ever experienced. I suppressed it as best I could. "Marie, honey, take down the number."

She shook her head.

"Marie, please."

She continued to sob, got up, went to the desk by the phone, and came back with a pen and paper. She scribbled the number.

I scooted to the edge of the couch. "Sit."

Marie sat. I stood and gently peeled Toby's arms from around my neck. He started to wake. I stopped and whispered in his ear, "Everything's gonna be all right, little man, here's your mom."

Marie took him in her arms. Toby glommed onto her without coming fully awake.

On legs weak with rage, legs filled with unrequited revenge, I walked over to the phone with the piece of paper in my hand.

The piece of paper that contained the phone number to the president of the Sons of Satan, the outlaw motorcycle gang.

CHAPTER TEN

A FEW MONTHS earlier during a trip to the States, a series of unfortunate incidents led me to discover evidence that took down the president of The Sons, Clay Warfield, as well as the majority of the Southern California chapter. They all went to prison for life because of me. I had enlisted an unwilling participant, an ex-outlaw biker by the name of Karl Drago, and with the help of my friend John Mack, we attempted a robbery of The Sons of Satan's clubhouse. A stupid, foolhardy move that got all three of us caught and severely beaten by The Sons.

Now they wanted their pound of flesh, and they'd conveyed that message by sending some members of the club to Costa Rica. Those members had waited for their opportunity and somehow caught Toby alone. They sent their message to me in the form of a phone number written in black ink on the back of poor little Toby.

I stood at the table in the entrance hall of our house, the phone in my hand, the dial tone loud in the quiet room. Was this the best path to take, the best solution for the problem? What good would calling these animals do? Why play their game, call them, let their smugness further enflame my rage? I should walk straight into the bedroom, pack my bags, and take off after them. Go handle this the BMF way.

As detective on the Violent Crimes Team, I'd made my bones, proved my loyalty, and the team bestowed upon me the team logo

in the form of a *BMF* tattoo on my upper right arm. I'd been proud
of it in a time when I was young and dumb. Later on, after I shot
and killed Derek Sams, my son in-law, and saw the law from its ugly
backside, I became ashamed of that tattoo. I kept it, though, as a
reminder of how the misguided could think and act.

Now I wanted to channel those wild days working on the Violent
Crimes Team, where I'd crossed the line into the gray area of the law
again and again, and did whatever it took to take down a violent
asshole. Took them down the *BMF* way.

Because back then we were *Brutal Mother Fuckers*.

I had no intention of treading lightly with these assholes, men
who'd hurt a child like that, and worse, one of our children. These
men who'd threatened my family.

My past experience told me to take a step back and think it
through—that same experience that had kept me alive through
some pretty hairy violent confrontations. I tried to force down my
rage in order to think more rationally but couldn't. All I wanted
was to get my hands around the throat of the man responsible for
this.

A member of The Sons had to be in Costa Rica, right there in our
village. That put my family at risk. How could I leave to go take care
of this problem and still protect my family? Who could I trust for
such an important job?

My brother, Noble.

He owed me, and I could trust him. Sure, I'd call Noble.

With that problem solved, I got right back into my unchecked
rage, a comfortable place to be. I let the rage creep back in and
slither around in my gut. I dialed The Sons' number. The phone on
the other end rang once.

Someone picked up, a male with a raspy cigarette voice. "Took
you long enough, Mr. Watermelon Man. Oh, but I forgot. Mud

People are none too bright. Ain't that right, Mr. Bruno The Bad Boy Johnson? You're of the mud persuasion, right? Negroid."

I took a deep breath and checked my anger. "What do you want?"

"Let's not pretend I'm some kinda fool here. You know exactly what we want, nigger. We want you back here so we can lynch your lying black ass. That's what we want. And if you don't make the trip, we'll be glad to bring it to you. We've already proven we can do that. The Sons have put up a twenty-thousand-dollar reward on your sorry ass. And believe me when I say someone's gonna try and collect it no matter where you go to hide."

"You're making a big mistake. I come back there this time, there won't be one swingin' dick in your organization left standing. That's not a threat, that's a promise. And this time I won't be nice and use the law. You understand my meaning here?"

Raspy-voice laughed. "You're threatenin' *me*? They said you had a set a balls on ya. If you're dumb enough to bring 'em here, I'll make you eat 'em."

I lowered my voice so Marie couldn't hear. "Just tell me where and when and I'll be there."

"When you get here, you call, and we'll set up a nice little meet and greet, if you know what I mean."

"I'm on my way."

He hung up.

No scenario existed where this would end any other way but violent.

CHAPTER ELEVEN

I CALLED NOBLE in Spain. He didn't balk or hesitate, he jumped right on a plane. I couldn't leave until he arrived, in fifteen hours or so.

I took my father to his chemo appointment. He had stomach cancer and had been fighting it too long. The battle had eaten his body from the inside out. He'd retired from the United States Post Office with forty years of service, never using one sick day. Now it seemed those accumulated illnesses he'd dodged throughout his life caught up with him all at once. As a child I remembered him as the biggest, strongest father in the neighborhood, with his narrow waist and broad shoulders and thick biceps. A man who took no guff off anyone, especially not gang members trying to recruit his two sons.

I helped him out of the cab and decided I could, if need be, and without difficulty, pick him up and carry him the entire way. He couldn't weigh more than ninety pounds. He couldn't afford to lose any more. His once-glistening black hair, now turned pure white, reflected the bright sun and stood out in stark contrast to his black skin.

I held his arm and we did a shuffle-step down the flagstone walk to the clinic. His frail arm brought me back to another time, a graveyard shift at Lynwood, on White Street, and another old man whom I had failed to protect at the time.

"Somethin' happened last night," Dad said without looking at me, his full concentration on his foot placement.

"I'm sorry, did we make too much noise?"

"No, I didn't hear you, but this morning at breakfast you could serve up the tension in the air with a spoon. What's going on, Son?"

We stopped at the bench under the shade of a Spanish Feeder tree and sat, the morning fresher than usual after a recent rain.

I knew better than to lie to him even if I did it to protect his feelings. "I have to go back again."

He didn't reply right off and tried to catch his breath from the exertion of the short walk. "I can't for the life of me . . . imagine what would be so bad . . . or so demanding that it would draw you back to that ugly world. Not when you have everything right here. This is paradise, Son. You of all people know that."

I nodded and fought down the rage that started up again, rage fueled by my inability to live a life like Dad described, rage fueled by ignorant and violent people who couldn't leave well enough alone, leave me or my family alone to live quiet lives.

"Yes, I agree this is paradise, Dad, and if I want to keep it that way, I have to go back to keep the ugliness from following me here. Believe me, if there were any other way, I wouldn't be going."

He nodded. "If Marie is letting you go, then I trust her judgement. She wouldn't unless there wasn't any other way."

My jaw sagged open. "Oh, is that right? You trust that Marie could make a sane and cognizant decision, but me, you think I can't?"

He chuckled and patted my leg with a frail hand. "No, Son, I just think . . ."

He hesitated.

"What?"

"I just think that you have something inside you, a kind of hunger that every now and then needs to be fed. A need to right a wrong, no matter whose wrong it is, to better the world even if it means stepping on someone's neck in the process." He paused a long moment and swallowed hard. "And I worry that, during one of those feeding times, something will go horribly wrong, and you will not be allowed to come back to us."

"Huh. I never thought of it exactly like that. I mean what you said about fulfilling a need . . ." My voice trailed off. His words evoked great emotions. I scrambled to examine those words to see if they held even the smallest bit of truth.

Unfortunately, they did, and that made me uncomfortable.

"You know, you're some kind of wise old man."

A tear filled his right eye and threatened to spill over the edge. "This is gonna be a bad one, isn't it?"

I tried hard to force out the lie. Tell him how I'd take care of this thing and be back in a couple of days, only I couldn't. I said nothing, and in that non-response, he'd easily glean the truth.

I needed to change the subject. "Noble's coming to stay for a while, until I can get all my business taken care of."

"It'll be good to see your brother again." He smiled, but it came out crooked; too many of his facial muscles had melted away with the cancer.

"Come on, Dad, let's get you inside."

"No, no, not just yet. Let's just sit out here a little longer. You need to tell me what's bothering you. There's something else that's got you all worked up. You don't need that kind of thing hangin' over your head when you go back to deal with the likes of what you gotta deal with."

He'd again caught me unaware. The man had an innate sense when it came to reading people.

I looked away from him, back at the street to the passing cars, not unlike Toby at the park, watching for that evil to catch up to him.

He waited for me to tell it. I wouldn't get away with a lie or an excuse. He'd know.

I shook my head, fought tears of my own, and then just let it out. "I wasn't a good father."

I didn't look at him. He patted my leg again. That simple contact meant the world to me.

I turned back to him and asked, "How did you do it? How did you know how to be such a good father?"

Before he could answer, I continued on, "I know I wasn't so good at it back when I worked the street raising Olivia. I admit I screwed that up. I did. I screwed it up something terrible. And I live with those regrets every day."

He still said nothing and let me continue at my own pace.

"But now, Dad, now I'm really trying. I'm focused and really paying close attention. I am, and somehow I keep screwing this up." I didn't want to tell him that some evil I'd been watching for had penetrated our defenses and that poor little Toby became the victim of my ineptitude.

I waited for him this time.

"Are you kidding me?" he said. "Those kids wouldn't have had one chance in hell. Not one chance in hell if you had not interceded and taken them from those dangerous homes. Have you ever thought about that? You *are* doin' the best you can and no one can ask more of you. Not without dealing with me first. And you damn well know I'm not someone to trifle with."

I thought about that for a moment and let it sink in. What he said made sense. The first part anyway.

"And as far as Olivia," he said, "I won't lie to you, Son. You could've done better with her. But you were nothing more than a kid yourself. Keep that in mind. You didn't have any life experience back then. You were living a violent life making the streets safer for everyone, and doing it for the better good."

"Dad, that's not a good enough excuse for being a bad father. In fact, there's no such thing, there's no excuse that works."

"I won't disagree with you there, but think about this. Could you have done what you did, pulled all those children out of those horrible homes, brought them all down here where it's safe, had you not had all those experiences working on that special team with the sheriff's department?"

What he said warmed my soul. It made a lot of sense and helped, to some degree, to assuage the guilt and anguish eating away at my core values. Only it wouldn't take all of it away. No way it could.

I needed to feed the beast he'd described, and do it soon. And in doing so, keep my family safe.

"Son, you've made great sacrifices and you've done an admirable job in the process. So when you tell me this time that there's no getting around going back, then I believe you. I say go ahead. You go with my blessing. Just keep your head down and get back here as soon as you can. We need you, Son. We need you here with us."

CHAPTER TWELVE

I MOVED ABOUT the bedroom preparing for the trip, dreading it. I didn't want to go. Well, a large part of me didn't want to go. The other part, the one that Dad described—the beast—couldn't get there fast enough.

Marie wore sandals with shorts and a pink t-shirt she'd made special just for me that read, "Bruno's naughty little girl." She kept her chin up and didn't talk about my trip, even though the topic smothered the room the same as if a fat elephant sat on the entire house.

I put an old, banged-up leather grip on the bed, and beside it I laid out the few clothes I intended to take. Each time I went to the closet and came back with another shirt or a pair of pants, the clothes I'd just put down prior had disappeared. I spun around and Marie returned with a different shirt and a different pair of pants, clothes *she* thought I needed. She set those down and returned to the closet. I picked up what she'd set down and took them back to the closet and again retrieved the first set I wanted originally.

She stopped mid-step with more clothes in her hands, looked at me, looked at the clothes on the bed, and said, "You know I'm only asking you to do one thing for me, just one. You know that, right?"

I walked over and took her hand. I guided her to the bed and sat down with her. "I know," I said, "that this is difficult for you, I really do."

She gripped my hand hard until her hand blanched. "You didn't answer my question, Bruno Johnson."

I'd been so focused on the task that lurked in both our minds that my thoughts remained jumbled in regard to the simple things like packing, as well as the most important ones, like consoling my wife. I'd forgotten what she'd said and didn't want to hurt her feelings by admitting it. "I promise to bring you home something special. You name it, whatever your little heart desires. A Mercedes coupe, seven Coach bags, one for each day of the week, Chanel Number 5, or maybe just one red rose."

She let go and socked me in the chest. "You never listen to me, do you?"

"Of course I do."

"What'd I say, then?"

I tried to play back our one-sided conversation in my head and nothing popped.

Nothing except the memory of that raspy voice on the phone, the one that menaced my family.

I took her hands and pulled her up, brought her around and sat her on my lap. She nuzzled my neck, her breath warm and comforting. She whispered, "You know I can't go with you, and I want to more than anything in the world. But I can't. I have a responsibility. Bruno, all you have to do to make me the happiest woman in the world is to come back here."

She reached over, took my hand, and placed it on The Bump.

I nodded, acknowledging her one request. "Kiddo, there's no way I'd let you go anyway, end of story," I said. "Not this time, not with what has to be done."

"That's just it—" Her voice caught. "I've tried to think of any possible way this could work out. And I can't, not without a lot of people getting hurt." A little sob snuck out. "Bruno, this is an international outlaw motorcycle gang who wants you . . . Who wants you . . ."

"Hush, now. Have you ever known me not to take care of business and come right home afterward?"

"How then, Bruno? Just tell me how you intend to take care of this monumental problem."

I had no clue as to what I'd do once I got to the States. And she wasn't far off the mark. I, too, could not think of any solution, not yet anyway, and I hoped like hell one would come to me before too long. I wished my old boss Robby Wicks, the leader of the Violent Crimes Team, were still alive. He'd know exactly what to do. He wouldn't hesitate for one second. He'd simply say, "Saddle up, Bruno, let's go kick some white-trash ass."

I kissed her cheek, tasted the salt in her tears. "Listen, as soon as I land and I get things started over there, that'll be the distraction we were talking about. I'll give you a call, give you the code word, and then you pack up our little circus here and get on the road. Find a safe place in Panama. Then I'll catch up to you there, later on after I finish my business."

"You didn't answer the question, Bruno."

Rosie came to the open bedroom door. "Meester, there's someone here to see you."

"Thank you." I stood, lifting Marie with me and gently sat her down as if she were a delicate porcelain doll.

"That'll be Salvador. He's going to watch over you until you get settled in Panama."

"Salvador?" she said. "You don't worry about us. No one, and I mean no one's going to come within miles of us without having to reckon with me. And Noble's coming, too. We don't need to spend that kind of money with Salvador. We'll be all right."

"Noble is coming, but this is just a little redundant insurance. Humor me, okay, sweetie?"

I went over to the nightstand, picked up a book, and headed for the front door.

When Marie and I left to go back to the States to deal with Jonas Mabry, I hired a local private security company to watch over Dad and the kids. Salvador, the owner of the security company, and two of his operatives did a fantastic job. An ex-pat local by the name of Jake Donaldson came for me while I was gone. Salvador did not hesitate and engaged Donaldson in a gunfight that ran Donaldson off.

The open front door let the bright sunlight outside into our home. Salvador stood in our entrance hall wearing a white linen suit, his black hair slicked back. He could've been the actor Andy Garcia's twin brother. He smiled wide when he saw me. He offered his hand when I got close. I knocked it away and gave him a hug. My arm bumped his automatic in a shoulder holster under his suit coat. "Good to see you, my friend," I said.

"Yes, good to see you as well, amigo."

I held out my arm toward the kitchen. "Please, have a beer with me."

He nodded and followed along. I closed the front door, went through the dining room and into the kitchen. I took out two brown bottle beers, took the caps off, and handed him one. We stood by the center island in the middle of the kitchen. I took a gulp and he took a meager sip, drinking more for the ceremony.

"I need you to do a job for me," I said.

He nodded. "No problem."

"No, this is . . . this will . . . please, come with me."

I led him out to the back patio off the kitchen and closed the double French doors. Salvador lost his smile and turned professional. "What has happened, my friend?"

"I have to leave. I have to go back to the States, and there isn't any way around it."

"I understand. You want me to protect your family? I can do that. You can trust me with your family, you know this."

"I know, my friend, and of course I trust you, but that's just a part of it. Something happened. I need your . . . ah, your best people on this, you understand?" I didn't know how to ask him such a huge favor.

"What has happened?"

"Some people came for me, the kind of people who'll stop at nothing."

He smiled. "This is not a problem. You don't have to worry anymore about it." At that moment I recognized in him what Dad had described. Salvador had a beast as well, and it needed feeding.

"I know," I said, "I do, but here's the deal. You know my son Toby?"

"Yes, you have a lot of sons."

I nodded. "These people are in town." I pointed down at the ground. "I mean right here in *our* town. And somehow they got to my son—"

Salvador put his beer down on the picnic table, his smile gone. "Is your son Toby okay?"

I nodded again. "You see, we watch our children very closely because of their past. They can't have anything more happen to them. And I failed at this. I failed miserably. Someone, somehow, got to Toby. They wrote a message on his back, a challenge and a threat."

"Is your son okay?"

"Physically, yes."

Salvador caught my meaning and looked toward the house. "These people, you say they are in our town right now?"

"Yes. I have strong reason to believe that they are and that my family is in danger because of their presence."

"And they hurt your son?"

"Yes."

"Now I understand your meaning. For this I will get Jose Rivera. He and I will handle it personally."

I took from my pocket one of the two-karat diamonds my brother, Noble, gave me not three weeks before. "Here, this is appraised at twelve thousand dollars. This one is for the protection of my family. I will give you three more just like it if you take care of the problem in town."

He took the diamond and held it up to the sunlight, not really interested in the quality, and used it as a distraction to ponder the contract. "This is more than satisfactory for the protection of your family. And three more for the problem in town is too much, especially since they have already harmed your son. Ticos look out for their own. And you are Tico, my friend. One additional diamond will be satisfactory."

"Thank you, Salvador. I will rest easy now with you on the job." I shook his hand.

I held up the book. "This is my brother's book, *A Noble Sacrifice*." I turned it over and showed him the photo of Noble and me sitting on the front porch of our house on Nord in South Central Los Angeles. "He'll be here in a few hours. Other than Noble, no one is to come within fifty feet of my family."

"I understand."

"I don't know who or what the people look like who hurt my son."

"That won't be a problem, I promise you. I know all the people in our village, and they will talk to me. No one can hide."

I stuck out my hand and we shook on it. I felt better already.

The doors leading to the kitchen opened. Marie stood there, angry. "Telephone for you, *Bruno*."

"Who is it?"

She let go of the doorknob and put her hands on her hips. Anger flared in her eyes, anger unlike other women's, anger rooted in her hot Puerto Rican blood.

This was going to be a bad one, real bad.

"The woman you told me was *dead*," she said. "Sonja Kowalski."

CHAPTER THIRTEEN

Sonja Kowalski?

A wave of nostalgia shook me to the core and almost took me to my knees. I flashed back to my patrol days at Lynwood, the hot summer nights working a black-and-white with Sonja. Her beautiful eyes, the soft touch of her alabaster skin, her red hair, and most of all, her scent. Twenty-five years later I smelled her scent all over again, the same as if she stood inches away, that unique combination of woman and green apple shampoo, with a hint of hibiscus left over from her perfume.

"Bruno?"

"What? Oh, yeah." I snapped out of my funk and turned to Salvador. "Thank you, sir." I shook his hand again like some kind of absentminded professor.

He smiled. "I'll see myself out. It appears you have other more pressing business to attend to."

Glad he didn't shoot me a knowing smile, the one I knew he kept in his pocket.

I followed along behind him, my mind racing far out ahead. He passed Marie, who stood in the doorway. I bent down to kiss her on the lips, and she turned away. "You need to get the phone. Then, little mister, we're going to talk."

Not "the little mister" routine. She only used that term in severe cases of misconduct by the children.

I tried to think back to the conversation Marie and I had about Sonja. We only spoke of her once, as far as I could recall, when she'd asked about Olivia's mother. I winced at the memory. The words I'd used might've been a little misleading.

No, there had been no question about it. I had implied that Sonja was . . . I'd said that Sonja was . . . "Sonja's dead." That's what I'd said. But what I had meant to say, and didn't finish, was, "Sonja's dead *to me*." I'd cut out two small words, and now I'd pay dearly just for those two little words.

My thoughts shifted back to the problem at hand. How had Sonja found me? How had she gotten the phone number?

Marie followed along in bare feet. I couldn't hear or see her and didn't want to look back to confirm it. I just knew she'd be close in tow, her jaw set firm, her eyes angry beyond belief. I fought the urge to contract my shoulders in self-defense for the blow that was sure to come. I didn't know how she'd kept from hitting me with some object close at hand. I deserved every bit of her anger.

In the entrance hall, I picked up the phone's receiver and held it against my chest, where my heart beat out of control. I tried to compose myself.

Sonja, of all people—why would she be calling me now? I hesitated for a couple of those heartbeats to examine my emotions, to see if I still held out some fire for her, no matter how small or how unlikely.

And I did. I still did.

And it wasn't that small.

Guilt for that feeling swept over me. I loved Marie beyond the other side of forever and would never do anything to hurt her. I didn't want anything to change in our relationship, not when things hummed along so well. I knew when I had it good, and Sonja could only complicate matters. Could? She already had.

Marie stood close, staring up at me, her arms folded across her chest, her eyes a beam searing a hole right through me.

But Sonja had been my first true love. You never forget your first love. She and I had worked a patrol car together, one of the most intimate things a man and woman could do. Yes, I held something in my heart for her. Only now, that affection came out tarnished and old in comparison to what I had with my sweet Marie. Ours was new and fresh, something that would never tarnish or get old no matter what happened, even if an old flame suddenly interjected herself into our lives. I wouldn't let it.

With my mouth drier than dry, I swallowed and said, "Hello." The word came out in a croak.

"Bruno, is that really you?"

"Sonja?"

"Yes, it's me, Bruno. Sonja."

"What's going on? Why'd you call?"

"Oh, it's good to hear from you, too, Bruno, I'm fine, thanks for asking."

Same old Sonja.

Marie went up on tiptoes to listen in.

"I'm sorry," I said. "No, you're right. How are you doing? It is good . . . no, great, to hear your voice again." I looked askance at Marie just as she socked me in the shoulder.

Marie whispered, "*Great*? You had to say *great*?" Then, louder, she said, "I'm pregnant, Bruno." She held up her fist. "And hormonal." I nodded that I understood.

Back in the phone, Sonja said, "Not great, Bruno. I've got problems I can't handle. Believe me or I wouldn't be bothering you. Not now, not after all these years."

"I wish I could help, really I do, but right now I'm into something myself that's taking all of my . . . ah focus and . . ."

I didn't want to brush her off, but I'd never felt more boxed in. *Cannons to the left of me, cannons to the right of me, cannons in front of me.*

"Okay," she said, "I understand."

We both let the silence over the line tear at our emotions. The nostalgia, just hearing her voice, threatened to choke me. Then she said, "You think I would have called if this wasn't of the utmost importance?" Her tone turned angry at the end. Even though I loved Marie dearly, I didn't want to make Sonja mad at me, either, and that wasn't fair to Marie.

Sonja composed herself and took a deep breath. "Listen, about us, now that I'm older and some time has gone by, I'm willing to admit I was the one who had the problem. I was the one who broke us up even though you'd been the one to say the words. And I'm sorry for that, Bruno, really I am. I've needed to tell you that for a long time now. It was all my fault." Her voice caught with tears.

Marie socked me again, lower this time. She stomped off down the hall. She slammed our bedroom door.

"Sonja, I'm married now and I have . . . I have ten children who rely on me."

I wanted to tell her that I had a child on the way, but couldn't get the words to materialize. I stopped to think, to figure out why I'd not said those words. Was it because I didn't want Sonja to know how serious it was with Marie, or was it because I was ashamed at having a child at my age?

"My wife's pregnant," I said.

Sonja said nothing for a long moment, enough time for several thousand beats from my out-of-control heart. At least it seemed that long.

Then, "Congratulations, Bruno. I know you'll be a great father."

I didn't know about that. I was about to leave on a mission that, in all likelihood, wouldn't allow me to ever return to my family.

"Thank you," I said, without much behind it.

"I'm going to only say one more thing to you, Bruno, and then I'm going to hang up." She paused. "After that, you do what you think you need to do. All right?"

"Yes, I understand."

"What I have to tell you needs to be said face-to-face. And, Bruno, hear me when I say you're really going to want to hear this." She paused again to let it sink in, then she said. "It's Tuesday the 13th, and it was a blue Chevy."

Click.

She'd hung up.

CHAPTER FOURTEEN

I LOOKED AT the phone in my hand. "What the hell could she have to tell me that I'd want to hear?" I said to no one. I stood there a moment, then put the phone down and headed back into the master bedroom.

The last part about *Tuesday the 13th and it was a blue Chevy* was a code we'd used together when we worked patrol. The prime place to hunt for felony arrests was in the projects: Nickerson Gardens, Imperial Courts, and even Jordan Downs. But those areas belonged to LAPD, and by strict edict, sheriff's deputies from Lynwood Station were not allowed to "poach" there. The idea was to let LAPD clean up their own messes. But if it was a slow shift and we hadn't snagged our felony arrest for the day, then we'd swoop in and cherry-pick an easy one in the projects. If the shit ever went down heavy and you got separated from your partner before you could get your story together, then you needed to know only the day. On odd days, the probable cause was a blue Chevy that we followed in from our area. On even days, a green Ford.

When she said, "*Tuesday the 13th and it was a blue Chevy*," she meant that this was serious and not to talk about it to anyone else until we had a chance to talk first.

Who the hell would I talk about it to? She didn't tell me anything to talk about.

In our bedroom Marie moved back and forth from her bureau to an open suitcase on the bed as she packed her clothes. When I entered, she stopped and pointed a loaded finger at me, her eyes fierce. "I'm going with you, and you better not so much as say boo about it or I'll be all over you like white on rice. You understand me?"

I bowed a little, not knowing what else to do, and made my exit. I knew Marie well enough not to even attempt a counterargument. I went back to the entry hall just outside the living room, to the small table with the phone. I dialed another number. It rang once. Someone picked up but didn't say a thing.

I said, "We're coming, and I'm going to need your help in a big way."

"Hey, it's my Negro friend, my only Negro friend. Good hearing from you. Perfect timing. I need someone of your talents to gimme a hand with something . . . something of a sensitive nature, if you know what I mean? Gimme a call when you get into town. Can't talk right now, I'm ass-deep in a caper. We'll catch up when you get here."

"Thanks, man, you know I wouldn't call unless I needed help in a bad way."

"Who's *we*? You said, 'we.'"

"I'm bringin' Marie."

"Excellent. See you soon, bro," he said with a smile in his voice. He hung up.

I steeled myself as I walked back to the bedroom. Marie stood on the bed and squatted as she tried to sit on the suitcase to get it closed enough to latch. Before she could point that dangerous finger at me again, I said, "It's not what you think. I haven't talked to that woman in twenty-five years."

Marie jumped off the suitcase, which sprang open, and hopped off the bed. She came right up to me, her eyes angry and sad at the same time. She stuck her finger into my chest and poked hard again and again. "That right? Then how did she know how to get a hold of you? Huh, cowboy? Tell me that. How in the holy hell did she know where to find you? You're in Central America, little man. And only three people in the world know—Mack, Barbara, and Noble. And you and I both know they wouldn't tell a soul. You and I both know those friends of ours don't even know about *Sonja Kowalski*. So how could they tell her, huh?"

Her words struck me like a sword slicing straight through my heart. I'd been too worried about the fallout with Marie to put two and two together. Marie, in her hyper-hormonal state, jumped to the conclusion that I'd gone off the reservation and violated our wedding vows. And then she asked the question I should've asked, the how instead of the why. How had Sonja found me? I moved in a daze, straight-legged over to the bed, and plopped down.

Marie followed along. "What, Bruno? Are you okay? What's the matter? Tell me. Are you having a heart attack? What?" She sat and held my hand, putting her other hand on my forehead. "What is it, you feeling sick? Tell me."

I looked at her. "There *is* someone else who knows exactly where we live."

"What? What are you talking about? Who?"

"The Sons. They know. The Sons of Satan know."

CHAPTER FIFTEEN

TWO HOURS LATER, Marie sat next to me in the first-class section as the plane lifted off. Noble had arrived on time, loaded with presents for all the kids, and instantly hit it off with them. Toby even opened up just a little, a glimmer of his old self when Noble gave him a baseball, glove, and a bat all his own.

Noble still carried a bad limp from the injuries he'd sustained breaking out of prison, and he relied heavily on a cane. I feared he'd be crippled like that for the rest of his life.

He and I had feuded for many years. Growing up, he'd taken a different path. He'd gone to the dark side and sold rock cocaine for Papa Dee in South Central Los Angeles. While working patrol out of Lynwood Station, I caught the trail of a murderer, a trail that led right to my brother. I arrested him. I hung the case on him and put him away for life without the possibility of parole.

A little more than three weeks ago now, Marie and I, with the help of John Mack, broke Noble out of prison. In the process, I found out Noble had a *noble* reason in his mind for selling the dope. The shooting of the gangsters that sent him to prison had happened out of self-defense. He'd done it all for the love of a woman.

Marie had not said one word on the drive from the house to the airport. And now she sat in the seat with her arms crossed, her jaw locked tight, and her eyes straight ahead.

"You going to be like this," I asked, "for the rest of the trip?"

She didn't answer.

"I'm unjustly accused here," I said. "I swear I have not talked to the woman until just a little while ago with you standing right next to me. That was the first time in more than two decades."

Nothing.

The flight attendant came by and gave us warm towels to wipe our faces and hands. I leaned over and used mine to wipe down Marie's arms and face and neck. I kissed her gently on the lips.

I leaned back in my seat. She turned, her eyes wet. "You lied to me."

I found it hard to swallow and wanted to look away but didn't. I nodded.

"Why, Bruno?"

"I don't know."

"I believe you when you say that you haven't talked to her until now, but it's the lie that hurts."

"I'm sorry. I didn't think it would matter. I didn't think that this would ever come up again. And to tell you the truth, I honestly don't know why it has come up, even now."

"Well, it did come up, and it hurt me deeply."

I took her hand. "I know that now, and I'm sorry. Please forgive me. Babe, I love you and only you." I reached down and rubbed her "bump."

Her eyes softened. She leaned over. I met her halfway and we kissed. She leaned back. "I told you it would be this way."

"What way's that?"

"That I'd be hormonal."

I knew better than to say anything. My dad didn't raise any fools. She would've fired up the same way over what happened, hormones or not.

I didn't blame her. I deserved it.

We held hands for about an hour, ate a nice in-flight meal of steak and baked potato, and after the flight attendant took our trays and again handed us hot towels, Marie turned to me. "Tell me."

"Tell you what, my love?"

"Tell me all about Sonja."

"You sure you want to know?"

"Bruno."

"Okay, okay. Let me think . . . ah." Talking about it with her would come hard. "I'll start with the night I was going to tell her we were through."

"Going to tell her? You never told her?"

"Hold on. It got a little complicated. The whole thing got so damn complicated. You'll understand in a minute after I tell you."

"We have a six-hour flight, cowboy," she said, "and I'm not going anywhere, so spill it."

My body started to hum with tension. She wanted me to dredge up old memories I didn't like and hadn't thought of for many years. The kind of memories that took a chunk out of me that never healed.

"Okay," I said. "Remember the story I told you about the old couple on White Street, the one where the old man opened the door to two thugs who clubbed him and went in to rob and maim them?"

"Yes, but now you're telling me that Sonja was your trainee when that happened?"

"Ah, yeah."

"When you told me that story, you neglected to tell me that part."

"Did I?"

"You know you did." Marie raised her voice. A woman with updo hair, red lipstick, red nails, and heavy eyeliner next to Marie looked over.

I leaned in to Marie. "Keep it down, and I'll tell you the whole thing."

She pinched my arm.

"Ouch."

"You're going to tell me the whole thing anyway, without any of your conditions." She smiled.

Her smile warmed me a little.

We both scrunched down in our seats, our heads together. I told her again about getting the call on White, about how the old man shot two gangsters in self-defense and the way Sonja reacted to it. I told Marie about what happened when we got back to the station with Good, and how I'd decided to break it off with Sonja.

Then I told her the rest of it.

PART THREE

CHAPTER SIXTEEN

THE SAME NIGHT the two punks from the Trey-Five-Seven robbed
the Abrams' home on White Street in East Compton and Mr.
Abrams shot them both, I worked overtime with Sonja and intended to tell her we were through at the end of shift. I loved her,
but the white-on-black issue remained an insurmountable hurdle,
one I could not force upon her. Not in clear conscience. I'd convinced myself she didn't understand and that I knew more about it
than she did.

An hour before we got off shift, we caught a Four-Fifteen-V—a
violent domestic.

On the way to the call I hung my arm out the patrol unit window,
let the air rush in to cool the heat in my face generated from the idea
of telling Sonja. When the time came, at the end of shift, I didn't
think I would be able to get the words out. I was sure I wouldn't. I
guessed telling her would be a lot like suicide: the mind says to do
it, even has an overwhelming desire to, and the body's survival in-
stinct won't let it happen. Intelligence and logic pushed me to break
off our relationship, but my love for her, the more powerful of the
three, ruled the day. I was being torn in half.

Sonja said, "Can we swing by White Street on the way back, check on those old folks?"

I took my eyes off the road and looked over at her. She kept her eyes straight ahead, watching the streets. She didn't want to talk about the thing between us. She now did her job diligently and paid attention to the street. The crooks in the neighborhoods would take the street signs down in an attempt to thwart law enforcement. The deputies had to know the area by landmark or memorize the streets as they passed and used made-up acronyms. That's why she watched so intently, her lips moving silently as we passed each street corner, mouthing the names from the acronym. One of the most dangerous aspects of patrol is not knowing where you are in order to call in backup. One of the biggest fears for any deputy was lying in the gutter, gut-shot, and no one knowing where to even start to look for you.

"Sure," I said. "No problem. We can go by the Abrams' house, but I don't think they'll be back from the hospital yet."

She nodded. "We get off shift at three. Can you call the on-call OSS deputy and give him a heads-up to watch over the house? Maybe try to take the temperature of the Trey-Five-Sevens, see if OSS can do their job and intervene?"

"No problem, I already said I'd do that. You okay? You got your head in the game, because we're going Ninety-Seven."

She looked at me. "I'm good, Bruno. You don't have to worry about me. You never have to worry about me." She picked up the mic and said, "Two-Fifty-Three Adam is going Ninety-Seven tag fifteen, Two-Five-Three."

I pulled up and stopped on Cherry, one of the more violent streets in Fruit Town, a section of Willowbrook. Two o'clock in the morning, most all the houses remained dark, except the one with the Four-Fifteen-V.

I recognized the house. "Watch yourself, the guy in here is bad news. He gets pumped up on rock and there's no talking to him."

We moved up the steps to the porch.

A decorative plaster horse lay in the debris of shattered glass.

We peered in through the broken front window and whispered, "That's Douglas Howard and he's Three-Ninety for sure, flyin' high on rock and drunk on his ass."

Sonja whispered, "Oh my God, Bruno."

"I know, he's huge. It's going to take a while, but we can talk him down. We gotta fight him, it's gonna be a problem."

"No, not him, look at the woman."

Over in the corner of the living room, Doug's wife, Norma, cowered as she cradled her arm. Blood from a long, deep laceration on her forehead ran into her right eye, down her cheek and her neck, soaking her blouse. Doug Howard stood over her, fists clenched as he yelled, berating her.

"Have you talked him down before?" Sonja asked. She didn't wait for my reply. Instead, she drew her baton and stepped into the debris-strewn house through the open door.

Doug heard the crunch of her boot. The giant spun around and roared, his mouth wide, his lips pulled back, displaying yellowed teeth. He was shirtless, his muscles twitched, and sweat gleamed off his black skin.

I took long steps and caught up to her, put my hand on her shoulder to keep her from engaging him. "Go to the car and ask for the Sam unit to respond with a taser. We're gonna need a taser."

"Like hell I will. I'm not leaving you in here with the likes of him."

"Get out of my house." Doug yelled intelligible words this time as he took a step toward us. Sonja pulled back her baton into the ready position.

"You hit him with that," I said, "it's only going to piss him off." I held up my hand. "Doug, wait, it's me, Bruno Johnson. You know me, we played B-ball in high school."

I didn't know him in high school and hoped that he at least attended one year so it would make him stop and think that what I said might have a bit of truth. "What's going on here, man?" I said. "Why all the drama tonight?"

He'd expected orders to "get on the ground" or "turn around and put your hands behind your back." He visibly calmed a little, but kept his fists up at the ready. "I know you?" he asked.

"Sure, sure it's me, Doug, Bruno Johnson, I grew up over off Nord, over in the Corner Pocket. My brother's Noble."

"You're Noble's brother?"

Sonja slowly eased around, trying to flank him.

Bad move.

Not with this guy. I couldn't stop talking, or even look at her, or Doug would, too, and all hell would break loose. Doug could flick her aside, throw her head-on through a wall if he wanted to.

"Sure, sure, Noble's my brother."

"You got any cane? Your brother slings the best cane in the hood." He brought his fists down. Now I knew with a little time I could talk him into the cuffs.

Sonja saw his defenses come down as an opportunity and moved quick as a mongoose after a snake. I yelled, "No."

She came in behind and sapped him in the head with her blackjack.

Doug acted as if someone flipped off his power switch. He wilted to the floor face-first, his eyes unfocused and half rolled up. He hit with a thud and caused a wave to scatter the detritus of fast-food wrappers, empty Old English forty-ounce bottles, and broken-up furniture.

Norma struggled to her feet, still cradling her broken arm. "My husband. My husband. You bastards, what'd you do to my husband?"

Sonja straddled Doug, pulled his hands behind his back, and cuffed one hand with one set of cuffs and had to use her second set to cuff the other because of Doug's size. Then she cuffed the two sets together.

"You shouldn't have sapped him," I said. "I could've talked him into the cuffs."

Sonja, in a half-crouch, looked up, a little startled. She pointed to Norma, who now knelt by Doug and keened. "We have to get her medical aid, and fast. We don't have time to dick around with this guy. Besides, you said before we walked in here that there was no negotiating with this guy."

Sonja stood up the rest of the way. We stared at one another. Something passed between us; at least I thought it did. She, too, knew our relationship had just shifted direction, moving on down a bad road. Maybe she'd known before that moment and took her anger out on the back of Doug's head.

She'd sapped him too hard.

"Go, put out a Code-Four," I said, "and call for medical aid." She waded through the debris of broken furniture, never taking her eyes off me. I went and checked on Doug.

She *had* hit him too hard.

She came back minutes later, got a towel from the kitchen, wet it, and tended to Norma's face, daubing away the blood from her eye and cheek and neck, the towel turning crimson. Norma sat on her knees next to her man and rocked back and forth, her eyes distant, on the razor edge of going into shock.

Medical aid got there fast, or at least it seemed quicker than normal. It took six of us, including paramedics and the fire fighters, to get Doug up on the gurney. He overlapped the sides. The paramedics treated Norma for a broken arm and lacerations to her face, the largest of which would need a plastic surgeon's delicate hand. They transported him Code-Three to St. Francis while we followed along in our patrol car with Norma. No one spoke. Norma quietly moaned.

The doc determined Doug to have a depressed skull fracture and transferred him to LCMC, Los Angeles County Medical Center. By the time they admitted him to the jail ward, I had one hour to make an 8:30 a.m. subpoena in Compton court. I had to leave Sonja writing reports in the briefing room. I didn't want to tell her the kind of trouble she'd be in if Doug didn't make it. Instead, I looked around to make sure no one was around, then I bent over and kissed her forehead. "See you in a few hours, kid." We still had to work our regular shift at two in the afternoon. She looked up and smiled. For a brief second, the old Sonja shined through, then her face closed up again.

My heart ached for her. I wanted more than anything for her to be happy. Maybe fatigue clouded my good judgment; I no longer wanted to tell her we were through. I wanted to tell her that, no matter what happened, we could stand together and weather through it.

I sat in court waiting to be called until noon, when the defendant from an armed robbery, Deshawn Simpkins, who'd shot an Asian clerk for looking at him wrong, finally took a plea. I made it back to the station in time to grab an hour-and-a-half nap in the bunkroom downstairs. Sonja wasn't at the briefing table, and I felt hollowed out inside and a little lost not seeing her. We'd been inseparable for the last three weeks. A glorious three weeks.

CHAPTER SEVENTEEN

"Hey, Johnson, get your black ass up. Come on, man, you're late for briefing."

I struggled up out of a bad dream, one with a tree and a rope and white hoods, one with Sonja standing by, restrained, wanting to stop it but unable to. Her beautiful face filled with anguish. I'd done that.

I opened my eyes to see Good Johnson standing over me. At first I didn't know where I was and thought maybe I was still in the nightmare. Then everything flooded back all at once. This *was* a nightmare after all. Good Johnson really did populate the real world: the one I lived in. And now he stood next to my bunk in the Lynwood Station basement bunkroom.

He nudged me in the hip with his polished boot a little too hard. "Come on, man, Cole told me to come in and wake up your sorry ass. I did what he asked and now I'm leavin'. You go back to sleep, it's on you."

"Partners of all things, of all days for this to happen, son of a bitch."

"What'd you just say?"

He didn't turn around. He just walked out, muttering, "What'd I ever do to deserve this? Huh? Nothin', that's what. They fucked me over but good this time, that's what they did, fucked me over but good. Saddling me with the likes of you." He walked into the light of the open door at the end of the bunkroom and, like an apparition, disappeared into it.

I swung my legs over the edge of the bunk and tried to decipher what he'd just said. *An hour and a half sleep, what the hell.* I just closed my eyes not two seconds ago. I rubbed my face hard, trying to wake up. I stood. Every muscle ached and cried out for more rest. I reached to the top bunk and took down my Second Chance vest-body armor. I put it on and then my uniform shirt over it. Good thing I had the sense to take my shirt off and not sleep in it. Still, the shirt looked like I'd already worn it for a week. I took down my gun belt, didn't swing it around my hips, and carried it slung over my shoulder.

I shuffle-stepped out and held my arm up to the bright light as I crossed the hall and into the briefing room. All of early swing shift sat at the table, waiting for me to arrive before Sergeant Cole started. I sat at the opposite end of the table from Sergeant Cole. My eyes adjusted as my mind continued to wake up.

Over to the right, at the trainee table, Sonja didn't look at me. She wore a fresh uniform, her hair clean and combed. No one would know she'd only had a couple hours' sleep unless they looked close and saw the small fatigue wrinkles at the corners of her eyes.

Cole smiled. "Nice of you to join us, Bruno."

I held up my hand, not trusting my voice, sure a croak would come out instead of words.

Cole started to read off the watch list.

Johnny Cane sat next to me and slid a folded piece of paper over. I opened it.

Did you notify OSS about the Abrams on White Street?
—Sonja

I looked up. Sonja now directed her attention at me and saw her answer by my expression. Her jaw locked tight and her eyes narrowed. There'd be hell to pay once we got in the cop car this afternoon. I started to turn angry and wanted to say, *Hey, when did I have the time?* But Sergeant Cole broke into my thoughts.

"You hear that, Bruno?"

"What's that, sir?"

"You're riding in Two-Fifty-Three-Adam tonight with Good."

"That's not even funny."

"I'm not joking."

"What're you talking about?"

"Lieutenant Rodriquez's orders. You have a problem with it, see me after briefing." He gave me the look that said this wasn't the time or the place to argue about it. He said, "Your trainee is riding with Joe Lopez."

I could guess what happened. Lieutenant Rodriquez caught wind of the feud between Good and me—the thing that happened in the briefing room, the way I had C-clamped Good, and shoved him up against the wall. And in their typical old-school way of thinking, they put us in the same car to work out our differences. Only in this case it wouldn't work, and we'd only end up killing each other. Or it could be something else. Rodriquez had a hard-on for Good, thought he was a sadistic racist, and may have put him in the car with me to provoke an incident. Kill two birds with one stone.

Rodriquez didn't like blacks either. At least not at his station.

What a screwed-up mess. At least Sonja now rode with someone decent. Indian Joe was one of the best training officers at Lynwood Station.

Cole started going over the day-shift log, the calls for service and the extra patrols. I'd also not had enough time to write up the extra patrol on the White Street address and waited for an opening, for Cole to pause long enough for me to jump in and tell the shift deputies about it.

Cole said, "Oh, Bruno, that call last night, the one on White?"

"Yeah, I'm going to put that house in for an extra patrol."

Everyone froze at the table. Good Johnson chuckled. "Little late for that, dumbass."

"What? What happened?"

I looked over at Sonja. She slowly stood, her mouth sagging open in shock.

"Shut your mouth, Johnson," Cole said to Good.

"What happened?" I asked, already knowing, my stomach going sour, the guilt heavy enough to smother me.

"At about twelve hundred hours this afternoon," Cole said, "suspect or suspects unknown firebombed 16637 White Street. Both occupants perished. The occupants couldn't get out the bedroom window because of the wrought iron."

Sonja picked up her aluminum posse box and slammed it down on the table. She spun and shot me a glare that wilted me right down to the bottom of my boots. She left the briefing room and ran up the stairs to the parking lot.

Good said, "Huh, probably her time of the month."

I stood to go after her.

"Bruno," Cole said, "give her some time."

I started to sit back down but changed my mind. "The hell with that."

I went after her anyway.

CHAPTER EIGHTEEN

I CAME OUT of the stairwell, the afternoon sun almost too bright to see. Sonja had disappeared. I went through the garage area where maintenance worked on the patrol cars, two of them up on racks. I went by the station gym, around back to the two trailers that housed narcotics and gangs. She stood by the ten-foot-tall back fence, fingers intertwined in the chain link. I moved up beside her and put my fingers in the fence and remained quiet. We both watched the street.

"They killed them, Bruno."

"I know."

More silence. I watched her out of the corner of my eye. Tears streamed down her face, and her body gently trembled.

I wanted in the worst way to take her in my arms and whisper how it would be all right, that I was so terribly sorry that things worked out the way they did. But I couldn't; we both were wearing uniforms. We both stood out in the open for everyone to see. Cole had admonished me to keep our relationship on the down-low and he'd been right. Still, it hurt something fierce not to console her.

She said, "I've got nothing to say to you, Bruno Johnson."

"I understand."

"I don't think you do."

"I'm sorry."

We stood there for a moment, not talking.

"I guess I do have something to say," she said, "and I'm only going to say it once so you better listen."

"I'm listening."

"Once I say it, there won't be any discussion. I'll say my piece and walk away, no discussion, end of story. You understand?"

I nodded, a large lump growing in my throat, and a pain in my chest. I didn't know if she saw the nod, but she continued anyway.

"In part, I blame you for what happened to those poor folks."

"I understand." Right then I'd made a promise to myself to track down the Trey-Five-Sevens and get a little street justice for the Abrams couple. I normally didn't believe in that sort of thing, but did now. Saw it plain as day.

"I don't think you do," she said, "not entirely. You can't possibly understand or you wouldn't have screwed up like that." She lowered her tone. "Trust me, you don't understand all of it. And you won't, not until I tell you."

I looked at her. She still wouldn't look at me, but instead watched the street on the other side of the chain link.

"Then tell me."

She turned, her eyes hard. "Not now, after shift." She wiped her face with both hands and headed back to briefing.

I couldn't move for a long moment. I just watched her walk away. An emptiness as wide as a canyon yawned open inside me. When the shift ended, she'd do it. She'd end it with us. At the end of shift, she'd say the words that I couldn't say, not in a million years. Words I didn't want to hear.

I went back to the station, my legs moving all on their own, the world turning without notice, the sun moving lower in the sky as the day slowly died, the same as it did every day. It would die quietly as it handed off to darkness.

* * *

I carried my war bag and gear out to the car, following along behind Good, who seemed abnormally cheerful. He tended to feast
on other people's hardship; that's why he worked in the ghetto.

We stopped at the unit assigned to us. Good opened the trunk
with his key.

I set my bag in the trunk. "What's with your polished boots?"

Good turned, his expression a scowl. He always kept his hand on
his revolver in his swivel holster so the stock canted the gun back,
ready for a quick draw. He did it unintentionally all the time. He
imagined himself a ghetto gunfighter.

"Hey," I said. "And your badge is polished, too. What's going on?"

"Don't you worry about it. You don't stand a chance in hell anyway, so don't you worry your pretty little head about it. I'm drivin',
you're bookman."

He had seniority on me, so I went along with his orders. Normally,
deputies would flip a coin. I didn't want any trouble. I just wanted
to get the shift over with so I could talk to Sonja.

As the driver of Two-Fifty-Three-A, he got to choose all the pedestrian checks and car stops we'd make and get us to the calls. My
job as bookman meant I'd keep up the unit log on all of our activ-
ities and write all the reports for the evening. I didn't mind—the
reports would keep my mind busy.

I opened the passenger door and took out the shotgun. I racked it
and checked to make sure the firing pin had not crystallized, something the Ithaca Deer Slayer was notorious for. I loaded it with my
own double-ought buckshot shells while I watched Good over the
roof of the car. Good smiled.

"What?" I asked.

He got in. I did, too. He turned on the overhead red and blue lights and then the siren to check them.

He smirked.

"What?"

He turned to me with his shit-eating grin. "You sure picked a perfect day to look like you slept in that uniform."

"Why, what's going on?"

He shook his head. "There's a guy, a sergeant who just promoted outta homicide. He's a lieutenant now. He's starting up a special team. They're calling it a Shotgun Team. They handle major crimes, all violent crimes. The team is going to chase the worst of the worst. He's goin' around all the stations in The Devil's Triangle—The Stone, Lynwood, and Carson—to check out the deps, see which ones he wants on the team. Word is he gets whoever he wants, and it's an automatic promotion to detective whether you're on the list or not."

Good started the patrol unit, stuck it in drive, and pulled out of the parking lot onto Bullis Road. "And in that uniform, you look like a sack of taters, not that you'd have a chance anyway. I'm guessin' it's gonna be an all-white team, 'cause of who they'll be huntin' the most. If you know what I mean." He bumped his eyebrows up and down.

"You think I care about something like that right now? Well, I don't. I have more important problems to deal with."

"Yeah, I know. I'd say a little bit of that animal love is messin' with your mind. What's it like to bury that radiator hose of yours in—"

I shoved his face all the way over to the doorpost and kept pushing. He slammed on the brakes. We stopped right in the middle of the intersection of Bullis Road and Century. Horns honked.

"Take your hands off of me, nigger." His words were muffled by my hand mashing his face.

"I'll make a deal with you," I said. "You don't say another word about me and Sonja, and tonight I'll do my best to make you look good in front of this lieutenant. But if you continue to screw with me, we are going to do battle. You understand?"

I eased off a little at first, then sat back in my seat. He came right back and shoved me. "Keep your dick beaters off me or I swear to God I'll cap your black ass."

"That right?"

"You bet your ass I will. I'll do it. I swear to God I'll do it."

"That's exactly what Lieutenant Rodriquez wants to happen. He'd like nothing better than to launch both of us back to the jail."

He took a moment and calmed down a little. Took a couple of deep breaths. "Yeah, I know about Rodriquez gunnin' for me. I've been tryin' to stay off his radar, but the man's some kinda asshole. He's always watchin', always tryin' to rack me up for the least little thing."

"Then let's try and work together tonight, huh? Let's just get through this. Then you can go your way and I'll go mine."

He didn't answer, and instead, put his foot back on the accelerator. We drove west, headed through Lynwood to our patrol area in Willowbrook.

After several minutes Good asked, "Where you goin'?"

"What?"

"You said you'd go your own way. What'd you mean by that? Where you goin'?"

We drove on as I thought about what he said. I hadn't meant anything by it, but maybe I had. "When we get back to the station tonight, I'm putting in for a transfer."

"Hallelujah, finally. Please do, get the hell outta my station."

CHAPTER NINETEEN

WE CLEANED UP the reports hanging over from day shift. I caught two residential burglaries: a door kick and a window smash. Then a missing person. I kept my head down in the car log and on the face pages of the first reports, only looking up to catch a landmark as the sun settled and cast a faded yellow that turned everything to a reddish-orange. I followed the calls Two-Fifty-Five, the unit with Sonja. They, too, had a slow night, taking a purse snatch, an attempted rape, and a strong-arm robbery that sounded more like a civil problem.

"What do you say we grease?" Good asked.

"I'm not gonna eat, but go ahead."

"What, I'm not good enough to eat with you?"

"Stop it. I'll have a little something, I'm just not hungry."

"Where you wanna go? Stops, Lucy's. What?"

I couldn't believe he just didn't go where he wanted and actually asked me. "Doesn't matter."

He headed north on Wilmington. Stops was up off Wilmington and Imperial Highway across from the Nickerson Gardens projects. He slowed in front of MLK—Martin Luther King hospital.

"Hey," he said, "look at that."

I looked up from the car log. "What?" I didn't see any sort of violation.

"That, right there." He pointed. "You're actin' like a boot with your head up your ass."

"What?"

"That van's parked in the red."

"You got to be kidding me, a parker?"

"Yeah, a parker. Get your ass out there and cite it."

Now he just wanted to wield his power as the driver over the bookman. I didn't care. Whatever it took to get through the night with this guy.

He edged the patrol car up closer to the van, double parked, and turned on the amber overhead light so no one would hit us as dusk continued to descend. I got out and walked up to the van, which was painted a rust primer with a large spot of gray at the back. I peered in and was startled to find a driver, an old black man. "Roll down your window." He complied. An old and pungent odor of marijuana wafted out.

He looked to be in his seventies, his brown eyes going a little milky with cataracts.

"License and registration please?"

"Oh sure, sure. What'd I do, Officer?"

"You're parked in the red, sir."

"Oh, my, I am sorry. Can't you give me a break today? I'm waitin' on my wife. She's inside gettin' some work done. She's got the cancer." He handed over his license and registration.

"It's only a parking ticket. It doesn't mean nothin', so don't worry about it. I'll be right back."

"Thank you, Officer."

I moved back toward the patrol unit. Good stood outside his open door, ignoring the traffic that zipped by too close for safety's sake. "You gonna cite him or not?"

I ignored him, stopped between the patrol unit and the van. I looked at the registration and then back at the plate. The plate numbers matched, but something niggled at the back of my brain. Something wasn't right. Good had a chance to move up close and look at the registration in my hand and then at the plate. "What's the matter with you? It matches, cite the motherfucker, and let's get this show on the road. I'm hungry."

I let my mind relax and tried to think about something else to let the problem in my subconscious bubble to the surface. And bingo. "Look at the taillight pattern."

"What kinda shit you talkin' now?"

I held the registration up for him to see. "The taillight pattern is two years older than the year listed on the reg."

"You've gone off your nut. Cite the bastard and let's get goin.'"

I went back up to the side of the van. "Mr. Freeman, please step back here and talk with me."

He opened the van door and stepped out. "What's the problem, Officer?"

"Just step back here, please."

"Okay, Officer, take it easy. Take it easy, I'm doin' it."

When he got up to me, I put his hands on the van and patted him down. I escorted him around the back and set him down on the curb.

"This is bullshit, Johnson," Good said. "I'm hungry. Quit your messin' around and let's go."

"Watch him, this is a G-ride."

"What? The hell you say?" He pulled his gun and stood behind the old man.

"You don't need your gun."

"You work your way, I'll work mine. Just confirm it."

I shook my head and hesitated. I didn't want to leave the old man alone with Good, not when Good had his gun out. Nothing I could do about it. I went back up to the driver's side of the car. A dash carpet covered the VIN, the vehicle identification number. I pulled it back and checked the number on the dash and compared it to the number on the reg. They didn't match, not even close. The van had been cold-plated. I wrote the number down and walked back.

Good holstered his gun and pointed at the notebook in my hand. "That the VIN?"

"Yeah."

"Here, give it to me." He snatched my notebook from my hand before I could move away. I started after him but checked the move. I just needed to get through the shift and that was all.

Good took up the mic hanging off the outside spotlight and ran the VIN. When it came back Ten-Twenty-Nine-Victor, like I knew it would, he wanted his name associated with taking down a rolling stolen.

Big deal, let him have it.

Seconds later, the dispatcher said, "Two-Fifty-Three, Ten-Thirty-Five," Ten-thirty-five being the code section for "stand by for confidential traffic."

Good smiled that shit-eating grin. "Go ahead with the Ten-Thirty-Five."

"That VIN is Ten-Twenty-Nine-Victor."

"Ten-four," Good said, "I'm Ten-Fifteen with one and start a tow to our location." He pointed to Mr. Freeman. "Hook him up, he's going to the can, and then get the One-Eighty started on the van."

I didn't care that he told me what to do. I'd have done it anyway. If it somehow made him feel better, more power to him. Regular partners didn't work that way. One would fill out the tow sheet while the other started the booking form. We weren't regular part-ners and never would be.

CHAPTER TWENTY

IN THE PATROL car on the way to Lynwood Station jail, I worked under the map light attached to the dash, filling out the booking application. "Sorry about your wife, Mr. Freeman," I said.

He'd moved his face up to the black metal screen that separated the back from the front, the whites of his eyes stark against the dark background. "Dat's okay, Deputy. I wasn't waitin' on my wife. I'm not married. I jus' said that ta try and catch a little rhythm from ya all. I bought that van offn a dude two years back. I knowed it had somethin' wrong wit it, especially at that price."

"Mr. Freeman, do you have anything medically wrong with you?" I asked.

"I got the trumberkulosis."

Good hit the steering wheel with his hand. "Aw, shit."

Now we couldn't book Freeman at Lynwood Station, not when he had tuberculosis. We had to divert and transport him all the way downtown to LCMC, the same place where Sonja and I had spent most of the entire last shift booking Doug Howard, the guy with the depressed skull fracture.

I picked up the mic and advised dispatch of our detour.

"Now I'm never gonna get ta eat," Good said.

From the back, Mr. Freeman said, "I could eat."

The signal changed, and Good stuck his foot on the accelerator. "Shut the fuck up." To me he said, "I'm gonna stop at Taco Quicky on the way and I don't wanna hear any shit outta ya."

I said nothing and worked on the booking app. When transporting a prisoner, policy dictates that you don't make any stops, no exceptions. We were responsible for the safety of the suspect in the back of the cop car.

Good turned left on Atlantic from Century and then immediately turned right into the parking lot of Taco Quicky, a place that popped full price for anyone in uniform. Good pulled around into the drive-thru and ordered three tacos and a cup of coffee. He didn't ask if I wanted anything.

I turned in my seat to talk to Freeman. "What would you like?"

"We're not gettin' that asshole shit. He's a felony suspect."

"Mr. Freeman?"

"I doon usually eat the Mex, but I'll have whatever you're havin', Deputy."

"Fine." I leaned over into Good's personal space and yelled into the restaurant drive-thru mic, "Two bean-and-cheese burritos with extra cheese and two more coffees, please."

"How's he gonna eat?" Good asked. "The asshole's handcuffed."

I didn't answer him and went back to my booking app.

Good pulled up in line. We had one car in front of us.

The other patrol cars started to get busy; the radio traffic increased. Those other units would now have to cover our area probably for the rest of the shift.

Mike Ciotti, a Lynwood city unit, came over the radio and asked for Two-Fifty-Three to go to Charlie, the secondary talk-around channel. I switched our radio to listen as Good pulled up to the window, accepted a cardboard box with his three tacos, and set them on the seat between us.

Ciotti asked, "Hey, what was the description of that two-eleven, two-oh-seven vehicle broadcast earlier?" He wanted the information on a kidnap and robbery suspect vehicle.

Two-Fifty-Three said, "It was a silver AMC Hornet four-door with four male blacks, all armed with sawed-off shotguns."

Ciotti came back, his voice anxious. "Go back to primary, I have the vehicle."

I switched our radio back to channel 22. Good muttered, "Son of a bitch. We got this dickhead and can't jump into it. We're gonna miss all the action."

The woman at the drive-thru window handed Good a cardboard tray with three coffees.

Ciotti came up on channel 22. "Ten-thirty-three."

Dispatch said, "Ten-thirty-three go."

"Two-Fifty-One, I have a ten-twenty-nine Frank David, eastbound Century at Atlantic. A silver AMC Hornet wagon occupied four times."

"What the fuck?" Good said. He leaned forward closer into the windshield to look around the corner of the drive-thru, to see the intersection at Century and Atlantic not more than two hundred feet from us.

The Hornet sat at the limit line waiting for the light to change with Two-Fifty-One right behind him in the black-and-white patrol unit. Good shoved the cardboard coffee tray out the window. The cups spilled out onto the ground. "Put it out, we'll back him," he said to me.

"No, we can't, we're ten-fifteen." I hooked my thumb, indicating Freeman in our backseat.

He eased the car forward. The intersection now came into full view. He grabbed the mic. "Then I'll do it." He keyed the mic and said, "Two-Fifty-Three-Adam, at Atlantic and Century, we'll take the back."

I said, "This is not a good idea."

Good ignored me.

Freeman, in the backseat, said, "I don't want any parta this. Come on, leave me off right here. Right here's good, Deputy Johnson. Let me out." He'd grown up on the street and saw the disaster in the offing.

The signal changed, and the Hornet continued east with Ciotti right on his tail, riding him too close, a rookie move. Good pulled out, went onto Atlantic in opposing traffic lanes, and got behind Ciotti as he went by.

The crooks had been playing it cool with one cop car behind them, not knowing if the cop had tumbled to them, but now with two behind them they knew the jig was up. The driver made the first right, which was Platt Avenue. We followed along behind Ciotti.

Good said, "We'll back him until the other units get here. We can't leave Two-Fifty-One alone."

His way of justifying his out-of-policy decision.

Sonja, in Two-Fifty-Five, came up on the radio. "Two-Five-Five is two minutes out."

My heart gave a little skip with the sound of her voice.

Ciotti had just gotten off training, a brand-new rookie with six months total time. He really didn't know what the streets were all about, not yet. Maybe it wasn't such a bad idea backing him until the closest unit arrived on scene.

I said to Good, "Okay, we back him until he's Code-Four and another unit shows up."

"Yeah, yeah." Good waved his hand. Then he said, "He's made us. He's gonna rabbit."

"Good, we can not, repeat, can not get in a pursuit with this guy in our car."

"Sit back and take a pill, *bookman*, cool your jets. I'm the driver."

CHAPTER TWENTY-ONE

THE HORNET SPED up in the first two blocks, getting up to sixty-five in a residential twenty-five. The first stop sign came up fast. The driver in the Hornet braked hard and the front of the car surged down. Their speed bled off to about thirty. The right rear passenger took the slower speed as an opportunity and bailed out. He hit the asphalt hard and spun like a top. He got up and ran, looking over his shoulder, sure a bullet from a deputy's gun would take him in the back. Los Angeles County Sheriffs didn't work anything like LAPD. They still shot fleeing suspects who presented a danger and a threat to public safety.

Ciotti pulled his car to the right, his driver's door held open with his foot as his car came to a stop. He intended to chase the guy. I opened my door, held it with my foot, and drew my revolver, ready to jump as soon as Good stopped our car.

The Hornet let off the brake and hit the gas.

Good said, "Fuck that guy, we're gonna take the car." He hit the gas, too.

I let the sudden momentum close my door. "Hey, hey, we need to back Ciotti. He's by himself with an armed suspect."

He ignored me and spoke into the radio. "Two-Fifty-Three-Adam, we are now primary in the pursuit, still southbound on Platt Avenue. Two-Fifty-One is in foot pursuit."

I'd not taken my eyes off the suspect or Ciotti, now out of his patrol car and running, trying to catch up. The suspect, still looking over his shoulder, couldn't see what came in front of him. He ran head-on into a block wall and fell to the ground just as we drove on by.

We entered the Freeway Corridor off Fernwood. The State of California had bought or condemned all the houses for the new 105 Freeway, which when finished would run east and west and transect all the north–south freeways, connecting them all to the Los Angeles Airport. The project had been in the works for the last twenty years. All the houses had been razed. The area now looked like one long, giant park with trees and shrubs, concrete foundations and curbs and gutters.

The area turned darker, more ominous without houses. If the suspects bailed out here, they could melt into the background and we'd never find them. Maybe these guys knew the area and that's what they intended.

The Hornet turned east from Platt onto Fernwood, went two quick blocks, and turned north again right into the heart of the Freeway Corridor.

One block north, the driver braked hard. This time the driver bailed out of the Hornet, which was still moving at thirty miles an hour. Driverless, the car now contained two suspects, one in the right front and one in the back left, two crooks now just along for the ride in a ghost car.

The driver rolled two times and came up running like some kind of circus acrobat. He ran right across our path, headed westbound.

Good gunned our car and jerked the wheel, trying hard to hit the suspect. He just missed him. The patrol car banged over the curb. I bounced and hit my head on the ceiling. Mr. Freeman moaned, "Lordy, lordy."

Good brought his gun up with his right hand crossed over his left arm and rested it on the windowsill as he horsed the steering wheel one-handed. He lined up on the running suspect and fired. The noise exploded in the interior of the car. Bright light from the muzzle flashed the night in a strobe as he fired again and again until his gun clicked empty.

Mr. Freeman moaned and moaned, only now it came out muffled. Behind us, more shots went off. I spun in my seat.

To our rear, the Hornet, without a driver, veered off and crashed into a block wall. A Lynwood black-and-white came up in the street we'd just left, and slowed. The deputy stood on the sill of his open passenger door shooting at the occupants of the crashed Hornet.

Good jerked the wheel hard. A split second before I turned to look forward, my mind clicked in and identified the deputy doing the shooting.

Sonja.

Good gunned the big Dodge Diplomat, spinning the back tires in the grass, trying to gain traction to run down the suspect in front of us.

Cordite filled our car like a fog bank, bitter to the taste.

I held on to the spotlight handle and the upright shotgun in the rack. I needed to get free of this crazed man, to get back to Sonja, to see if she was okay.

We gained speed, dodging full-grown cypress and pine. "Stop. Stop."

Good paid me no mind, his eyes intense, his mouth a straight line. He only took in one thing: the man who ran in his headlights, the car eating up the distance in between.

I braced for impact.

The suspect juked at the last second and disappeared into the darkness off to the left. Good missed him by no more than a breath.

Good jerked his head to look over his shoulder, his third or fifth mistake of the evening.

Without the driver's attention, the car hit a dip, a deep one. The bottom dropped out of my stomach as gravity grabbed hold and pulled. The next second, I turned weightless.

The engine roared.

The tires spun free.

The car came down on something hard and immovable. I crashed into the ceiling. The world flickered on and off, then stayed on.

We'd come to a complete and abrupt stop. I didn't know how. Everything had gone quiet except for the ticking and hissing car. I opened my door and fell out onto the wet grass that had once been someone's front yard. I switched on my flashlight. Steam and smoke roiled out from the undercarriage.

Good yelled, "My gun, my gun. I can't find my gun." He floundered on the ground in the wet grass on his hands and knees on the other side of the car.

The suspect might not have run off. He might've stayed close and now lurked in the area looking for a little retribution. And Good didn't have his gun. Worse, he'd told everyone within hearing range he didn't have a gun.

I stumbled around the front of the car. For some reason the headlights stood out higher than normal. The car teetered a little. I looked underneath. We'd come down on the stump of a huge tree. The entire undercarriage looked mangled and shoved to the back, the transmission and drive train in ruin.

I grabbed onto Good, shook a little sense into him. I pulled my backup gun from my ankle holster and told him, "Here, cover us, I'll find your gun."

"No, gimme your service weapon." He reached to grab the larger gun in my holster. I shoved him away. "Kiss my ass. Now cover. I'll find your gun."

He hesitated. I put my flashlight into his face. He flinched and brought his arm up, the distraction enough to pull him out of his crazed funk and back to reality. He brought his arm down, his eyes going wide. "Hey, hey, you better back me up on this. You hear me? Come on, let's get our story together."

He'd gotten caught up in all the excitement of the chase, the adrenaline of the violence, and violated ten or fifteen department policies, several of which carried enough weight for termination and even criminal charges: involvement in a pursuit while transporting a prisoner, shooting from a moving car, shooting with a transport in the car, crashing said car with a transport, totaling the car, leaving a deputy involved in a foot pursuit. The list went on and on.

"I'm not backing you on this. There's nothing for it. It is what it is."

He grabbed my arm. Something evil flashed in back of his eyes. For a moment I thought he might raise my own backup gun, point it at me, and shoot. I put my hand on the stock of my gun. "How," I asked, "are you going to make this something it's not? Not with a witness in our backseat."

His head jerked to the side, to the back window of the patrol car. His mouth made a little "O" as he just started to realize the full ramifications of his actions and the mess he'd stepped in.

"Bruno, hey, buddy, you gotta back me up on this. You gotta help me out here or I'm totally fucked."

CHAPTER TWENTY-TWO

Sirens from all directions started to converge on our area.

I moved the flashlight around in the front driver's compartment, which smelled of fresh hamburger grease and hot sauce and shattered tortilla. It looked like a taco bomb had gone off inside. Bits of lettuce and taco shell stuck to everything, the ceiling, the dash, the windshield, and the upright shotgun. I couldn't find Good's handgun. I backed out and shined the light on my already wrinkled uniform, now further soiled with ground hamburger grease and taco sauce. I went to the back door and opened it.

The back seats in all the cop cars are not secured to the bottom bulkhead like in civilian cars. Every shift, the deputies are required, by policy, to look under the backseat to ensure that no suspect left any contraband, weapons, drugs, or—many times—identification. Without identification, they can't be identified when booked and can give a false name.

The backseat sat on top of Mr. Freeman. He must've really banged around when the unit went airborne and landed violently. I lifted the bench seat off and helped him struggle to get out. Good's revolver sat on the floor underneath Mr. Freeman. I opened the carriage, kicked out the expended shells, and reloaded his gun with my speedloader. In the back of my mind, I worried about putting my fingerprints on his weapon. I handed him back his gun and grabbed my backup out of his hand.

I took the handcuffs off Mr. Freeman and helped him sit down cross-legged on the ground. "You okay? Are you hurt?"

Good stepped in close, grabbed my arm, and in a harsh whisper said, "You idiot. If he's not hurt, you're gonna give him the idea that he could be. He'll sue our ass off whether he's hurt or not."

I jerked my arm away. I went down on one knee and said, "If you're hurt, it's okay, we'll get you some medical aid."

He rubbed his wrists where the handcuffs had chafed him. "I think I'm okay, Deputy Johnson. My back aches a little, but it ain't nothin' a little *E and J* won't take care of."

E and J, the brandy of choice in the ghetto.

I stood. "Excellent, that's good. I have to go over there for a few minutes. You sit here, I'll be right back." I needed to go check on Sonja.

He grabbed the material to my pant leg. "Don't leave me here." He looked up at Good.

"Yeah," I said. "You're right, that's probably not the smartest idea."

Good flicked his hand in the air. "I wouldn't do nothin' ta the puke. Don't insult me. In fact, I'm all for letting him go."

"What, and add an escaped prisoner to the long list of offenses?"

My words stunned him for a moment, but he recovered quickly. "Nah, we just say we never had him."

Mr. Freeman struggled to his feet. "I'm good wit dat."

I shook my head. "Good, you told them on the radio you were ten-fifteen with one for GTA. It's on the log and recorded on the radio."

"Oh, yeah, you're right."

I took my cuffs out and handcuffed Freeman in the front instead of the back. "Come on, you can come with me." I grabbed my posse box with all my report forms, and we headed back to the street we left when Good started his Wild West show, shooting from the window and playing cowboy and Indians with the patrol car.

Good fell in beside us and shifted his tone to gracious, which did not work for him at all. He said, "Hey, Mr. Freeman, what exactly did you see from the back? I mean, you were under the seat and all when we found you."

"It's Mista Freeman now? What happened ta puke?"

"Well, you don't have to be an asshole about it."

I stopped. "Good, go back and wait by our car. There's at least one suspect on the loose, and we left the shotgun in the rack."

Good looked at me and then at Mr. Freeman.

Through the trees we'd dodged while trying to run down the suspect, red and blue lights from the arriving cop cars reached out to us. Good nodded, turned, and went back. I gently took hold of Mr. Freeman's arm and started walking.

After a few steps, I said in a quiet tone, "What exactly *did* you see?"

He stopped before we got any closer to the mob of cars building over on the street. "Whatever you want me to 'ave seen, Deputy Johnson."

"No, I don't want you to lie. I want you to say exactly what you saw."

He hesitated. "Ahite den. Nothin'. I ain't gonna throw my dog in ta this fight. In all dat mess back dere, bouncin' all round, all I saw was dat metal cage and da flo and the roof and the flo."

I nodded. "Maybe it's better that way."

He pointed back the way we'd come. "But dat man, back dere, he's got an ugliness inside, an awful bad ugliness."

"I won't argue with you on that one."

We made it to the street. Trainee Woods came running by. "Hey," I said.

He stopped, looked at me, and then at the mess on my uniform. He looked up the street where the Hornet sat mashed into the wall, surrounded by uniforms. He wanted to go see and be a part of it all.

"Sorry, man," I said. "I need you to take this ten-fifteen, put him in the back of your unit, and stand by the car. You understand?"

"Yes, sir."

I pulled out the booking app from my posse box. "Here's his booking paperwork. He can't go to Lynwood and has to go to LCMC."

Woods' face fell even more. He knew what that meant: hours and hours at the hospital when all he wanted to do was get into the action.

He took hold of Freeman's arm and escorted him back the way he'd come.

Now it was my turn to be conflicted. I looked up the street at the mashed-up Hornet and Indian Joe's unit right behind it. Bullet holes in the Hornet stood out in the bright light from all the sheriff units' spotlights. Four hits out of six—not bad shooting with both cars moving.

Sonja had been in an officer-involved shooting. I had to see how she fared. She'd be emotional. I looked back at the departing Freeman and Deputy Woods.

Down by Fernwood Avenue, an ambulance turned up the street. Someone was hurt. Maybe Sonja.

"Hey, Woods?"

Freeman and Woods stopped and looked back. "Yeah?"

"You gotta cite book?" Of course he did, all trainees did. I hurried over to him.

"Yeah, sure." He smiled.

"Then cite him for GTA, grand theft auto. Cite him for CVC, California Vehicle Code 10851 with a regular in-custody court date."

His smile disappeared. "Can we cite for that? It's a felony. I don't think we can cite for felonies."

"We can't. Put my name on it."

"You sure?"

"Yep."

"Mr. Freeman, I'm crawling way out on a limb for you. You better show up on that court date or I'll be mad as hell and I'll personally hunt you down. And you won't like me when I'm mad."

"No, no, I'll be dere, I promise. Thank you, Deputy, thank you."

I uncuffed Freeman. "You got this now, Woods?"

"Yes, sir."

The two paramedics from the ambulance hustled by, pushing a gurney that rattled and shifted under the wheels. I quick-walked alongside them. "Who's hurt?" I asked.

The older one with thinning brown hair said, "It's a deputy."

"Which one?"

"All we know is that there's been a shooting and that a deputy's down."

Sonja.

I didn't wait for them. I ran on ahead.

CHAPTER TWENTY-THREE

I CAME UP on a concerned Joe Lopez, who stood over a deputy on the ground.

Sonja.

I went down on one knee. The first thing I noticed was breath. Her lungs expanded and exhaled. The second thing I noticed was her expression: anger. Her eyes blazed.

"You okay? What happened? You shot?"

"Ah, Bruno, I fucked up. I did. I really fucked up this time." She rocked back and forth, both hands holding her foot. I knelt and put my arm around her. It felt good to touch her. The relief that she wasn't hurt made me almost giddy.

Indian Joe leaned down, took hold of my arm, and pulled me away. "Come on, come on, we gotta talk." His eyes dropped to my shirt. "What the hell happened to your uniform?"

Oh boy, I didn't like his tone. "I'll be right back, kid. I'll just be right over here."

I went with Indian Joe to the other side of the patrol car. "What happened? She shot in the foot?"

"No, no, nothing like that." His words came out a little harsh, angry, and in a rush. "I don't think she's hurt bad, maybe a sprained ankle. I don't think it's broken. We were coming up the street and—"

Johnny Cane came hustling by and didn't slow. He hooked his thumb over his shoulder and said, "Lardass's here. I'm grabbin' my trainee and we're splittin.'"

Lardass was Lieutenant Rodriquez's nickname.

"Quick," I said to Indian Joe. "Tell me what happened."

The paramedics caught up.

"Right here," I said to them. "It's her ankle."

They stopped, took their gear off the gurney, and set it down by Sonja and went to work. She said, "Leave me alone. Get the hell away from me."

Indian Joe said to me, "I'm tryin' to tell ya."

I didn't look at him. I couldn't take my eyes off Sonja. "Okay, so tell me."

Indian Joe talked and moved his hands as if they came attached to his words. "Like I said, we were coming up the street right here. There was a unit in front of us, right behind the suspect's car."

"That was me and Good."

"Right, but I didn't know it was you. I thought it was Ciotti. I couldn't see what you guys were seeing because we were still tryin' ta catch up. All of a sudden your car veers off and shots were fired. I couldn't tell if you guys were taking rounds or if you did the shooting. But you couldn't've been shooting. Not from the moving car, right? Tell me you didn't shoot from your moving unit, right?"

"No, I wasn't."

"Ah, shit. Good. Good, that dumb son of a bitch. You gonna cover for him?"

I ignored his question. "What happened?"

"All right, so I was paying too much attention to what happened at my left, looking at you guys as your shots went off. My trainee—"

"Sonja."

"Right, Kowalski. All of a sudden shots went off right in my own car. In my own damn car right next to me. I look to my right and Kowalski has her door open. She's standing on the sill shooting over her open door. Shooting at the suspect vehicle as it crashed into the fence. I swear it happened in two seconds. That's all, two, nothing more than that."

"Ah, shit."

"Yeah, exactly. I say what the hell and slam on the brakes. Kowalski gets shoved into the door and falls to the ground. She's moanin' like she's hurt. I don't know if she's been shot. So I put it out. I put out officer down."

"Ah, man, I didn't hear that go out over the radio. No wonder we got us a full-blown circus here."

"Yeah, and I don't know how I'm going to cover this, Bruno. She was shooting from a moving patrol car. I can hear Lardass now: 'This ain't Custer's Last Stand, what the hell you doin' lettin' your trainee shoot like that?'"

"You gotta cover for her. She probably heard Good shooting and thought the shots came from the Hornet."

"Yeah, that's what she said."

"Well, that'll work, she did what she thought was right. She'll just take a hit on the policy violation, maybe a letter in her training file. At the worst, a written reprimand."

"What about me, Bruno? What about me? She was in my car. I'm gonna take a hit for failure to supervise. They'll take away my bonus status."

"No, you won't. Rodriquez is gonna have his guns loaded and aimed at Good. What Good did is gonna overshadow everything else, by far."

Indian Joe finally smiled. "Really? Did he really screw the pooch that bad?"

I hit him on the shoulder. "Worse. You got nothin' to worry about. Not with Good on the job."

Only I had a larger problem. I had to work as a street cop and depend on the other deputies to back me up. If I didn't back Good on his Mr. Toad's Wild Ride, I'd be labeled a snitch. No one would work with me, and on the street I'd turn into a danger to myself and others. Department supervision would eventually label me a hazard and ship me back to work MCJ, Men's Central Jail, to toil the rest of my career in that dark, smelly hole.

I moved back around to Sonja. The paramedics helped her onto the gurney. I took her hand. She shoved me away. "Not now, Bruno. We'll talk later."

I nodded to no one and looked at the paramedic. "How's her foot?"

"I think it's only a sprain, but we won't know until we get an X-ray. We're going to give her a ride in anyway."

"I don't want to go, Bruno. Tell 'em I don't wanna go."

I leaned down close to her ear. "You need to get out of here until things cool down a little. And it wouldn't hurt any if your ankle was really broken."

Stunned, she sat back in the gurney. She held up her hand to hold back the imaginary crowd. "Oh, stand back, girls, this one's all mine."

I kissed her on the forehead. She tried to push me away, but I jumped back.

I helped load her gurney on the ambulance and closed the back doors just as Cole broke away from the throng of uniforms surrounding the Hornet and headed my way. I watched him come, his expression grim.

He stopped in front of me. "Rodriquez wants you back at the station ASAP."

I nodded.

"He also said he doesn't want you talking to anyone on the way. You are not to talk to anyone until he talks to you."

I nodded as I watched the ambulance drive away with Sonja.

"Bruno, did you hear what I said?"

"Huh? Yeah, don't talk. I'll catch a ride to the station, or maybe I'll just walk."

"I told you to be careful around Good."

"I'm not supposed to talk about that."

Cole smiled.

"How many of the four did we catch?" I asked.

"None. They all got away, and *that* only makes things worse."

"None?"

"Yep, those guys made us all look like a bunch of monkeys trying to fuck a greased football. Come on, I'll give you a ride back to the station."

I walked with him down the street along all the parked cop cars. We stopped at his. I opened the passenger door. Cole stood about five-eight and peered over the roof of the car. "Just so you know, before this little rodeo kicked off, I got a call from LCMC. The guy with the depressed skull fracture, Doug Howard?"

"Yeah?"

"He didn't make it."

CHAPTER TWENTY-FOUR

I SAT IN one of the two chairs outside the watch commander's office waiting for Lieutenant Rodriquez to come in from the field, where he must've been trying to get the lowdown firsthand about what happened. After an hour I stood and paced, the whole time worried about Sonja and not thinking clearly about anything else. I should've been thinking about what I was going to say. The interview with Rodriquez could easily bust my career into little pieces. The bad part about it was that I wasn't at all sure I cared.

Another twenty minutes passed.

The side door around the corner opened and slammed shut. I watched the end of the hall. Good appeared, looking harried. He quick-walked right at me, glancing back over his shoulder, as if the boogeyman chased him. "Hey, hey, listen. The dude that jumped from the car had a sawed-off shotgun, okay? You good with that? That's why I cranked those rounds off at him, okay? He was going to unload on us, and I wanted to keep his head down, okay?"

I walked back to the chair in front of Rodriquez's door and sat. "I've been ordered not to talk to anyone."

"I know, me, too, but you gotta back me up on this one, pal. I'm toast if you don't. You understand, right? You don't back me, I'm sunk."

The door around the corner opened and closed again.

I said, "You got about two seconds to get your ass outta here."

"I'll owe ya forever, pal, if you back me up on this."

"I can't do it."

"You son of a bitch."

Rodriquez came around the corner in time to hear it. "Deputy Johnson," Rodriquez yelled.

I stood.

"Not you, this other asshole right here. Get your ass out of my sight. Now."

Good scuttled off.

Another man, dressed in a dark-brown sports coat and tan slacks, accompanied Rodriquez. The man's expression, along with his blue-gray eyes, gave off a solid aura of confidence and something else I couldn't quite place. His smile made you instantly want to like him.

Rodriquez stopped in front of me. "I believe you were ordered not to speak with anyone?"

"Yes, sir."

He hooked his thumb in the direction Good just disappeared. "You talk about what happened out there?"

"No, sir."

"Come in my office."

He unlocked his door and went in. None of the other watch commanders kept the office door closed, let alone locked. The others had an open-door policy and wanted the deputies to wander in and talk.

Once inside, he pointed at a chair that faced his desk and said, "Take a seat."

I no longer felt like sitting, but did as ordered.

Rodriquez sat in the big chair behind his desk and took a tape recorder from the drawer. He set it down and turned it on. He recited the date and the time and then said, "Deputy Bruno Johnson, tell me what happened out there tonight."

So much for small talk.

I looked from Rodriquez to the man in the brown sport coat, who stood off to the side, his hands casually crossed at his waist.

Rodriquez said, "This is Lieutenant Robby Wicks. He'll be observing and advising."

I nodded.

"Go ahead," Rodriquez said.

I hesitated a long moment, weighing my options.

"Deputy Johnson, you'd better start talking right now or suffer the consequences."

"I rode in Two-Fifty-Three-Adam as the bookman tonight. Good—I mean Deputy Johnson—drove. We picked up a rollin' G-ride out in front of MLK, and we were transporting the suspect to LCMC. The suspect claimed to have tuberculosis. Two-Fifty-One called out an armed and dangerous vehicle occupied four times at the same intersection where we were. He was in a one-man car. We decided to back him until backup could arrive."

Rodriquez held up his hand to stop me. "So you had someone in custody in the back of your unit?"

"Yes, sir."

"Was this your decision or was it Johnson's?"

"Both."

"What's the suspect's name and where is he now?"

"His name is Freeman and he was cite-released at the scene."

Rodriquez let his pencil drop to the pad. "You cite-released a suspect involved in a rolling stolen?"

"Yes, under the circumstances, with all that was happening I—"

"That's out of policy, mister."

"Yes, sir."

"Go on." He picked up his pencil and made a note on his legal pad.

I hesitated.

He looked up. "Go on, Johnson, then what happened?"

I looked at Lieutenant Wicks.

"Johnson." Rodriquez raised his voice. "You have two seconds to tell me what the hell happened out there before I bust your ass. You understand me, mister?"

I snapped back and looked at him. No one talked to me that way. I'd only slept an hour and a half in the last two days. I was worried about Sonja. And Rodriquez, the pompous ass, pushed me that last little bit right over the edge to where I just didn't care anymore.

"As I said, we had a ten-fifteen and I was completing the booking app, filling it out under the map light. The car hit a hard bump and . . . and I guess in all the excitement I dropped my pencil. I reached to pick it up. I heard some shooting. When I looked back up, it was all over."

Rodriquez' mouth dropped open, his eyes wide in stunned shock. I glanced over at Wicks, whose smile was even wider than before.

Rodriquez recovered. He must've realized the recorder now memorialized the fat silence that suffocated the room. "Is that the way you're going to play this? Really, Deputy Johnson?"

"Play what, sir? I dropped my pencil, reached to pick it up, and didn't see any part of the shooting."

He pointed to his desk, his face flushed red. "Badge and gun now."

I stood, knees weak. I couldn't believe my career ended just like that. Just that easily, after all those hard years of work. I unhooked my badge and set it on his desk.

"Look at your uniform. You're a disgrace."

I fought that bad self of mine and its desire to piss Rodriquez off even more, and lost. I did a quick draw of my Smith and Wesson model 66 .357, twirled it like in the old western cowboy movies, and finished with the butt facing him. What did I have to lose? He didn't take it. I set it down on his desk, turned, and headed for the door.

How would I tell Dad? He'd been so proud that his son worked the same streets we both grew up in, streets I worked as a Los Angeles County Sheriff's deputy.

I made it to the door, hand on the knob. "Johnson?" Rodriquez said.

I turned.

"I'll give you until tomorrow noon to change your mind."

"How can I change my mind from the truth, Lieutenant?"

He locked his jaw, his eyes going narrow. "Kowalski resigned tonight. I guess you fucked her figuratively and literally."

PART FOUR

CHAPTER TWENTY-FIVE

Current Day
Los Angeles Airport

MARIE SNORED HER dainty snore. I didn't know at what point in the story she'd fallen asleep. There'd be plenty of time to talk about it again as long as we continued to talk. She'd scared me. I'd never seen her so angry. I couldn't blame her, though. My fault. I did imply that Sonja no longer walked the earth. Stupid.

The constant drone of the plane's engines lulled me to sleep, and I woke with the pilot's announcement of our final approach into LAX. I gently nudged Marie. She came awake with a start. Her fists shoved into my chest in a wild-eyed, desperate attempt to defend herself, to escape, to flee.

"Hey, hey, it's okay. It's me," I said.

"Oh, Bruno, jeeze." She leaned over and hugged me, held on, end-of-the-world kinda tight. "I had the most horrible nightmare."

I'd been the cause of that nightmare. Our trip back to the States to handle a problem without a solution, a problem that could only end in violence, had eroded our confidence. It forced us to stare down the barrel of a gun, waiting for it to go off. That kind of stress would give anyone a nightmare. Factor in the baby and no wonder she had bad dreams.

The flight attendant came by and said, "Please put your seats forward. We're about to land. Thank you."

I reached over and moved her seat forward and kissed her forehead. "Tell me all about it when we get in the car, okay?" Better if she cooled down emotionally first, instead of reliving it again so soon by telling me now.

She nodded and gripped my hand, waiting for the plane to touch down. I watched her closely.

The impending doom hanging over my head, the unknown resolution in how I'd handle the untenable situation with The Sons, helped me to cherish each precious moment.

* * *

After we grabbed our bags off the carousel, we took the shuttle bus to the rental car office and checked out a sleek new Ford Escape, "Bronzit" in color. To me it looked more like the copper from a penny. I liked the way the car handled. I drove, heading toward Burbank and the hotel. Marie sat in the passenger seat, staring out the window, her feet up on the dash, her open window letting the warm, dry Southern California wind blow on her face.

"Hey," I said, "why don't you tell me about what you're going to buy at the Galleria Mall? We're going to be staying about two blocks from there."

She looked at me, this time without anger, only sadness.

"Bruno, in the plane when I fell asleep, I had this real bad dream and it scared me."

"Don't worry your pretty little head, missy. Big Bad Bruno Johnson's here to protect you. It was only a dream. Dreams don't mean a thing, darlin'. They're just a product of your pent-up anxiety."

She nudged me, a little too hard. "Hey, how come you don't want to know about it? Dreams are the window to your soul. Don't you at least want a glimpse at *my* soul?"

Boy, I sure didn't want to throw my dog into that fight. "Hey, when you go to Macy's, buy an extra suitcase for all those clothes you're going to buy and bring home with us."

She socked me with her little fist, crossed her arms, and stared forward.

"I'm sorry," I said. "Please tell me all about your dream."

She let me stew a few moments more. The dream bugged her too much, and she had to get it out.

"Really, babe," I said, "tell me. I really want to know."

She twisted around in her seat, swallowing hard before she started. "In the dream, I went into the bathroom on the plane. You know, one of those little cramped jobs with no space at all. And . . . and somehow this huge yellow life raft inflated with this loud hiss while I was in there. It shoved me right up against the wall. It pinned me against the wall so tight that I could hardly breathe. And . . . and the odor, it smelled terrible in there. Like moldering butt."

I looked out the side window, trying my damnedest not to smile.

"Then I realized," she said, "that the plane was in distress and going down. Going down in this corkscrew that made me sick to my stomach." She put her hand up like a plane and moved it downward in a swirling motion. She turned to me, truly upset. "What do you think it means?"

I took a deep breath and tried to stay focused. I looked from the road to her and back again as I spoke. "Well, a good psychoanalyst, for which I think I qualify, would say that the dream was symbolic of feelings deeply rooted in your subconscious and points directly to your adoring and loving husband, the man soon to be the father of your darling little boy."

Her expression went from serious to a half-grin. "That right, cowboy? Why don't you lay it on me then? What does my psychoanalyst, with his degree from the University of The Sorry-Assed Street, think?"

I looked at her for a moment, trying not to smile, then back at the road. "It's obvious. This dream indicates a deep-seated desire to have hot—"

She grabbed my arm. "Careful, Bruno."

I hesitated. "Okay, look," I said. "The airplane is this long, a cylindrical aluminum tube that resembles—"

"Bruno!"

"Okay, okay, you want it in a nutshell. Your dream, simply put, means you want to have hot, randy sex in a small bathroom in San Francisco."

She giggled and stared at me for a moment.

"That's what you got from what I just told you?"

"Sure did, babe. It's obvious."

"So when you say San Francisco, you mean like in Ghirardelli Square?"

I fought to stay in character. "Exactly. Chocolate indicates that you want to do it in that San Francisco bathroom with a tall, handsome black man."

She laughed for the first time since we discovered the phone number written on Toby's back. I hadn't realized how much I needed to hear her laugh. It warmed my heart.

She calmed. Her laugh petered off. We rode in silence for a while. She said, "Hot, randy sex, huh?"

"That's right, the hotter and the randier, the better."

"You mean like with Randy Travis, that kinda Randy sex?"

My head whipped around, my mouth dropped open. She'd blind-sided me with that one.

My turn to laugh.

We drove some more. "Why Randy Travis? You don't like country western."

"I don't have to like country western to—"

"Okay, okay, I get it, that's enough."

I thought about it for a moment. I took my eyes from the road and looked at her. "You haven't been thinking about Randy when we . . . I mean . . . ah, jeeze. You haven't . . . you know, been thinking about him while we've been . . . you know?"

"What's that Bruno?" She shot me that impish smile I loved so much.

"Ah, jeeze."

"Bruno?"

"Yeah."

"Your 'Ah, jeeze' is stuck again."

CHAPTER TWENTY-SIX

WE CHECKED IN to a nice hotel, the kind with monogrammed towels, at a price of three hundred and fifty a night, and unpacked. Neither one of us spoke. Our time together started to wind down from hours, shifting to minutes, the time before I'd make the phone call to The Sons of Satan and put in motion the game they had in mind for me.

Marie went into the bathroom and closed the door.

I sat for a long time and worried about the kids back home. I picked up the phone and punched in the number. My brother, Noble, picked up, his mellow voice a comfort. "Hey, Bruno?"

"How'd you know it was me?"

"Huh?" he said. "What? Oh, who else is going to call? And I figured you couldn't be away too long without checking in on the children. They're fine. I told you, with me on the job you don't have to worry about a thing."

"Thank you, Brother, it means a lot. How's Dad?"

"Same, gettin' by, you know. You just pay attention to what you got going on there. You need to stay focused. Get all that done and get on back here."

I wanted to talk to each of the children, hear their voices, but thought it might be better not to, for their sake.

"Man, oh, man these kids sure can eat. It's like feedin' an army. You can't just slap together some sandwiches for lunch. Well, you can but it's a loaf and a half a bread, a jar of grape jelly, and a jar of peanut butter."

The image of Noble slathering sandwiches for ten kids made me smile. I needed that smile.

"Bruno?"

"Yeah?"

"I know you're busy and I wouldn't ask if it wasn't important."

I sat up straighter on the bed. "What? What's the matter?"

"No. Nothing, take it easy. I think it's just an old man's paranoia, that's all. You know, a paternal kinda thing. You know what I mean?"

"Is there something wrong with my nephew? Is he in trouble?"

"No, nothing like that. Really, it's just a silly old man's worry, that's all. I can't get a hold of him. No big deal. He's a kid. He's busy. I know that. If you have a minute, while you're out there, can you check in on him? It'd really give this old heart a mine a break if you know what I mean."

"You know I will. I'll do it right away."

The long pause sat between us over thousands of miles of phone line. I'd known my brother well when we were kids, but now he felt emotionally distant when he shouldn't be. Twenty years in prison could do that to a couple of brothers. I'd be sure to fix that when I got home. I'd reconnect with him. "We'll be back soon," I said. "Give the kids a kiss for me."

"You bet."

I hung up.

I sat on the bed and turned on the television with the remote for a little mind-numbing news.

The woman newscaster, Asian, with intense eyes and wearing a nice blue blazer, said, "Bizarre and scary footage tonight caught on a hospital security camera that picked up the action at a residence not far down the street from the hospital."

The CCTV footage caught my attention. I recognized the location even though the footage came across a little vague and indistinct in black and white.

A large man in a ski mask walked through a hole in a wrought-iron fence. The FBI had mowed down that gate a few weeks ago when they served a search warrant on The Sons of Satan's international clubhouse. I'd seen it firsthand from the rear seat of an FBI Suburban, and had given Special Agent Dan Chulack the probable cause for his affidavit in exchange for my freedom. That search warrant was the reason for The Sons coming to Costa Rica and threatening my family.

On the television, the large man in the ski mask set down a hard plastic milk crate loaded with glass soda bottles. Cloth wicks sprouted from the tops of the bottles.

Only the parking lot separated him from the clubhouse, the lot about fifteen or twenty yards wide.

Bikers came out of the clubhouse wearing their regalia: black leathers, tall black boots, chains hanging from their pants pockets, and denim jackets with the sleeves cut off. Groupthink, in this case "group" being a bunch of apes. Together they yelled obscenities and pointed at him. Two started walking toward him. Their actual words didn't come through on the broadcast, but no one would mistake the threat.

Unperturbed in the least, the big masked man took out a small butane blowtorch. One at a time, he lit the rags hanging out of each bottle. He threw them hard in a high arc, their flames fluttering in the wind. Some landed against the walls, shattering in a whoosh of bright flame. Some landed on the roof of the clubhouse to spill yellow flame in a rolling puddle. The wood and stucco structure caught fire and immediately turned into a blazing inferno. More bikers ran out, two of them firing guns.

Chaos.

The big man spun around and fled.

I didn't hear the rest of the news broadcast. My laughter took over. I rolled on the bed. I laughed until tears came to my eyes. The scene had not been that funny, but I'd needed the diversion more than I knew.

Even with the ski mask, I recognized Karl Drago. He'd been instrumental in helping me take down the Southern California chapter of the SS, The Sons of Satan. Twenty years or more earlier, Drago hid the loot from an armored car heist inside The Sons of Satan clubhouse, a melted-down ring of gold. Now he'd come to reclaim it. Only he couldn't go into the hornet's nest with the hornets still at home so he burned their nest down. Brilliant. Absolutely brilliant.

I leaned over and picked up the phone and dialed Drago's number. He answered on the first ring. "Where are you?"

I told him.

"Be there in fifteen." He rang off.

Marie came out of the bathroom naked. Steam billowed out behind her. "I was just going to take a shower," she said, "and wash off some of this travel grime."

"You looking for the Man From Ghirardelli to help you out with that?"

"Sure, Randy—I mean Bruno—"

She turned and ran into the bathroom with me in close pursuit.

CHAPTER TWENTY-SEVEN

THE LOUD KNOCK came just as I turned off the water in the shower. I grabbed a towel, wrapped it around my waist, and headed out, anxious to see my friend Drago. I stood to the side of the door and leaned over to look in the peephole as I dripped water on the carpet.

Someone out to do you harm on the other side of the door might be watching the peephole from his side, see the shadow shade the hole, know someone stood in front of it, and fire through the door. Caution, not paranoia, ruled the day.

I couldn't see much other than a man the size of a small planet that filled the outside hall.

I swung the door open. "Hey, buddy."

Drago's smile lit up my world. He shoved his way in, wearing a huge black with white lettering Raiders jersey and aqua sweatpants, just as Marie came from the bathroom, a towel wrapped under her arms and another one on her head. She looked radiant.

Drago shook my hand, but his attention went to Marie. "Howya doin', kid?" he said to her.

She made a circular movement with her finger. "Turn around. I'm not presentable to the public."

"I'm not the public, I'm a friend."

I closed the hotel room door. "I'll second that."

"Drago," she said.

"All right." He turned around and away from her. "Please tell me you two weren't taking a shower at the same time?"

"You just wandered deep into the personal zone, pal," I said. "Hey, I saw you on the news last night."

"That ain't normal. How long you been together now, what four, five years?"

"Five and some change," I said.

"This far into your relationship you're supposed to hate each other and barely be getting along. Not still scrubbin' each other's privates in the shower."

"Haven't you heard, California's in a drought," I said. "We're just doing our part to conserve."

Behind him, Marie grabbed some clothes from the dresser and scurried back into the bathroom.

"I only say that"—Drago lowered his voice—" 'cause I was hopin' she'd finally come to her senses and dump your sorry ass."

"What, like you'd have a chance with her if I'm outta the picture?"

"Damn straight. I know I could satisfy the woman in ways you couldn't even imagine. And don't get the wrong idea, I'm talkin' emotionally here."

I went to the dresser and took out some clean clothes. I felt a little self-conscience dropping the towel in front of Drago but did it anyway. I stepped into some underwear.

He raised his eyebrows. "Confirmation, bro. I wouldn't have a problem keeping her happy."

"You know, I should've shot you a little higher up on your leg than I did, like maybe in the hip."

Drago laughed. When he walked over to the bed, his feet shook the floor a little, and it made me less secure with the building's structural integrity. He didn't show any sign of the injury from the bikers' beating or from the gunshot wound to the leg I'd given him.

When we first met, and before I got to know him, I kidnapped Drago at gunpoint right out from under the nose of the FBI. Then, when he wouldn't tell me where he'd hidden the money from the armored car heist, and because he lunged at me, I shot him in the leg.

He stomped his foot a little, his hand on his leg in the area of the wound. "Yeah, I still owe you for that one, darkie." He smiled.

He used to call me much worse.

I pulled my pants on and went over and shook his hand. "We're even."

He wouldn't let go of my hand, and instead, stood and pulled me into a hug. He held me there a second or two longer than what felt normal for a couple of dudes.

Marie came out of the bathroom dressed in slacks and a red peasant blouse. "You boys have something you wanna tell me? Do I need to go downstairs, get a coffee and a scone, let you have some quality time alone?"

Drago let go of me and took a couple of quick steps over to Marie. He picked her up and swung her around. "Nope, we were just talking, and I just gave Bruno ten bucks. He said I can have you. He sold you off just that quick."

"Careful with her, big man. Take it easy," I said.

Drago lost his smile, his expression turning to concern as he gently set her down. "What's the matter? You hurt or somethin'?"

"Oh, don't listen to Bruno."

She'd avoided his question. He turned to me and said, "What, Bruno? Tell me."

"It's not that, it's just . . ."

"Bruno?" Marie said.

We'd agreed not to tell him, and now I'd gone and screwed that all up.

He held on to her shoulders. "What's wrong, kid, you sick or somethin'?"

I said, "Now you have to tell him."

"All right. I'm pregnant."

It took a second for this information to process before his face lit up with a huge smile. "That's wonderful." He picked her up as if she were made of delicate porcelain and set her on the bed. He sat on the bed next to her, and it tilted like a ship going down in the ocean.

His short hair pulled back in a tight ponytail stretched the skin on his flat, pie-tin face. He used to have a shaved head. Every square inch of skin on his exposed arms contained jailhouse ink, tattoos depicting Vikings, shotguns, and big-breasted women, and mirrored his violent life. His presence, picking Marie up and setting her on the bed—which bothered neither of us in the least—made me think we'd somehow crossed over into a parallel universe. In the real world I'd never let someone who looked like he did get anywhere close to my Marie.

"Ho, ho," he said, "you poor girl. You're gonna have a kid with the likes of this poor ugly slob?"

She smiled. "No, no, no. I never said he was the father."

His expression fell. "What?"

She'd gotten him good with that one.

"No, just kidding."

I sat on the bed.

Drago asked me, "What's that all about?"

"Inside joke. You weren't here a little while ago," I said. "My lovely wife was goofing on me about Randy Travis."

"Randy Travis? Solid dude, great voice."

"Don't tell me you listen to that crap? Never mind," I said. "Let's get down to why we're here."

"You came to help me get the gold from the clubhouse, right? For the money, right? That's why I torched it last night. You'll get half of the gold once we go dig it out of that foundation. Like I told you before. I'm a man of my word. Your half 'll help raise this new little Bruno bambino."

"No, that's not why we're here. And we wouldn't take your money anyway. You've sacrificed far too much for it already."

"Oh, now my money's not good enough for you?" He grinned.

"Stop it."

"Okay, then spill it, why are you here?"

"The Sons are mad over what happened and they want a piece of me."

He jumped to his feet and spun around to face us. The bed rebounded from the weight. "The hell you say. They'll have ta go through me first. So what'd they do to you? What happened?"

I couldn't talk. Just thinking about it made the ire rise up inside me.

Marie spoke in a calm and controlled tone. "They came down to Costa Rica. They got to Toby, our little Toby, and wrote their phone number on his back. Bruno called them. They want Bruno back so . . . so . . ."

Drago's hands turned to fists the size of canned hams. "You two go on back home. You don't have ta worry about this anymore. Not for one minute do you have ta worry about this, you understand me? You should've just told me over the phone. I'll take care of this. No problem. I got this."

I stood and took a step toward him. "They didn't ask for you, they asked for me. And I'm not going to ask you to do something that I have to do myself."

He raised his hand and pointed his finger at me. "You get no part of this. You're going to be a daddy. This falls squarely into the middle of what I'm all about. This is mine. This is my gift from me to you."

"Bruno?" Marie pleaded. I knew what she wanted. She wanted me to go along with Drago. Only it wasn't the right thing to do. And I knew she really didn't mean it. Not after she had a moment to think about it.

I turned to her and shook my head.

She gave me those big eyes, hesitated a moment, and then nodded in agreement.

Drago saw the nonverbal communication between Marie and me. "Then what?" he asked. "Why did you call me?"

"I need you to stay with Marie and keep her safe."

Marie stood and stomped one foot. "No. No. I won't have it. He's going with you. You have to have someone backing you up."

"He stays here with you," I said, not leaving any room for interpretation in my tone.

"Drago, what do you say about it?" she asked.

"Ah, I wanna go with Bruno, but I think I should stay with you. No question, stay with you. But, then again, I, ah, also think I need to go with Bruno. That's where the action's going to be, that's where the fun's gonna be."

She moved closer to Drago, picked up his hand, and looked up into his eyes. "I'm asking you as a friend to go with Bruno and keep him safe."

His mouth dropped open a little as he nodded. She went up on tiptoes and kissed his cheek. "Thank you."

He turned to me. "Looks like you lose, pal. I'm going with you."

CHAPTER TWENTY-EIGHT

DOWN IN THE lobby, I stepped out of the elevator with Drago, stopped, and visually checked all the patrons, the people coming and going, looked for someone out of place, a predator, one who resembled an outlaw motorcycle gang member dressed down in sheep's clothing.

I didn't like Marie being left alone with no one covering her. I wouldn't be able to focus with her at risk.

With Drago at my side, though, I started to get a glimmer of hope that this thing might work out. Drago knew how to influence people.

We could do what we did the last time with Jonas Mabry; we could get a chunk of money from somewhere and offer it up to The Sons as a form of reparations. The Sons worshiped only one thing: their false idol, money. They had a price, like everyone had a price, and I'd gladly pay it as long as the number didn't come in too large. The big drawback, even if we got the money and gave it to them, was that they couldn't be trusted. I didn't want to use Drago's gold, but that might be the only way out. If we did use it, I'd swap the menace to my family for an oversize dose of guilt over the debt I'd owe him.

We moved slowly through the hotel lobby to the centerpiece fountain. With Drago dressed in aqua sweatpants and a football jersey, everyone took a second look at us. Not good. We stood out too much. Drago didn't seem to notice. He took out a cell phone and hit a speed-dial number. "Yeah, it's me," he said. "I got a job for you and Dill. You handle this for me and we'll call it square. You screw it up, and I'm gonna introduce you to my blowtorch, you understand?"

He listened for a moment and then said, "Yeah, that's right, a clean slate, you won't owe me a damn thing after this. I want you at a hotel in the next twenty minutes, you understand? One of you will be in the next room to the woman and the other down in the lobby. Nothing is to happen to the woman in 1410. I'll give you the entire lowdown when you get here. I'll text you the name of the hotel and the address. She's not to know you're on the job."

"The threat?" Drago raised his voice. "Yeah, there's a threat or I wouldn't be talkin' ta your dumb ass. It's The Sons. They want ta hurt her and her family and that's not gonna happen."

He listened some more.

"Yeah," he said, "that's why I'm not watchin' after her myself. I'm gonna have a sit-down with The Sons. Be a day, maybe two at the most 'til I get all this sorted out and then you're done."

He rang off and used his big thumbs to text the hotel name and the address.

"Thanks," I said, "that makes me feel a lot better."

"No problem."

"Can you trust these guys?"

"Yeah, one of 'em's my brother, and they're both cops."

"You got a brother who's a cop?"

He waved a beefy paw. "It's a long, sad story without a happy ending. But you don't have to worry, these guys are solid. So whattaya got in mind? You want to systematically hit every one of The Sons' stash pads, safe houses, satellite clubhouses, torch 'em to the ground, keep it up until they yell 'uncle'? That's what I'm thinkin' we do. We start up our own little program of crimes against The Sons."

We moved together to the side of the lobby by the couches and watched the doors and the valets out front taking care of the cars. Watched the kind of cars, the kind of clientele.

"We do it that way," I said, "uninvolved people could get hurt."

"Well, yeah, maybe. Maybe no," he said. "But that's the basic idea—you make an omelet, you're gonna break a few eggs. A body count is the only thing The Sons will stand up and take notice of. You gotta get 'em rubbin' their ass sayin' ouch, that hurt, or you're not gonna get anywhere with 'em."

"I don't want any innocents to get hurt."

He looked at me a little stunned. "What happened to the guy with the huge balls? The guy who walked into The Sons international clubhouse with me and pretended to be a cop? What happened to that guy?"

"We got caught, remember?"

"You're gonna have to get wet on this one if you wanna take care of the problem. That's the only thing they know. You answer violence with violence; it's the only rule in the jungle. I don't know how many different ways I gotta say it."

"What if we tried to buy them off?"

"They'd take the money and come right back at you. They wouldn't even wait a week. And then you'd be right back where you started. Minus the money and a huge chunk of your credibility gone, flushed right down the toilet."

"Who's callin' the shots for The Sons?" I asked. "Did they nominate a new president?"

"No, Clay's still callin' the shots, only now it's from Pelican Bay."

"You've got to be kiddin' me. After all the evidence he kept stashed? The same evidence that put all of his brother bikers in the can for life? He betrayed them with his huge ego and ignorance."

"Clay told everyone that the feds planted that shit, that he had nothin' to do with it."

"*All that evidence?* Are you kiddin' me?"

My voice rose. Drago grabbed my arm and tugged us over to a huge ficus in a pot next to a marble pillar. "No one said these guys would win any spelling bees."

"That's amazing, simply amazing. You know, maybe if we can prove he did keep all those trophies and photos, the membership would turn on him. That might be our way out."

Drago got a faraway look in his eyes. "You know, if we could cut off the head of the snake, the snake might die."

"Take out Clay Warfield? I thought you said he was in Pelican Bay. That's not just a regular prison, it's a supermax, and he's on the inside, and we're on the outside."

"No, no, we get someone on the inside to do the dirty for us."

I didn't like the idea of hiring a thug to take care of my problem. It went against the grain. It was also against the law, murder for hire, one of the most heinous crimes you could commit. No matter how bad Clay turned out to be, if I hired someone, I'd be stooping to his level. I'd been a cop too many years for that.

Drago's theory on life came from a much simpler point of view: you fuck with the bull you get the horn. And in this case, Drago thought Clay more than deserved the horn.

"Let's think about it," I said.

Drago shook his head. "I'm sorry, pal, there just aren't any other options. I think you're gonna have to sack up, my Negro friend, if you wanna get this thing done the right way."

"I'm gonna think on it. Right now I have to make a phone call and meet with a friend."

"Oh no, you don't. You're not gettin' rid a me that easy, pal."

"It has nothing to do with this thing with The Sons. It's something else altogether."

"Really? You tellin' a brother true?"

"Yes."

He waved his hand in the air. "Say, old hoss, listen. I think you already got enough on your plate. Let's get this first thing sorted out first before you go 'round socializin'."

"I won't be long."

He looked confused at my resolve and didn't know which way to jump. "I'm goin' with you," he said, though not as firmly this time.

"That's fine, no problem, but who's gonna wait here and cover Marie until your two friends show up?"

After a time, he nodded. "Then you can just wait 'til they get here, and we can both go."

"By the time they get here, I could've gone and come back. And we're going to need some guns, probably sooner than later."

"I can deal with that."

"Here, gimme your cell phone, let me make a call."

He handed it over.

I dialed Sonja.

CHAPTER TWENTY-NINE

THE POMONA FREEWAY eastbound at two thirty in the afternoon started to bind up with go-home-from-work traffic. In another fifteen minutes, as folks got off work, the clumps of cars would turn into long moving bodies, and fifteen minutes after that, it would shift to stop-and-go. Another fifteen minutes after that, it would be more *stop* and a lot less *go*.

Without any distractions—like a car crash—I could make it to Chino in forty minutes and get back to LA in thirty. The westbound traffic for the return trip would be opposite, everyone trying to get out of LA, not too many trying to get in. I drove with the window down, the warm wind on my arm and blowing in my face.

I noticed the air the most, the difference between the humid, thick air in Costa Rica compared to the dry, light, and smoggy air of So Cal. Too bad I liked the So Cal air better, even with its smog.

I left Drago in the lobby of the hotel, waiting on his security people. He said that he'd have some guns delivered. I asked him to take one up and give it to Marie and reiterate to her not to open the door for anyone.

The phone call to Sonja turned out just as cryptic as the last one with her coded message about Tuesday and the blue Chevy. This conversation didn't start out with any, "Hello, how are ya?" Just, "Meet at the barbeque place on Pipeline east of Central in Chino."

"When?"

"Now, right now."

"Thirty minutes."

Click.

She'd hung up. I couldn't blame her. We'd not left on the greatest of terms. That last time, we'd hardly spoken, the night I laid my badge and gun on Rodriquez' desk, the night I'd watched the paramedics load Sonja on a gurney and into an ambulance.

And then nine months after that she'd just dropped Olivia off. She walked up the stairs to my apartment and knocked on the door. When I answered, she tried to set her in my arms without a word, not so much as a hello. I didn't even know she'd been pregnant. How could I have known? She never told me. My entire life shifted that day, tilted out of control. I had a child, a baby girl. I knew absolutely nothing about raising a baby, let alone a baby girl.

Sonja said, "I can't handle a girl. A girl, of all things, can you believe it?" I thought that's what she said, anyway. I'd slipped into a kinda groggy shock with that warm, squirming little child in my arms. Her tiny hand reached up and gripped my nose. Sonja simply turned and walked away, still talking, words that drifted into the wind.

I found out later, from a friend who said it wasn't that uncommon, that Sonja probably had a bad case of postpartum depression. From my experience working the streets, with postpartum depression, sometimes it was better for the child's safety if the mother and child were separated. Olivia needed to be with her mother. I only took the child because I thought it would be for a short stint, until Sonja felt better. Sonja would one day suddenly snap out of it and say, "What the hell did I do? I gave up my daughter." Then she'd come running back and snatch Olivia away just as abruptly as she'd dropped her off.

Only that never happened.

With each passing day that Sonja didn't show, I lost a little more of what I had in my heart for her, until that day I finally hit the peak of my emotions. By that time I didn't want Sonja to show up anymore to take away my daughter. In fact, after six months, I'd have fought her over custody. That never happened either.

Seventeen years after I received Olivia, I again contacted Sonja and told her that she was now the proud grandmother of twins. Olivia, only a child herself, gave birth to little Albert and Alonzo. On the phone, Sonja sounded indifferent, but said she'd buy some gifts and come right over. She never showed. It saddened me that a grandmother wouldn't want to meet her grandchildren. I never told Olivia about it.

Out of nowhere, three Harley Davidson motorcycles zoomed up on me, growing large in my rearview. Outlaws for sure, all the chrome, the ape-hanger handlebars, the rumble of their engines, the blue denim of their cuts. They yanked me out of my nostalgic funk.

I didn't have a gun. I should've gotten a gun from Drago, first and foremost. What was I thinking?

How had they gotten on to me so quickly?

Okay, okay, I still had the car. I could use the car against them. Motorcycles didn't do so well against cars, especially with someone who knew how to use one as a weapon. In my days on the Violent Crimes Team, I ran over three suspects, three different times, suspects who'd chosen to fight rather than go to prison for the rest of their morally corrupt lives.

All three bikes gunned their engines and came around on the driver's side. I watched their hands in the side mirror for weapons as they made the move. Their hands never left the handlebars. I braced for impact, ready to jerk the wheel to the left, shove my car right into them. What a dumb maneuver, to come up alongside me like that.

In the last second, I caught a glimpse of their colors, the words embroidered on their cuts: *Visigoths.*

Visigoths, and not The Sons of Satan.

As far back as I could remember, the Goths had warred with The Sons in a blood feud, the original reason for it long forgotten.

All three bikes continued to accelerate and changed lanes until they rode in the lane right in front of me. Only four more miles until Central Avenue where I needed to get off. I kept it cool. My pulse calmed. No cops, no Sons, I didn't have any problems.

Coming from behind, two cars caught up to us and rode side by side. Teenagers not paying attention—a little yellow VW and a brown Honda Civic. The passenger in the Honda, a girl, smiled and tried to yell an address or phone number or email address to the blond girl in the VW Bug. Both had their windows down, the wind blowing their hair, their skin tanned and smooth, eyes clear and bright, a vibrant display of youth in its most innocent form.

The Honda swerved—unintentionally—into the other girl's lane. The girl in the yellow Bug overcompensated to keep from smacking into the Honda, and in doing so, her tires crossed into the Goths' lane. All three Goths swerved. They yelled and shot the young girl the finger.

The expression of the girl in the yellow Bug shifted from a smile to pure panic. The Goths slowed in front of me, causing me to slow. They came across and got behind the Bug.

I didn't like this at all. The older Goth, with long, dirty brown hair flowing from under his helmet, came up beside the Bug and kicked in the driver's door, denting it. The older Goth recoiled from the strike, swerved, and almost went down.

What a fool.

The girl screamed, now frantic to get away. The next Goth came up beside her, pulled a ball-peen hammer from a loop on his belt, and whacked the top of her car again and again, the metal-on-metal thunk easily heard over the loud roar of the bikes. He eased back and broke out her side back window. Safety glass sprayed everywhere.

The girl screamed again, her eyes wide in terror.

I put my foot on the accelerator to move over and ram them just as a siren from behind us lit off with a squeal.

I checked the rearview. A black-and-white California Highway Patrol car—red and blue lights flashing—coming up fast. I'd been so involved in what transpired right beside and in front of me that I'd not kept up my constant vigil for law enforcement. In this case, it worked out. The patrolman didn't want any part of me. He'd seen what the Goths did to the VW and the terror they inflicted, the threat they caused to the safety of the drivers on the freeway.

I backed off on the speed.

The Goths looked back. They nodded and yelled something to each other as the CHP got in behind them. In one large group, the CHP and three motorcycles moved across the two lanes over to the shoulder.

I didn't intend to follow until I saw the driver, the CHP officer, a petite woman with a blond pageboy hair cut. I fell in behind and pulled to the shoulder, stayed several car lengths back, my intent being to remain until her backup arrived.

But the Goths figured the same thing about the back-up.

The bikes stopped. The kickstands slammed down.

Things started to happen fast, too fast to think twice about leaving.

CHAPTER THIRTY

IN A REALLY screwed-up sort of way, outlaw motorcycle gangs mirrored the Boy Scouts. The bikers earned patches to wear on their cuts, their denim vests. Each patch or "rocker" symbolized an accomplishment they'd achieved. Dirty, ugly achievements like having sex with a cadaver, armed robbery, rape, murder, and even assaulting a police officer.

Two of the young Visigoths wore new cuts without any patches. They had everything to prove. The older one with the long brown hair, his cut hung heavy with soiled patches, supervised the other two. He would bear witness to their accomplishments. The young ones would want to make a good show for the older one, and that made the situation that much more dangerous.

They all got off the bikes and stood in a group. The CHP officer stayed too long in her car calling out the stop. If she wanted any chance at all of controlling the situation, she needed to get out right away and start giving orders before the Goths had time to develop a plan and work up their nerve. Patrol tactics 101.

I got out and moved around to the shoulder and stayed by the rental.

The CHP got out. She looked to be about five-one or -two and weigh a hundred and twenty-five with all her equipment on.

The old biker with the dirty brown hair and one of the young ones looked white-Caucasian, but overly tanned to the point of looking Hispanic. The third one took his helmet off to show curly red hair. He wore his gunfighter handlebar mustache bushy and untamed against a dark complexion. He didn't look ugly like the other two; his angular features and his freckles made him handsome in a boyish kind of way. He displayed an innocence that didn't jibe with his costume or with the men with whom he rode. All three stood at least six feet and weighed in at a buck-eighty at a minimum. Any one of them, alone, would be a handful for the officer.

As soon as she got to the front of the patrol car, the group of bikers started to move on her. She froze, hand on her gun, and pointed with her other hand. "Please step to the shoulder of the road." Over the roar of the traffic on the freeway, I could barely hear her.

Hundreds of cars zipped by, all those drivers unaware of the disaster unfolding on the side of the freeway.

The bikers didn't obey but instead continued to step closer to her. I didn't have any doubt. They were going to take her on. I ran a few steps up to the side of her car. The older biker saw me and hesitated. The young bucks followed suit and stopped. The CHP officer chanced it, took her eyes off her threat to look at what had caused the bikers to react.

I held up four fingers and mouthed the words "Code-Four?" to let her believe that I was a cop, and at the same time ask if she was okay.

She barely moved her head, indicating she wasn't Code-Four, the fear plain in her eyes yet not in her expression. I moved up to the front of the patrol car and stood three feet from her, about six feet from the bikers.

She yelled to the bikers, "I won't tell you again, step to the shoulder of the road, and I want to see some ID."

The two young bikers looked at the older one for guidance. The older one locked eyes with me. "Who the hell are you?"

"I'm just the guy standing here on the side of the road, trying to keep you honest."

"You better step off, nigger. You don't want any part of this."

I shifted my footing, taking a combative stance. "Not gonna happen."

"Move to the side of the road. Do it now," the officer said.

No one moved for a long, fat moment.

Then the old lion took a step toward us, his hand on the side of his belt under his cut.

"He's got a ball-peen," I said. "I saw him use it on the VW."

"I know, I saw it, too." She drew her gun and pointed it at him center mass. "Show me your hands. Do it now. Do it right now." Her other hand moved down to the top of her radio and pushed the red emergency button. Her action changed the whole game. Now every cop in a twenty-mile radius would be responding Code-Three to assist her.

Except that we stood on the side of a busy freeway without easy access, not with all the traffic. Backup would take longer than normal.

Too many cops would arrive in minutes. When they came on scene, they'd ask for *my* ID. One of them would surely recognize me from all the bulletins put out over the last two years. The FBI wanted me for kidnapping and various other felonies. I'd walked head-on into a no-win situation. I couldn't leave and I really needed to get out of there.

The older biker smirked at the officer. "What, the split tail's got the balls to drop the hammer on me? I don't think so. Take her, Dirk."

The young one called Dirk hesitated, then leapt forward, hands outstretched, shoulder down. I took two quick steps to intervene, planted my feet, and gave him a roundhouse right. He saw it coming, dodged a little, but not enough. My fist struck right on his ear and skull and vibrated up my arm. I followed with a quick uppercut to his chin that landed solid, jammed his teeth together, and mashed his lips. He stumbled, shaken to his core. He went to one knee to shrug it off.

The older biker, at the same time, took hold of the young redheaded biker and shoved him into the fray. Both junior bikers acted as cover so he could make his move on the officer.

The redheaded biker shoved hard into me. My footing ended up out of position from the punches I'd just thrown. He hit me at waist level. I backpedaled. We landed on the hood of the car, his chin close to mine, his breath minty fresh. He flailed his arms, trying to slug me, inexperienced. I took hold of his ear and pulled with everything I had, while I watched, helpless to intervene, as the older biker made his move on the officer.

The older biker swung the ball-peen high and wide. The officer, distracted for a brief moment with the fight on the hood of her unit, saw the assault too late. The hammer came down on her arm, the one holding the gun. The bone snapped with a crack. The gun flipped in the air. The older biker watched it as it fell to the ground. If he got to the gun, the bad guys would win with smoke and blood and two broken bodies left to die on the side of the road.

I kneed the redheaded biker in the belly again and again as I yanked on his ear.

The officer yelled, not in pain but in anger over the loss of her weapon. She charged, shoving forward, her head down, her good arm cradling the shattered one. She torpedoed her head right into the older biker. He saw the move, chuckled, and sidestepped her. He swung the hammer again and caught her on the back of the head.

She dropped to the ground face-first, absolutely still. Her breath puffed the dirt.

I shoved the kid off me and dove for the gun down in the grit and broken asphalt.

CHAPTER THIRTY-ONE

I LANDED ON the gun, a Glock nine, groped for it, fumbled it. The older biker kicked me in the face. The world wobbled, the air turned thick like a heat wave. The redheaded biker grabbed my foot, tried to pull me off the gun and came away with my shoe. He fell back on his ass. The older biker kicked me again. I moved my face out of the way this time and took it on the shoulder. I rolled off the gun when he came at me with the ball-peen. Had to, no choice. His swing took him off balance. The blow struck me on the left arm. White pain shot up to my shoulder and turned my arm numb. Still on the ground, I swung my leg wide and hard, kicking his legs out from under him. He flopped onto the ground.

I struggled to my feet, looked left to the gun on the ground. I didn't have time to make a move toward it. The redhead crouched and sprang at me. I let him come, grabbed onto his denim vest, and fell backward as I stuck my foot in his chest. His eyes went wide as he saw the move unfold. He said it fast, pleaded with me, "No, mister, please don't. Don't."

Three against one didn't make a fair fight. I had to even the odds or die. I flipped him high overhead, right out into traffic.

A black Honda Accord took him. Snatched him right out of the air. He smashed the windshield, flew in the air again, and landed on the hot concrete. The Honda with the shattered windshield skidded out of control and crashed into the three motorcycles on kickstands parked on the shoulder.

I rolled over to the gun and scooped it up just as the older biker came in fast with his ball-peen.

I shot him in the forehead.

Flipped off his lights.

Sirens, still miles away, reached out to me. They'd be on scene in minutes. I didn't feel sorry for killing the older biker. He'd called the game and lost. The redheaded biker, though, bothered me a great deal. His eyes, his voice, the way he pleaded. And I'd gone ahead and done it anyway, flipped him out into oncoming traffic.

I struggled to my feet, my knees weak, not wanting to cooperate. I hurried over to the downed officer and took a set of cuffs from the handcuff case on her belt. Dirk, on his hands and knees, spit teeth and blood onto the sandy earth. I put my foot on his shoulder and shoved him over. I pointed the Glock at him. "You saw what I did to your partners. You want some of this?"

He held up his hand and said, "No, man, no. I'm done."

I put the gun in my waistband, cuffed his hand, and dragged him over to the patrol unit. I ratcheted the cuff to the pushbar, securing him until backup arrived.

I went back to the patrol officer and eased her onto her back. Her eyes rolled open. "Hey, kid," I said, "it's all over. You're okay. You understand? You're okay and you're gonna make it just fine."

I unclipped her shoulder mic and keyed it. "Eleven-ninety-nine. Eleven-ninety-nine, shots fired, officer down, shots fired, officer down."

I took her gun from my waistband and stuck it back in her holster. A cop always felt vulnerable without her gun in her holster. "Help will be here in about two minutes," I said. "Just lie still and try to stay awake. It's real important that you stay awake. I don't need you going into shock."

Her color drained as I watched. Shock could kill her faster than any bullet. I needed to elevate her legs. I dragged over the older biker, the dead one, laid him on his side, and put her legs up on him. "It's the best I can do for right now, kid. I've gotta run. You gonna be okay?"

She gave me a barely perceptible nod.

I stood. Far off down the freeway, headed our way, a conga line of cop cars drove the shoulder, kicking up a huge dust cloud. All the cars on the freeway had stopped now. I hadn't noticed at what point that happened.

I ran for the Ford Escape, got in, slammed it in drive, and steered to the right side of the Highway Patrol car, to the far and extreme part of the shoulder, the only way out.

In the middle of the freeway, on the westbound traffic lanes, two Highway Patrol cars stopped parallel to the incident. The officers pulled their shotguns, jumped out of their cars, and climbed the center divider. They wove their way through all the stopped traffic, approaching with caution as I gunned the Ford Escape.

The black Honda Accord had shoved one of the downed choppers into my path, blocking my way out. I pulled the gearshift down into low and gunned the car. I drove right over the motorcycle. The Escape jerked and rattled. I banged into the right front of the Accord, shoved it out of the way, and made it clear. The driver of the Accord shot me the finger.

I took the speed up to fifty, too fast for driving on the shoulder, zipping past all the stopped cars on the freeway, but if I didn't get away, I would never see freedom again.

CHAPTER THIRTY-TWO

THAT REDHEADED BIKER, the kid, couldn't have been more than twenty-five or twenty-six. He had a smooth complexion, with a spray of freckles across his nose. I'd been too close to his face, no more than a foot or so in that split second before I flipped him. Pleading eyes. A grown-up Opie, the redheaded kid on *The Andy Griffith Show*, only with a little darker skin. Not so much a kid really. When I took hold of him, he had muscle under his biker vest, built stout like a weightlifter. A hidden strength most people would miss. I know I did. He didn't try that hard to take me down. As I played it back in my head, he didn't seem to have his heart in what the old biker told him to do. And yet he died for it.

The worst part about it, though, was his eyes. I couldn't shake his eyes. And his last words, as he begged me not to toss him into traffic. Those panicked words continued to haunt me. And they would for a long, long time to come. I needed to talk to Marie, tell her about what happened. She'd understand. She'd know just the right things to say to talk me down. Not to make what I did right but to make me understand this had to be done. And most important of all, to make me believe her.

Robby Wicks would've called me a pussy for not letting this caper just roll off my back. *No time for emotions, Bruno, not in this job. You want emotions, get a job as a nurse, you pussy.*

I made it to Central and turned south. I slowed my speed to blend in. Montclair and Chino police cars passed me going Code-Three—lights and siren—responding to the incident on the freeway with the downed CHP.

My arm still tingled with numbness from the blow from the ball-peen hammer. The fingers on that hand still didn't respond the way they should. The side of my face throbbed where the older biker kicked me. I realized my one foot registered a kind of draft. I looked down. My foot wore only a sock, the shoe gone. That's right, I'd lost it in the melee.

I dialed Marie on the burner phone Drago gave me. She didn't recognize the number and answered with a tentative hello.

"Babe, it's me."

"Oh, Bruno, are you okay? I haven't heard from you in a while. It seems like hours and it's only been a few minutes. Everything all right?"

"Yeah, sure, everything's fine. That's why I'm calling, to tell you I'm fine. Are you still in the room?"

"Yeah, and Karl's here with me." Her tone suddenly shifted. "That wasn't the deal, though, Bruno. We're both mad about you taking off like that. Hold on, I'm going into the bathroom."

I came to a stoplight and closed my eyes. I really didn't need a scolding right now, not with that kid's words burning a hole in my conscience, burning a hole right down to the bone. I'd done a bad thing. But I had to do it, right? What choice had they given me?

In the background, the bathroom door closed. "Bruno, you said we'd both go see Sonja together. That was the whole reason why I came along, remember?"

I heard the tears in her voice.

"I know, I know, but you're pregnant and don't need to be exposed to this kinda emotional stuff. I'll find out what she has to say and then we'll be done with it and we can move on to the bigger problem, The Sons."

She didn't say anything.

"Marie?" I wanted to tell her about the kid I'd just killed, but I couldn't get the words to come out.

The light changed. I drove in silence. Sometimes all I needed was to be connected with her even if only through the phone, the silence traveling miles and miles through the air. I made it to Pipeline and turned east.

"Bruno, what's wrong? What's happened? There's something wrong. Are you okay?"

Amazing. She'd sensed something through the quiet over the line.

"I'm okay."

"No, you're not. You're not telling me something. What's happened?"

"Your right, something has happened, but I can't talk about it over the phone. I'm almost to the meet, so I have to go now. I love you, Marie. You know that, right? And you don't have to worry about me. I'm good."

"I love you, too, Bruno. Be careful and get right back here."

We let the line hang open for a long minute. She never ceased to amaze me. She didn't continue to give me a hard time. She'd sensed a problem, assessed the situation, and backed me the best way she could under the circumstances, by letting the silence hang between us.

I hung up.

I pulled into Joey's Barbeque, the parking lot almost empty, the lunch rush over. An older woman, with sun-damaged skin and gray hair in a ponytail pulled through the back of a baseball cap, came right up to the front passenger door and tugged on the handle. She wore a khaki utility vest with a blouse underneath and Levi 501s worn soft from too many washings.

I waved my hand. "No, go away. Whatever it is, I'm not buying any."

"Bruno, you son of a bitch, quit fuckin' around and open the door."

What?

I looked again at her.

Sonja.

Life had not been kind to her. I looked at her a second more, and some of her old beauty reappeared, mostly through her eyes.

She jerked on the handle again. I hit the door locks. She opened the door and jumped in. She still washed her hair with that green apple shampoo, the scent fleeting but there.

"Hey," she said.

"Hey." We checked out each other for a moment, top to bottom.

She said, "What the hell, Bruno, you look like someone just put the boot to you. Are you okay?"

"You look great," I said, my voice coming out lower than I wanted.

She smiled. "You always were a poor liar, Bruno. Your dad ruined you that way. Go ahead then, don't tell me what happened. Come on, start this thing up, let's get goin'. You're late and they're going to be waitin' on us."

"Where we going?

"I'll tell you how to get there."

I didn't put the Escape in gear and I waited. "No, tell me what's goin' on."

She looked at me long and hard and then said, "A very dear friend of mine is in trouble, bad trouble, and we need your help. So come on, let's quit doin' the dick-around and let's go."

"I told you on the phone, I've got something goin' right now. I don't have time for this right now."

She lost her smile. "I know all about your trouble, and if this works out, we can help each other."

"What? How can you possibly know what I have goin' on?"

"Bruno, just drive."

I hesitated as my mind spun, trying to put together any and every possibility, and nothing, I mean *nothing*, fit. I put the Ford in reverse, backed up, stuck it in drive, and headed for the street.

CHAPTER THIRTY-THREE

SOMEHOW THIS OLDER version of Sonja riding in the passenger seat of my car corrupted the youthful memory of her along with my version of the normal world. Something seemed broken. We'd slipped past that delicate edge of reality and into some parallel universe where time bent and curved backward.

She hadn't been in my car for going on . . . what, twenty-three, twenty-four years? Back when she did ride with me, I couldn't think about anything but her. And more important, how I thought that feeling would never change, that it was so strong *it could never* change.

She fed me directions and I followed them, snatching pecks at her whenever I could. Each time I looked, I caught her watching the street or checking the mirror, like some sort of predator. Yes, just like a predator. Was her behavior a carryover from our patrol days? She'd only been a cop for a few months before she hung it up. Had that been enough time to gain that predator mentality? Or had she somehow evolved into a criminal, as described in Robby's oversimplified classification system?

Robby Wicks broke the world down into two basic categories: predators and victims. Cops could be a kind of predator, but in a good way. Most were not. Most wrote citations and took drunks to jail. The real cop predators acted like the detectives on Robby's

Violent Crimes Team, and there were only a few of those in the entire world.

And criminals, of course, fit into the predator category, no question.

Everyone else, all the other humans, fit safely into the *victim* category. If Sonja wasn't a cop and she acted like a predator, then according to Robby's theory, she fit in as a criminal predator.

She gave out the directions in a devil-may-care tone, almost too late for me to make the turns, her mind chewing on something far more important. Within a few blocks, she guided us north out of Chino and into the county area of Pomona. Dinky houses on long, narrow lots turned older. They had large, majestic trees out front and poorly maintained shrubs. There was painted concrete and empty dirt where there should've been grass in the short front yards. Kadota Avenue didn't have any curbs or gutters.

The whole area looked oddly familiar. Not long ago, on the same Kadota but in Montclair, we'd taken down the serial kidnapper Jonas Mabry. Couldn't have been more than a mile from where we'd just pulled up and stopped.

When I worked the streets, I sometimes thought there might be a sort of malignant vortex that attracted criminals to a particular area. They'd swirl around and around in this toilet bowl until the justice system flushed them for good.

Out in front of the house, parked on the street, sat a Toy Box, a fifth-wheel trailer hooked to a one-ton truck. The camping trailer had a drop-down rear that turned into a ramp that allowed ATVs and motorcycles to be wheeled inside. The bumper of the truck sported a Good Sam Club sticker.

The house looked too squatty in comparison to the ones on either side, built out of two single-wide mobile homes put together to make one. The owner had covered over the aluminum sides with

wood siding and painted the whole thing a light blue in a feeble attempt to make it look like a normal house. A wind chime hung from
the wooden porch, giving off a pleasant sound. A sun-faded yard
gnome sat at the base of the two steps that led up to the porch, the
gnome incongruent without any grass or shrubs or anything even
green close by. The place worked too hard at trying to be quaint.

Sonja got out, didn't say a word, and walked down the long driveway toward the deep backyard. When I didn't follow, she turned
around and scowled at me. Still in the car, I said to no one who
could hear, "Jesus, just tell me what it is I need to hear, what you got
me down here for, so I can be on my way. I gotta get outta here. I
don't need the rest of this shit right now."

Emotionally, I had already started to transfer the stress from The
Sons of Satan problem and the death of the redheaded biker. The
kid. That's what Marie would tell me once I had time to call and talk
with her, that transference thing she continually warned me about.

Sonja had told me she could help me with my problem with The
Sons, otherwise I wouldn't have been there at all. And I'd never
have come upon *that problem* backing the CHP. I would have still
been back at the hotel with my lovely and sweet Marie.

"I'm coming, dammit." I got out of the car, slammed the door,
and followed along. My arm throbbed.

I stopped and looked back at the Escape when the brief thought
of fleeing returned, the need to move on to the next pressing issue
and leave this one far behind, the feeling almost too strong to resist.
The left front of the Escape no longer matched the right. I'd caved it
in when I rammed the Honda Accord out of the way on the freeway
in my mad dash to get away. How would I explain that to the rental
car folks? Why did I care? The damaged car problem was minute in
comparison to this one.

"Bruno?"

I turned back and said, "I'm coming."

The long driveway led to a prefab metal building large enough to house a small manufacturing operation: furniture, welding, auto repair, that sort of thing. The big roll-up door, once opened, looked wide enough to allow four cars side by side to enter at the same time.

I clumped alongside Sonja.

She looked down at my feet. "Hey, your shoe. What happened to your other shoe?"

"I don't wanna talk about it."

She nodded and kept walking as if my answer made perfect sense.

Sonja bypassed the big door and went to the smaller, pedestrian entrance. She didn't knock and went in.

The air conditioner mounted in the window cooled the place down too much. Chilled the air enough to instantly dry the sweat on my forehead. A large man with an unruly mop of curly brown hair sat behind a desk too small for his bulk. He wore a long-sleeve, blue chambray shirt, the arms tight like fat sausages. In the web of his right hand he sported a tattoo, a crude little black cross, the kind of mistake kids make. He looked at least fifty; only his long black eyelashes gave off a false impression of youth. Even in the overly cool environment, sweat beaded on his face.

A couch and two easy chairs sat along the walls in front of the desk. Above them, pictures in cheap frames depicted the inside of the manufacturing area just on the other side of the wall. Pictures of the design and manufacture of custom motorcycles, the sixty- to a hundred-and-twenty-thousand-dollar kind of bikes. Custom-designed frames, built from the ground up, with fat tires and sensational airbrushed paint jobs.

Sonja took a seat in one of the easy chairs as if she owned the place. The big man stood and leaned over the desk, offered his hand.

I took it. His grip rivaled Drago's, and I'd never experienced a grip like Drago's.

"M'name's Bobby Ray Kilburn. You can call me Bobby, Bruno. I've heard a lot of good things about you. Your reputation is legendary. Sit. Sit."

"Thank you, I prefer to stand. I'm not going to be here long."

Bobby Ray looked at Sonja. She shrugged.

"What the hell happened to your face?" he asked.

"I'm not here to talk about my face."

Sonja said to Bobby Ray, "Just come right out and ask him. I told you, Bruno's not one to do the dick-around. I don't know what happened to Bosco. He's late, he's not picking up his cell, so go ahead and get started. I know Bruno, he's not going to wait around much longer. Bosco can catch up when he gets here." She got it all out in one long, nervous string. What did she have to be so nervous about?

Bobby Ray looked back at me. "I heard about what you did with those kids in Los Angeles. Hell, everyone has. That's why I had Sonja call you. I need you."

"She's right," I said. "You don't need to blow smoke up my dress. Let's get right down to it. Sonja said you might be able to help me with my problem?"

"It's gonna be like that?"

"Yeah, it's gotta be."

He nodded and thought about his next words before he spoke. "My son has a kid; we call him Little Bosco. He's the love of my life." He picked up a picture from his desk. I didn't look at it. Couldn't, if I wanted to retain at least some objectivity. Kids could bore right into my heart and instantly take over all clear thinking.

I shrugged, tried hard for indifference, and couldn't pull it off. Not with a small child involved.

"All right then," Bobby Ray said, "here it is in a nutshell. My son's been arrested and has a case pending against him. He's out on bail for right now. He's lookin' at a lot of hard time in the pen because of that minimum sentencing bullshit. That can't happen, he's a good kid. He needs to be home to take care of Little Bosco. Little Bosco needs his father. I need my son. I want you to take care of this problem for me."

"I don't understand."

"My son, Sebastian, got popped by ATF for something he shouldn't have had anything to do with. It wasn't his fault. He's not guilty." Bobby Ray raised his right hand. "I swear to you on a stack of Bibles, my kid's innocent."

"How do you know for sure?"

He sat down, tented his fingers, his smile gone now, replaced with a grim expression filled with sorrow and regret. "Because the guns they popped him with belonged to me."

CHAPTER THIRTY-FOUR

"I DON'T KNOW what you think I'm all about or how I can help you with something like this, because I don't think I can."

He looked hopeful, as if I'd said, "*Sure thing, whatever I can do.*" But I didn't. I stood there in one shoe, a half-second away from walking out—running out—to the smashed-up car. I needed to get back to Marie, to hold her in my arms, whisper to her about the evil I'd done, ask her if she could forgive me. I needed Marie, of all people, to forgive me.

But she didn't have the ability, not to forgive me for the killing of that young man—forgive me for that horrible sin.

Bobby Ray came around the desk and went to the short dorm-sized refrigerator adjacent the desk. He bent over, took out a couple of ice-cold Corona beer bottles, popped off the caps, and offered me one. I started to refuse but realized my throat and mouth, which were beyond dry, begged for any type of moisture. I swallowed. No, not just dry, but arid to the point of dust. I took it, the glass cold and wet in my hand. He clinked his bottle with mine. I tilted the cold bottle back and glugged the beer. The cold liquid, the best I'd ever tasted, chilled my overheated body on the inside where the air conditioner couldn't reach.

He held out his hand and said, "Please, sit."

I again fought the anxiety to leave. I sat and drank down the rest of the beer, then set the empty on the desk in front of me. He handed me another that I drank half of as if I'd been stranded on a lifeboat without water. I gasped for breath and then wiped my mouth with the back of my hand. I looked up at him, shrugged. "It's a hot day."

He took a drink, watching me over his bottle.

"Why don't you go to the ATF," I asked, "and just tell them the guns are yours?" I knew why, but wanted to see if he did, or if he'd tell me the truth.

"I would," he said. "I would, no question. Wouldn't I, Sonja? Tell him I would."

That's when I saw it, when they looked at each other, the relation between Sonja and Bobby Ray. They'd been trying to conceal it and accidentally let it slip out from where they'd kept it hidden.

Why hide it?

Sonja nodded. "He would. Bobby Ray would pay in a heartbeat. He loves Bosco. His name is Sebastian but we call him Bosco."

Bobby Ray pointed his beer neck at me and said, "You were a cop a lot of years, so you know how it works. I turn myself in, they don't let Bosco go, they just take us both. The sons of bitches. But that's not it, not all of it anyway. This shitty little deal gets a lot worse. And I can't believe my son's all wrapped up in it. It's a nightmare. I love Bosco. You have kids, you gotta know what I'm talking about here."

I nodded.

He nodded, too. "Okay then, here's the deal. We also got this shitty little ATF agent thrown in the mix. This guy contacted us, said for fifty K, in fifties and hundreds, he'd lose some evidence transmittal forms, or some shit like that, and dump the case on a technicality. Bosco would walk."

I said nothing and sipped the beer.

"It's not about the money," he said. "I got that kinda dough, no problem." This time he pointed the bottle at me like a weapon as the anger rose in him. "My problem is that this ATF asshole will take the money and just ask for more, leave my Bosco sitting in the can holdin' his dick. Why not? What does he have to lose once he does it the first time, takes my money, huh? Am I right? Am I right here? Fucking cops. They're supposed to be the good guys. They're supposed to follow the goddamn rules."

"Honey, take it easy," Sonja said. Now she'd let their relationship out into the open as if proud of it.

"Why am I here?" I asked, "What is it you think I can do?"

Bobby Ray sat on the edge of his desk in front of me, too close, our knees inches apart. I put the cold bottle on my injured arm and flexed my fingers. Very soon I'd need the use of my fingers, and the tingling worried me.

"You're a cop, you can talk to this guy and find out if this 'losing the transmittal' thing is bullshit or if it's for real. You'd be our middleman, give him the money. Then you tell me if you think that's it, that he won't come back for more."

I nodded, curious now. What he said didn't make sense, not all of it anyway. He'd been too smart in what he said up to this point, describing my part in his little play. No way in hell would it work out the way he described, not with me involved.

"Not to sound too self-absorbed or anything, but let me ask this again. If I do this, how are you gonna help me with my problem?" I wanted to see if they really did know what kind of problem I had, let alone would be able to solve it.

Bobby Ray smiled, showing all his teeth, teeth big as Chiclets. A perfect smile, except for a gap on the right uppers where two had been knocked out. "'Cause," he said, "I can take care of your problem with The Sons."

They did know.

How did they know?

How could they possibly get The Sons to back down?

"How?"

He shook his finger at me and went to the reefer. He got out two more beers, opened them, and handed me one. I finished the second, though I knew I shouldn't have. I needed all my wits about me. I took the third. I just couldn't quench my thirst. I set the empty on the desk next to the first one.

He said, "You're just going to have to trust me on this." He looked over at Sonja for verification.

Sonja said, "Bruno, you have my word that he does have the ability to stop The Sons from ever bothering you again."

"Nothing personal, Sonja, but I haven't talked with you for over two decades, and I got a lotta skin in this game."

"You fix this," Bobby Ray said. "I don't care how you do it, and I promise to make it right with The Sons. That won't be no small job either, they really want a piece of you. But I'll do it, you have my word."

"Do it any way I can?" I said.

"That's right." He looked me in the eye when he said it.

Now I understood. They needed someone they could trust to do a job on a fed. Preferably someone already a fugitive, hiding out in another country, someone who'd leave this country after the job was completed. The trust part being the major factor.

Over the quiet rumble from the in-the-window air conditioner came the muffled roar of motorcycles echoing down the long driveway we'd walked in on.

Sonja smiled, the big smile that I used to know. "That'll be Bosco. Come meet him. Then you'll see. You'll see that he didn't have anything to do with this mess. You'll be able to tell by just looking into his eyes that he's innocent."

Bobby Ray and Sonja went past me to the door. I got up and followed, clumped along in my one shoe and holding the cold bottle to my face, more relaxed than when I came in thanks to the alcohol.

Outside, the bright sunlight blinded me. I held my arm up, the sun hotter than before.

My eyes adjusted. I stumbled back a couple of steps in shock.

In the driveway, not ten feet in front of us, sat four Harley Davidsons, all chrome, with ape-hanger handlebars. Just like the others on the freeway. The gas tanks were intricately airbrushed, painted with skulls and shotguns, Viking helmets and Vikings and their long beards. The bikes didn't shake me as much as the men who rode them.

Four outlaw motorcycle gang members, all wearing denim cuts, flying the colors of their gang. *The Visigoths*.

CHAPTER THIRTY-FIVE

HOW HAD THEY tracked me here? I couldn't run, not with one shoe, and expect to gain any distance before they brought me down. Not with three of them in the driveway, all young bucks. I backed up to the wall and slipped off the remaining shoe for better balance and traction. The cold, wet beer bottle, my only weapon, almost slipped from my hand.

I'd fight them.

Three of the bikers looked sheepish and wouldn't make eye contact with Bobby Ray. The fourth, the leader who wore the "Sergeant at Arms" rocker and the name patch "Monster," looked angry enough to chew nails.

Sonja keyed in on Monster. "What's the matter? What's happened? Where's Bosco?"

Bobby Ray put a less-than-gentle hand on her shoulder, eased her back, and at the same time stepped in front of her. "What's goin' on, Joe?" he said to Monster. "Tell me now."

Bosco? Oh, Jesus, one of the three I'd encountered on the freeeway belonged to Bobby Ray. His son? Two out of the three were too old to be his son. It could only be the one.

How absolutely awful.

What a horrible mess.

I didn't know the man, but I had kids, and couldn't imagine the pain he was about to experience.

Monster took his time removing his helmet, made a show of it. He rubbed his bald and sweaty pate with his free hand.

I didn't want him to talk anymore, to say the words. But he did.

"Sons of bitches killed ol' Hector."

Bobby Ray jumped forward and took hold of Monster's denim vest. "*Who*? Who killed ol' Hector?"

"The cops. On the freeway. Not that far from here, either. Right off Central. And they didn't do nothin' either, Bobby Ray. The cops just pulled 'em over for nothin' and started shooting. Gunned ol' Hector like a dog."

Sonja's hand flew to her mouth. A little "oh" escaped her lips.

"Tell me all of it," Bobby Ray said through clenched teeth.

I took a deep breath. I tried to relax but couldn't. These men didn't have their facts straight, none of them.

Good thing.

They hadn't followed me after all. It wouldn't take them too long, though, to figure out what really happened, who'd participated, and who did what. Now the three I'd confronted, the two killed, and the one beaten and cuffed to the bumper of the car, didn't turn out to be some random contact after all. They'd been on their way to this same meeting on Kadota at the motorcycle shop with Bobby Ray, Sonja, and me. But a freak set of circumstances had intervened. Our paths crossed en route. Bad luck for everyone involved.

Suddenly Sonja moved in, elbowed Bobby Ray outta the way, and took first position on Monster, her hands on his denim vest. "Where's Bosco? He was forbidden to ride with Ol' Hector. Tell me he wasn't riding with Ol' Hector."

Monster couldn't look Sonja in the eye, couldn't look anyone in the eye. Not with that big ugly question on the table.

Bobby Ray figured out the answer, one he didn't want. He roared. He knocked Sonja out of the way and slugged Monster, hit him right in the mouth. Blood spewed. Monster flew back, his out-stretched arms tried to keep Bobby Ray off him. Not today. Today no one person—not even five—could have kept Bobby Ray from exploding. Bobby Ray came in swingin', roaring like a bull.

Monster, the sergeant at arms, went down under a barrage of knuckles, not daring to fight back.

Bobby Ray must've been the president of the Visigoths.

The president, Jesus.

Under the emotional onslaught, my mind went into a sort of neutral, an almost out-of-body experience. An odd thought bubbled up all on its own. The president of the Visigoths probably could keep The Sons of Satan off my family.

I snapped back into reality. Bobby Ray spun around, not done yet. The other three young studs looked around, ready to bolt, and couldn't move, didn't dare move. Bobby Ray grabbed the closest one. He shook him hard until the biker's head jerked back and forth and his teeth banged together. "Tell me."

The biker closest to Bobby Ray's new victim held up his hands. "Wait, wait. I'll tell you."

Bobby Ray froze, let go of his victim. Everyone held their breath.

The young biker said, "The cops, they threw Bosco out inta traffic. He got hit by a car."

"Aieeee." Sonja wilted to the ground, sat right down on her folded-up legs and let out another mournful wail. One that I'd been the cause of, one that ripped my guts out. I rushed to her side with a load of guilt now impossible to carry.

How the hell could this have happened? I knew. I did. And in that same emotional funk I looked back on a lesson hard-earned for solace, solace in any amount.

Robby explained it once while we hunted a murderer. We'd come upon a fresh kill, a violent scene in an apartment.

We got the story from the one guy left alive, barely. The suspect we hunted, Gary Weems, had pulled a gun, then everyone else in the room pulled theirs. The ensuing gunfight resulted in six dead and one wounded, all in a ten-by-twelve apartment. I stood there in shock and awe over what humans could do to one another.

Robby stood at the edge of the clumped-up mass of bodies and blood. He saw my confusion, put his hand on my shoulder, and said, "Bruno, my man, you can't have any compassion for these shitheads. They don't give one shit for their victims when they're raping, robbing, and murdering 'em. If you live by the shithead code, eventually, more sooner than later, you're gonna get your ass stomped. By the good guys or like this . . ." He held up his hand. "By their own kind. It's part of their cycle of life, eat or be eaten. Ain't this absolutely poetic, though?"

Back then, in that apartment, in that moment, I caught a glimpse of the real Robby Wicks and realized he, too, lacked compassion of any kind. A true predator, without compassion, who chased other predators, ran them to the ground, and killed them. That's what he'd meant. That's what I'd done naturally out on that freeway, did it the way Robby trained me to. I'd played by *his* cycle-of-life theory.

Without any compulsion, I tossed a kid out into traffic. I hated Robby Wicks and his simplistic explanation even if it did ring true and fit the circumstances. I had not wanted to be eaten and had acted on one of the most basic rules of the jungle.

Down on one knee, I put my arm around Sonja. She leaned into me. Her course gray hair smelled strongly of green apples and shook me with a nostalgia that took me back to a simpler time. Tears wet her face.

A lump rose in my throat. "Was he your son?" I asked in a quiet tone, in a voice I didn't recognize.

She froze. Slowly, she looked up at me, her face turning from sorrow to anger. With her hand, she shoved my face away. She struggled to her feet and ran for the office.

Bobby Ray anticipated her move. "No. No, Sonja, don't." He ran after her. In three long steps, I made it to the door and looked in. Sonja yanked on a file drawer and pulled out a Sig Sauer 9mm.

Bobby Ray tried to grab the gun. She fought him over it. "I'm gonna shoot those bastards. I'll gun some cops today, I swear I will. They'll be out there on the freeway working the crime scene. All bunched up. Easy targets. Come on, Bobby Ray, grow a set of balls, huh? This is Bosco we're talkin' about here. Our Bosco. Let's go do this."

Bobby Ray yanked the gun from her hands. Tears streamed down his face as well. He pulled back and slapped her so hard the sound made a crack in the small confines.

I stepped into the office, tugged his shoulder around, and slugged him full in the face. His arms windmilled. He fell across the desk and slid over, taking all the tabletop contents with him, including my two empty beer bottles.

Behind me, Monster's voice whispered, "Say good night, you abba-zaba."

He clubbed me with something.

CHAPTER THIRTY-SIX

I WOKE TO semi-darkness, my head throbbing in time with my heartbeat. Some things around me continued to bang and rattle. The scent of oil and gas hung thick and heavy down low at the floor level where I lay on my back, my hands and feet duct-taped. I kept my eyelids closed to mere slits until I figured out what happened, where I'd landed. My head ached something fierce with a pain that bleated bright colors behind my eyes.

I remembered everything, including the cowardly whack from behind by Monster. More important, though, I remembered the motivation—plenty of it—for the Visigoths to take me out to the desert and bury me in an anthill up to my neck.

I moved my head around just a little. More pain that brought on a little nausea.

Next to me sat the highly polished chrome spokes of a Harley Davidson motorcycle. Then I put it together. They'd trussed me up and thrown me into the back of the toy hauler, the one I'd seen parked out in front of Sonja's house, the fifth-wheel trailer hooked to the one-ton truck. On the inside, all the windows looked taped over.

"Hey, you? I kin see you're awake. I can see you movin' around."

I didn't need to see him. I recognized the voice, Monster. I craned my neck and looked, followed his voice up toward the front of the trailer. He sat at a small dining table, just a dark silhouette. His face glowed when he took a pull on his cigarette. The cherry tip popped and snapped. Cheap weed with stems and seeds, or maybe laced with bits of rock cocaine. Or more likely some crystal meth, the drug of choice for outlaw motorcycle gang members.

I played dumb. "What's goin' on? Why am I all taped up? Come on, man, cut me loose. This isn't funny."

He took another toke, not in any hurry as the truck towed us farther and farther away from Marie.

"You slugged the boss. I had my way, I'd take your sorry ass out ta the desert, cut your balls off, and let you bleed out."

"But you're not the boss," I said, "Bobby Ray is, and you'll do as you're told. What were you told?"

He took another long toke, the air in the confined trailer filled with the sweet scent of marijuana. He held in a big breath, letting the drug permeate his lungs, enter his bloodstream, take the edge off the job he'd been given to do. He flicked on a small table light, his face mangled with purple and red and swelled-up lumps from the beating Bobby Ray gave him with his fists. Like me, he'd want to transfer some of that pent-up aggression, and I fit the bill perfectly.

The light illuminated the small confines. The back end of the inside of the travel trailer was left open for hauling off-road vehicles. Framed pictures hung on the wall, pictures of Bosco, no more than a child, riding dirt bikes too big for him in the desert. One picture depicted Sonja and Bobby Ray and Bosco sitting in lawn chairs in that same desert under a shade attached to the trailer. All three smiled as if there were no tomorrow. And there was none, not for Bosco, not once I came into the picture.

Monster finally exhaled in a long, slow breath. His eyes squinted from the smoke as he pointed his doobie at me. "I think you know where we're goin'. For an abba-zabba, you're not as dumb as most of 'em."

"Let's pretend that I am and you go ahead and tell me anyway."

"Bobby Ray said you'd know, and that there wasn't any need to explain it all again. Said you'd know exactly what was goin' down."

I did, but I had a suicidal need to hear my fate spelled out for me. I said, "Well, I don't know what he wants. Why am I here in this trailer all tied up?"

He got up, flicked open a knife, and came at me with slow, deliberate steps. I could do nothing but watch him come. My adrenaline pumped, my pupils dilated, and my heart beat hard. Every detail of his boots, his dirty jeans, his denim cut, stood out. I didn't want this pig to be the last thing I ever saw. He smelled of body odor and marijuana and of an acrid chemical.

He leaned down over me, his body shading the light from the lamp. I tensed, waiting for the knife to slide into my body, slip under the skin, past the muscle and rib bones into my chest, to my lungs and heart.

He cut the tape binding my hands. "Hit ya too hard back there. Didn't want ya comin' around when I wasn't lookin' and have a big smoke like you jumpin' me when I wasn't ready."

He pulled a chrome derringer from his pocket, made sure I saw it, and handed me the knife. "Here, you can cut loose your own gorilla paws."

I took the knife and rolled to my side. The small confines rolled like a ship's deck, and I fought the urge to throw up all the beer. The bastard did hit me too hard. I cut my feet loose, the knife razor-sharp.

I stood on shaky legs, braced one arm on the counter for support, the freedom swelling in my chest. "Now where are we going?"

He held out his open hand. The other held the derringer pointed at my belly. "Gimme my knife."

I folded the knife and, looking him in the eye, shoved it down in my pants pocket.

"What? Am I gonna get ta shoot your dumb ass? Goodie. Now gimme the knife, I won't ask nice again."

The trailer continued to shimmy this way and that.

I walked up to him until the gun stuck right in my gut, my nose inches from his. "You shoot me, how're you gonna explain that to Bobby Ray? Now sit down over there and tell me where we're goin'."

He held his ground a second longer, a move his testosterone demanded, then backed up to the table with the half-circle couch around it. He sat at one end and I at the other. I wanted to close my eyes to help quell the nausea.

He let his hand rest on the table with the gun pointed at me. He'd have to pull the hammer back in order to fire it, so it couldn't go off accidently with the shimmy and bounce of the trailer.

He nodded. "That bag over there on the stove."

"Yeah."

"It's for you. Bobby Ray said you'd know how to handle it."

I got up and reached the short distance to the bag. Opened it. In the dim light from the small table lamp, the rolls of beat-up cash looked like about fifty thousand.

"Bobby Ray still wants me to make the payoff?"

"How the fuck do I know? They don't tell me shit. I don't know about any payoff. He just said give you the bag, drive you ta Compton, and let you off at Atlantic and Alondra."

"And?"

"Said to give you his wheels."

He pointed to the Harley Davidson I'd been lying next to.

"No one," he said with contempt, "and I mean no one's, ever rode Bobby Ray's hog. He's gone and lost a lotta juice with our crew over it, too. I'll tell you that much for sure. Lettin' some no-account smoke ride his bike. That's a bunch of buuullshit."

I still didn't understand. "What about Bosco? Why are we making the payoff if Bosco's dead?"

"Bosco ain't dead. He's banged up for sure, might not ever wake up again, either, but he ain't dead."

I sat down, stunned, as post-traumatic stress from the incident on the freeway played the whole thing over again in my injured head.

I watched the look in Bosco's eyes as I flipped him in the air—the long, yet too-short, span when he just floated in the air.

The way the car snatched him with a screech of tire and a thunk as his body hit solid metal and glass moving sixty miles an hour. Speed plus steel, versus flesh and bone—the body comes out a loser every time. How in the hell could Bosco have survived that?

CHAPTER THIRTY-SEVEN

THE FIFTH WHEEL trailer slowed, made a turn, and bumped. The rig came to a stop.

"Where do I take the money?"

"Ta the back of the old Sears, on Long Beach, in the parking lot." Monster checked his watch. "You got about ten minutes."

I picked up my stocking foot. "Shoes?"

"Whatta bunch of buuullshit this is. I ain't givin' ya mine. No way in hell, not for some smoke ta wear."

I got up and moved to the small bedroom section of the trailer and opened a closet. Inside the confined space, some men's clothes took up half and women's the other. I reached in and touched the blouses. Sonja's, for sure. Her bras and panties hung on a hanger as well. I didn't touch those. Couldn't if I wanted to. I no longer loved Sonja, but felt the need to protect her from the likes of Bobby Ray. The fact that he could corrupt such a good woman still wormed its way in, and with it came the anger that needed a vent.

I leaned back and looked at the king-sized bed that encompassed the entire upper birth—the overhang of the trailer. I shook off the image it conjured and reached down and grabbed the only shoes there, a pair of rattlesnake-skin cowboy boots.

I went back into the kitchen area, sat on the couch, and pulled the boots on. I wore size thirteen. Bobby Ray, well, he didn't. For someone so large, he didn't have a big foot. My toes didn't like it one bit, but there wasn't anything I could do about it. I stood and stomped my feet into them the rest of the way.

The back gate came down as Monster undid the nylon stays holding the bike upright. The young biker whom Bobby Ray had shaken until his teeth banged helped Monster roll the bike down the ramp to the asphalt parking lot. I grabbed the bag of money and followed.

The sun sat low in the sky, maybe four or five o'clock. Where had the day gone? Marie must think I'd gone off and taken care of The Sons all on my own, never to be seen again. I had thought about it. Get it over with and leave her out of it.

But it didn't work out that way. I'd convinced myself I needed to see Sonja first, see what she had to say, and then all hell had broken loose.

Now I stood in a parking lot in Lynwood wearing too-small snakeskin cowboy boots, about to mount a hog with a paper grocery bag of money on my lap. What the hell?

I walked over to the bike, my toes screaming for relief.

The bike, all chrome and fat tires, reflected the orange and yellow from the fading day. The gas tank, a true work of art, depicted Peter Fonda riding a Harley, with the wind in his hair, his sunglasses reflecting the image of someone riding beside him on another bike. Probably meant to be Dennis Hopper, but the image lacked enough detail to tell for sure. One of the nicest bikes I'd ever seen.

I'd ridden a bike for a short time in my misguided youth. Then I responded to three fatal bike accidents in one week, none of them the fault of the bike rider, and I gave it up for good.

I went up to Monster and held out my hand, much like he did when he wanted his knife back.

"What?"

"I need a gun goin' into something like this." He gave me a hard look.

"If I come outta this whole, enough to talk," I said, "you want me talkin' smack to Bobby Ray about how you didn't do what I asked?"

He reached into his pocket, pulled out the little gun, and slapped it into my hand. I checked the loads, snapped it shut, and stuck it in my waistband for easy access.

"Now," I said to him, "gimme your helmet."

"No way in hell am I lettin' you put your nappy head in my brain bucket. No. I won't do it. I don't care if you do rat me to Bobby Ray. I won't do it."

I turned and looked at the young biker, who stood by watching. He hesitated, then went to the truck. He came back with one of the small helmets that barely met DOT regs. Not much protection, but without it I stood a chance of getting pulled over for a helmet-law violation. I took it. Now I wore too-small boots and a dumb-assed helmet that hurt my head all the more.

I kick-started the bike, which roared to life. Monster shook his head and said over the rumble, "You look like one of those bike-ridin' chimps in the circus."

I'd had it with him. "After this is all over, you and I are gonna talk."

"Look forward to it."

I stuck it in gear and took off. The power of the bike almost got away from me. The handlebars jerked, stretched out my arms, and all but peeled my fingers from the grips. I zoomed out onto Atlantic, a little out of control. A white Ford van honked and swerved to avoid me.

I took Alondra west over to Long Beach Boulevard and turned north. If my feet hadn't hurt and the helmet hadn't been too small, I might've even enjoyed the ride.

* * *

After years of sitting vacant, the old red-brick Sears had been con-
verted into a daily flea market. Lots of cars cluttered the entrance.
Farther out, the parking lot sported cracked asphalt and tall weeds.
I parked in the weeds and put the kickstand down. I sat on the bike
and waited. My brain wanted to shut down and sleep. I fought the
urge.

After ten minutes, a light-blue Chevy lowrider with four
Hispanic gangbangers drove through the rear parking lot. I sat
on what would be a highly sought-after bike with a brown paper
grocery sack filled with fifty thousand dollars on my lap. I must've
looked like a guy with a dead goat tied around my neck in the
county zoo tiger cage.

They gave me the stink eye. I stared them down. They drove on.
I gave the odds fifty-fifty that they'd be back. I undid the blue bandana Bobby Ray had tied to the handlebars and tied it around my
neck. I pulled it up to cover my mouth. With the helmet, I'd be
hard to identify if I had to shoot someone trying to take my lunch
money.

A white van with tinted windows pulled up and parked by the
cluster of cars. Two minutes later, a white Lexus with limo-tint windows cruised through and went back out onto Long Beach and out
of view. Two more minutes and the Lexus pulled in again, this time
from the south, and drove right over to me.

No one got out.

From ten feet away, I stared into the reflective windows. The
driver's window came down four inches, not enough to see inside.
"Who are you?"

"I'm the guy with the bag of money."

"That's not your bike."

"Give the man a cigar. You want this money or not? I'm not gonna stick around."

The window went up. The Lexus engine kicked up in RPMs as the air conditioner pulled more juice.

I flipped out the kick-starter and stood to fire up the Harley. The driver shut off the Lexus. The door opened and out stepped a skinny man with ears too large for his elongated head. This wasn't an ATF agent. I knew this man. John Ahern, AKA "Jumbo," and he knew me. He hated me, wanted me dead.

CHAPTER THIRTY-EIGHT

I PULLED THE bandana up higher over my nose, like a bandit about to rob a stagecoach. "My orders are to give this money to a fed. You a fed?"

"That's right, boss, I am." He pulled out his wallet and flashed it like the feds did, too fast to get a name or agency. Only I'd caught a glimpse of it, saw the California driver's license he'd tried to pass off where the tiny fed badge should've been. The dumbass played it like a kid would.

He wore a white linen suit with a baby-blue silk shirt underneath, open at the neck with a gold necklace.

"You're no fed."

"I'm not here to play games with you, asshole," he said. "Gimme the money."

"Tell your friends in the van to come out. I'll give the money to you as long as they identify themselves as feds. I need to know who I'm dealing with."

Jumbo didn't flinch. "I ain't gonna fall for any of that old bullshit. You can do better than that. Ain't no one in no white van that has anything to do with us. Cut the crap and gimme the damn money."

Jumbo lost his smile and pulled a small .25 auto from his pants pocket, a no-account lady's gun. "Give me the money or—"

"Or what? Just what do you think you're gonna do, little man?" I put the kickstand back down and swung my leg over the bike, let the sack of money drop to the ground.

"I'm gonna cap your black ass, that's what. Whatta ya think of that, huh?" He started walking toward me, using up the last essence of his bluster and bluff.

"You don't have the balls for it, *Jumbo.*"

He froze.

"I know you?"

"Damn straight. Put that gun away before I take it from you and stick it up your ass."

"You gonna go hands-on against a gun? You'll lose, pal, garunfucking-teed."

"Tell me who you're working for. Who are you here to represent?"

I'd figured it out. Some fed had arrested Jumbo for one of his illicit dealings and flipped him, forced him to come pick up the money for him. The fed watched from the van. Jumbo never did menial work like picking up the money, not for his operations. He always sent his flunkies.

A few years ago I'd done some train heists for him that turned out to be financially beneficial for the both of us, although he cheated me out of my last payoff. We never liked each other, and if I revealed myself to him, he'd know I'd take great pleasure in squishing him like a bug under the too-small snakeskin cowboy boots.

"I don't have to tell you shit, Negro."

"You'll tell me by the time *I* get done with you, Dumbo." He hated to be called Dumbo.

"Who are you, damnit?"

I advanced on him. He raised the gun again. "Stop or I'll cap your ass, I swear I will."

I stopped. "I don't think so." I pulled down the bandana.

He hesitated, then squinted. He dropped the gun and swayed on his feet. He whispered, "My God, Bruno, The Bad Boy Johnson. I . . . I heard you were dead."

I quick-stepped over to him, grabbed him by the throat, and backed him right up to the Lexus. "Wishful thinking," I said in a harsh whisper right up by his ear. "Now tell me who you're working for."

He choked and gurgled. "McCarty, John McCarty. He's a gun fed."

"Where are you supposed to meet him after this deal?"

"Said he'd call me."

I let him go. He wilted to the ground, choking. He smudged the knees of his white linen suit.

I wanted to shoot him dead. He and Robby Wicks had killed Crazy Ned Bressler, stuffed him in a trunk of a car, and laid the whole thing off on me in a near perfect frame. Not that Ned didn't deserve it. Robby took his payoff with a bellyful of buckshot, close range, from my friend John Mack. I never thought I'd see Jumbo again and had put him out of my mind.

I picked him up and held him against the car. "Where's the two hundred and fifty thousand you owe me?" The anger rose inside me as I thought about what he'd done and what he'd tried to do.

"I got it, Bruno, I got it. When you want it?"

I hadn't been ready for him to roll over so quickly. His sudden shift in emotion, his eagerness to give away money, a character trait he'd never possessed, brought me out of the anger and back to my senses. I held him by the throat with one hand and, with the other, ripped open his shirt. He wore a microphone high on his chest. Wired for sound by the fed running his game, monitoring the deal. He didn't trust Jumbo.

Smart man, this John McCarty, if that was his real name.

I spoke for the fed's benefit.

"Deal was to hand the money directly to you in exchange for assurances. You can't give me any assurances from that van. You got sixty seconds to start up and get your ass over here or the deal's off."

I shoved Jumbo hard. He bounced off the Lexus and fell to the ground, further smudging his white linen. I counted in my head a slow sixty seconds. I picked up the .25 and tossed it to Jumbo. He didn't catch it or even try to. He let it fall to his chest. "I warned you about that little popgun the last time, out in the desert, remember? Next time you pull it on me, you better shoot me because that's what I'm going to do to you. Put one right between those big floppy ears."

I looked up at the white van, which hadn't moved. I saluted in that direction and said, "See ya next time, asshole."

I started for my bike, turned my back on Jumbo, and froze. I turned, went back to Jumbo, leaned over, and ripped off the wire. "You tellin' me true about the name of this fed? Tell me now. No one's listening."

"Sure, Bruno, of course I told you the truth."

I took out Monster's knife, flicked it open, and stuck the razor edge down by his crotch. "Tell me his name or I'm gonna give Little Jumbo a haircut."

"Okay, okay, it's Larry Gerber."

I pushed the knife in a little harder, not hard enough to puncture the material, enough though to put pressure on his little brain, the one that ran the body.

"I swear on my mother's eyes, it's Larry Gerber. Guys on the street call him Pike. He said he'd put me in prison forever if I told you his name."

"What's he got on you?"

"I bought a load of guns I was gonna trade up for some dope. The guy I bought them from was working off a case for Gerber. Hey, you wanna job? I'll pay ya to take this guy off the board, ten grand. Whattaya say, huh?"

"Here's my answer." I stood and kicked him hard in the ribs. I walked over to Bobby Ray's Harley, picked up the worn-out sack of money, and kick-started the bike. I took one last look at the van and zoomed off.

CHAPTER THIRTY-NINE

I PULLED UP to the front of the hotel, parallel to the valet stand, and revved the engine. The valet, a college-aged kid with curly black hair, came around from his stand and ran over. He took a step back and admired the bike. "What a nice ride. But, I'm sorry, sir, we don't valet-park bikes."

I reached into the brown paper bag and peeled off two one-hundred-dollar bills from one of the rolls of Bobby Ray's money. "I've had a long day," I said. "A bad day. One of those kinds of days that gives you nightmares for weeks. And I need a little break here. Can you help me out?" I handed him the money.

He started to shake his head until he saw the money wasn't ones or tens, or even twenties. He looked around furtively and said, "Sure, man, no problem." He snatched the money and made it disappear.

I climbed off and he climbed on.

"Park it someplace where it won't get messed with or scratched." I handed him another hundred. It wasn't my money.

He smiled and nodded. "No problem." He gunned the throttle, clicked it into gear, and took off. He'd ridden bikes before.

My feet throbbed in the too-small boots. My face still hurt from the fight in the freeway incident, and I had a lump on the back of my head the size of a dodo egg where Monster cold-cocked me. At least the feeling had returned to my fingers.

I limped into the hotel. I needed a hot bath, some hot food, and to snuggle up to my little sweet Marie.

In the elevator I pressed the button for the fourteenth floor. The doors closed, and I realized I'd walked right through the lobby without looking for Drago's added security, the two cops standing watch. I needed sleep more than anything else.

I reached in my back pocket for the room card key. Not there. I checked the other pockets. Not there. No room key. In all the excitement of the day, I'd either lost it or someone liberated it.

Monster.

If Monster had the room key—

A new dose of adrenaline hit and woke me up. The numbers over the elevator door somehow moved slower now.

Marie.

What if the Visigoths came and snatched up Marie, held her until the deal went down to make sure I didn't run off with the money? The crumpled bag of money tucked under my arm turned warm.

The doors finally opened. I ran down to the room and pounded on our door. "Marie?"

The door across the hall opposite ours opened. Drago stepped out and took hold of my shoulder with one paw. "You all right, man? Everything all right?"

"Yeah, yeah, how's Marie? She okay?"

"Yeah, I told ya she'd be fine and not to worry about her. You shouldn't'a run off like that, you scared the hell outta her. Jesus, man. What the hell happened to you? You look like someone took you through a meat grinder. You better sit down before you fall down."

"No, I'm good."

"No, you're not, man, no you're not. You shouldn't've of left me like that. I coulda backed your play. You wouldn't look like—"

The hotel room door opened. Marie rushed out and wrapped her arms around me, buried her face in my chest and wept.

Her love for me made a lump rise in my throat and tears well in my eyes. Somewhere along the way I'd transitioned from a hot-shit violent crimes detective into an overly emotional old man.

I handed Drago the bag of money. "Here, keep this safe for me, okay?"

"You got it, bud." He gently ushered us both into our room. "You two need some alone time." He backed out and closed the door. Marie had not let go. We stood there a long time, holding each other, swollen feet be damned.

"Bruno?"

"Yeah, babe?"

"Whose boots are those?"

"It's a long, ugly story that I might tell you about someday if you're very nice to me." I pulled her away enough to kiss her. And I did just like there was no tomorrow, a long, wet kiss we both got lost in.

We came up for air, her face wet with tears. She looked at me. She immediately lost her contented smile. "Bruno Johnson, what in the hell have you been up to?"

"Sweetie, please." I tried to usher her over to the bed to sit down. "These boots are killin' my dogs."

"No, come into the bathroom, let me get a better look at you." She took hold of my shirtsleeve and dragged me along. "Start talking, mister. Tell me everything that happened."

The memory I had difficulty locking away instantly brought me back to the freeway, brought me the image of Bosco flying overhead, the Honda snatching him out of midair, the look in his eyes.

His plea for me not to do it.

The image made me sick to my stomach.

I couldn't talk about it. Not yet. And I didn't want to lie to Marie.

She stood me in front of the sink in the bathroom and turned on the light. My mouth dropped open. I hadn't seen myself since it all started. I didn't recognize the person who looked back at me.

Marie went to work cleaning the abrasions on my face with a warm washcloth and soapy water.

"Start talking, mister."

"Marie, honey, I really need to get these boots off."

"Come over here, sit."

I did, on the edge of the bathtub. She tried to pull the boots off and couldn't. "Here," I said, "turn around and put the boot between your legs." She did. I put my other foot on her bottom and pushed. Nothing, not even an inch. My feet throbbed, my head throbbed, I had a rhythm going.

I leaned to the side and pulled the knife out of my pocket. "My feet swelled up and we're gonna have to cut 'em off." I tried to hand her the knife. When she didn't take it, I looked at her.

Her mouth hung open, her eyes wide. "My God, Bruno." She started to cry again. With shaking hands, she probed the dodo egg on my head. "We have to get you to the hospital, baby, and I mean right now. You have to have this X-rayed."

"No, we don't; no hospitals and you know why." She knew part of the reason, the warrants, but not the most recent.

She took my head in her arms, pulled my face into her breasts, and hugged me. Her body shook as she cried. She spoke in broken sentences. "Can you see okay . . . you're not . . . seeing double, are you? Are . . . are you nauseous?" She pulled me away from her chest and looked me in my eyes, checking my pupils, at the same time watching for the truth. "Did you lose consciousness?"

"No." I spit out the lie quick so she wouldn't spot it, and I felt like a heel doing it. We couldn't go to a hospital; they would report the injuries to the police, who'd be looking for the guy on the freeway who'd fled leaving bodies in his wake.

She waited a long moment for my eyes to give me away. When that didn't happen, she helped me up. "Come on, you're going to bed."

"Oh, thank you, babe, but I'm not feeling particularly amorous right now."

"You're not funny, Bruno Johnson. And I already told you once I don't like being lied to."

She'd seen right through me. I knew better and shouldn't have even tried it. She eased me down on the bed. She disappeared. The room door opened and closed. I fought to stay awake. The door opened again. She put a wet towel filled with ice on the knot at the side of my head.

Aah.

Someone took hold of my feet. I looked down.

Drago.

He tried to pull the boots off, and I only slid further down the bed. "Ow. Ow, hey!"

"They're not gonna come off," he said.

"I know that, Karl," Marie said. "Go ahead and cut them off."

"You sure? These are custom. We probably got two grand in boots here."

"Drago."

"Yes, ma'am."

Drago cut. The first boot came off. My foot screamed with delight. When the second one came off, the world closed in as my body decided, all on its own, that it was time to rest.

CHAPTER FORTY

BACK WHEN I worked as a Los Angeles County deputy sheriff and had a little girl to care for, Olivia, I needed extra money. I signed up for special-duty assignments on days off or after shift. I worked events at the Eagles Lodge, weddings, quinceañeras, birthday parties, that sort of thing. The job didn't require much brainpower, more just a security post so that no one got stupid. That didn't always work, though, on either side.

The night of the accident, I stood just inside the entrance to the Eagles Lodge, monitoring the people coming and going to a wedding reception. Henry Espinoza sauntered in wearing a black bowler and gray trench coat. He'd tattooed a big double-barreled shotgun on his neck, a symbol of his life's work that made him easy to recognize. I'd thrown him in jail a few times, chickenshit cases he pled to and got county time. I'd just wanted him off the street to cut down on the murders and mayhem.

He came into the hall, stopped, and gave me the stink eye. I returned it. People attending the wedding walked by. Henry shoved one guy into another guy, his eyes still on me. The fight started among them and quickly grew. A common prison tactic, he wanted a diversion to pull me into the melee in order to shank me in the kidneys or liver.

I took out my mace and sprayed it over the tops of all their heads, tear-gassed the whole mob, as I kept an eye on Henry. I'd arrest him for inciting a riot, put the hurt on him this time.

People screamed and tried to get away from the mace. Half the group, with Henry included, pushed out through the doors to the sidewalk. I followed. Henry saw me and ran west. I chased him down the sidewalk.

Behind me came a woman's scream. I turned in time to see a man, still rubbing his eyes from the mace, run blindly into the street. A car took him at full speed, forty-five or fifty miles an hour. He thudded hard and flew in the air in a cartwheel, up and over the car. He landed flat on his back twenty feet from where he'd started.

I'd caused him to run out into harm's way. My fault. I ran to him to render aid. I called for backup and an ambulance. I got to him and didn't know what more to do to help him. I flagged cars to go around him and took a piece of lumber chalk I kept in my pocket to mark tires at scenes of car accidents and drew an outline around his body.

I felt like hell.

I'd caused this.

I went back to directing traffic, not knowing what else to do. The sergeant arrived first. He parked his car blocking the road in front of the Eagles Lodge. He hurried up to me and said, "What the hell happened, Bruno?"

"It was terrible, Sarge. I maced Henry Espinoza and contaminated this other guy who ran out into traffic. He got hit. He's bad off."

"Where is he?"

I turned around. The street lay empty, with only the yellow chalk outline of where his body used to be.

Later that same night I tracked him down, patient John Cruz at St. Francis. Not one broken bone. He'd been so drunk, with all his muscles relaxed, that the impact only gave him soft tissue damage and no broken bones, this according to the doctor.

* * *

I came to in the hotel room, thinking about John Cruz and how he flipped over the top of that car and landed on the asphalt twenty feet back. Saw that empty yellow outline of his body again. I didn't think Bosco was drunk when I flipped him over and out into traffic. He would've been tense. I know I would've been.

Marie said, "Look, he's awake."

An Indian man I'd never seen before probed my cranium. Every muscle in my body ached. Marie and Drago stood at the end of the bed. The doctor put a light in each of my eyes and took it away, checking pupil reaction.

He stood and spoke to Marie with a faint British accent. "Based on my examination, and the symptoms you described, I would say he definitely has a concussion. To what degree, I do not know. I strongly recommend he seek regular medical attention at a hospital where he can receive X-rays."

"That's not going to happen, Doc." My voice croaked from lack of moisture.

"Bruno, shush."

"Barring that," the doc said, "I recommend bed rest for the next five days."

"Doc," I said, "if nothing's happened in however many hours since I got hit on the head, doesn't that count for something? I mean, if it was an intracranial bleed, wouldn't it have manifested itself by now?" I looked at Marie because I never talked like that. I'd stolen all of that medical-speak from her, the benefits of being married to a physician's assistant.

"Yes, that is probably true, but there is definitely an injury there, and you cannot injure it further if you are restricted to the bed until you can heal."

"I feel fine, Doc. All I needed was a couple of hours' sleep."

"Bruno," Marie said, "do you know what time it is?"

I looked out the window to the dark night. I'd rolled into the front of the hotel about six o'clock. "Eight or nine?"

The doc shrugged and didn't comment.

"Drago?" I asked.

"Yeah," Drago said, "he got that right, it's eight fifteen."

"See?" I said

"Bonehead," Marie said. "You've been asleep for twenty-four hours. That's why I had Drago bring in the doctor."

"Twenty-four hours?" I tried to jump up. The doc restrained me.

Marie pointed a loaded finger, angry now. "Bruno, you stay in bed or I'll have Drago tie you down. And you know I'll do it."

I eased back onto the pillow and nodded. I didn't know if I liked Marie having a bulldog like Drago available to do her bidding.

"He's my friend, too. I don't think he'd do that, would you, Drago?"

"Sorry, bud."

"So much for sticking together, huh?"

He shrugged and smiled.

Marie escorted the doc to the hotel door, where they spoke in low tones.

"Drago," I whispered, "gimme your cell."

He reached into his basketball shorts, pulled out his phone, and tossed it.

I dialed Sonja's number. She answered on the first ring and didn't say anything.

I said, "It's me. How's Bosco?"

"Same, thanks for askin'. Where's our money? How come you didn't turn it over to the fed? That was the deal and you screwed it up. He's already called and he's mad as hell." She sounded tired and angry.

"You know John Ahern, aka Jumbo?"

"Yeah, he's a little pinhead."

"But a dangerous pinhead."

"I'm not afraid of him," she said.

"He was the one who showed up in place of the fed."

"That little bastard. Why's he got his beak dipped in this?"

In the background, Bobby Ray said, "What is it?"

She put her hand over the phone, but I still heard her brief Bobby Ray.

"Sonja?" I said.

"Yeah?"

"Do you know the name of the ATF agent you were dealing with?"

"The guy who called and gave us the deal for the fifty large said his name was John McCarty."

"Yeah, that's what I thought."

"Whatta ya mean?"

"Jumbo fed me that name, too." I almost told her about Larry Gerber, but information is power and I needed to keep some on my side of the board.

"That little bastard." She put her hand over the phone and told Bobby Ray.

Bobby Ray took the phone from her. "Thanks, Bruno, for handling this for us. I don't know what's going on with Jumbo in the mix, but thanks for not givin' that money away."

"I got it here."

"I figured. What took you so long to call us? For a minute there I thought you might've skipped with our dough."

"No, you didn't."

"No, I didn't."

"I had a problem I had to deal with."

They hadn't found out about my involvement with the incident on the freeway, not yet anyway.

"I'm sorry about Bosco."

"Thanks. The doctor gives him a fifty-fifty chance of comin' out of it. That's better than last night when they told us to get his affairs in order. What a fucked-up way to tell someone their son is going to die."

"Yeah."

I didn't know what else to say. "Yeah"? What kind of reply was that? The guilt came on again and started to smother me. I again thought about John Cruz and how he just got up and walked away. That helped a little, helped me to imagine that Bosco could still pull through, wake up, and just climb out of that hospital bed. Yeah, and pigs could fly.

"Hey," Bobby Ray said, "how do you think we should handle this other problem with the ATF? I still wanna go forward with it. Bosco's going to come out of it, I know he is, and I don't want him going to a hospital ward in a prison."

"You got your hands full there at the hospital. Let me make a call, then I'll get back to you."

"Call who?"

"I'm not gonna say over the phone, but there is someone I can call who owes me a favor."

Dan Chulack, Senior Agent in Charge of the Los Angeles office of the FBI, no longer owed me. On our last phone call, he'd made it clear we were even and not to call him again, that if we ever met again, he'd be forced to arrest me for the outstanding federal warrants.

"Thanks, buddy," Bobby Ray said.

"No problem. I'll hang onto the money until I see you next."

"I'm not worried about the money, I trust you. Get back to me as soon as you can. I really need to get this thing resolved. And thanks again."

He clicked off.

He wouldn't thank me once the word got out about what happened out on that freeway. He wouldn't call me buddy anymore.

Marie came back into the room. "Give me that phone. You heard the doctor."

The phone in my hand rang. I held up one finger, begging for just one more minute. Bobby Ray forgot to tell me something and had just called back.

I answered it. "Yeah, Bobby?"

"Bruno, this is Dan Chulack, we need to talk."

CHAPTER FORTY-ONE

"How did you get this number?"

But I knew. The FBI had a wiretap on Bobby Ray's phone. He was president of the Visigoths. Of course they did.

Marie came around the bed and grabbed at the phone. I dodged her and said, "Babe, it's the FBI."

She froze. Fear filled her face. She looked to the hotel room door as if at any second it would come down under the force of a ram. She ran the short distance to the window and looked down at the street.

"It's okay," I said. "It's Dan."

"Dan Chulack? How'd he get Drago's number?" She ran back, crawled across the bed, and put her ear to the phone next to mine. Drago backed to the wall and looked on. He didn't like the sound of the letters FBI, and he had to be fighting the urge to do something. With him it was never flight, it was always fight. Right now he had nothing to fight, a dog without his bone.

Dan said, "You there, Bruno?"

"Yeah, good to hear from you, Dan. It's been a long time. How can I help you?"

"Not on the phone. I'll meet you across the street at the mall, by the train." He clicked off.

I swung my legs over the edge of the bed. The world swerved as it took a moderate curve around a long, slow bend. I put my hand to my head to steady my ship.

"No, you're not going anywhere. You heard what the doctor said."

"Sweetie, the FBI knows we're holed up in this hotel. If I don't go down there, they'll have no choice but to come kick down our door with a warrant. This was a courtesy call Dan just gave me."

"You mean, you think he's going to arrest you?"

I stood and went to the closet for some pants, a shirt, and my spare set of shoes. "No, if he intended to take me in, he would've just said to come down to the lobby. He wants something from me."

"What could he possibly want?"

"He wants a piece of Bobby Ray."

"Who's Bobby Ray?"

"The president of the Visigoths."

"Ah, Bruno, what have you gone and stuck your big nose into this time?"

I dressed, with one hand on the closet for support. I brought the shoes over, sat on the bed, and put them on. The swelling in my feet still hadn't subsided, and my own shoes squeezed my dogs.

"Hey," I said, "you told me you didn't think my nose was all that large."

"Bruno?"

"Kid," I said to her, "really, I was just mindin' my own business."

That's what I'd always say when I was telling her a story from my past just before the shit got heavy.

"Riiight, minding your own business always includes you shooting someone or running them over."

"Really, what you must think of me."

I probably never should've told her those stories. They occurred so long ago they seemed like they happened to someone else. And more important, I wasn't that person anymore, not by a long shot.

"I'm going with you," she said.

"Me, too," Drago said. He had been standing quietly off to the side watching our interaction. The relationship between Marie and me, for some reason, intrigued him.

My head throbbed, and I didn't have the gumption left to argue. "Okay, stay way back, though. He knows who you are, what you guys look like, and I don't know if he's gonna be alone. I don't want whoever he's with to get a good look at you."

Marie ran to the closet, grabbed some clothes, and ran to the bathroom. I sat on the bed to wait the twenty or thirty minutes she'd just doomed us to. Dan wouldn't be happy.

"What's goin' on?" Drago asked.

"I'm married, that's what's goin' on."

He nodded with a dumb look on his mug, as if he understood. He didn't understand.

* * *

In the hotel lobby, I told my two shadows to wait five minutes and then follow. Drago went to two men who looked like cops dressed down in civilian clothes and quietly spoke with them.

Outside, I walked with my hand in my pockets, watching the street for a tail. I still hadn't told Marie about what happened on the freeway. Didn't have a chance to. Least that's what I told myself. After the incident happened, that's all I'd wanted to do. Now the shame of it kept the secret hidden a little longer and made it more difficult by the minute to bring it out to the light of day. I guess I didn't want her to think poorly of me.

I walked into the open quad area of the crowded upscale mall, home to high-dollar retail stores. A little train made its way around the inside perimeter with children and adults alike onboard. Among the smiling, happy faces, I spotted Supervising Special Agent in Charge Dan Chulack on a bench by the train station. He was alone, eating a large soft pretzel with mustard. The sight of the food made my stomach growl. When had I last slowed down long enough to eat? I stopped at the pretzel cart and purchased one along with an orange soda.

I sat next to him. He wore khaki pants, a salmon-colored collared shirt, and penny loafers. I'd never realized Dan's fashion sense remained stuck in the seventies. Even so, he still fit in nicely. I didn't detect a hidden gun, so he must have agents out and about backing his play. I couldn't see his eyes through his designer sunglasses.

"Good seeing you, Bruno. What happened to you? You grab onto a tiger's tail again?"

I took a bite and chewed, ignored his comment, took a drink of soda. The orange bubbles eased the nausea in my stomach, a little. The sugar gave me the rush I needed. "What's goin' on, Dan?"

"You kind of stumbled into our high-profile investigation, that's what's going on."

"That right?"

"That's right."

We both chewed our pretzels and people-watched for a moment.

Drago and Marie went into a store close by that sold only purses. An entire store that just sold purses. I hoped Drago didn't tell her about the bag of money.

Drago stood out like a blimp among toy balloons. Security had already keyed on him as trouble. Two uniformed security guards stood by a decorative light post, watching him through the store window, ready to pounce. They just didn't realize that if it came to pouncing, they'd need four or five more beefy dudes if they wanted to have any chance at all.

"What investigation is that, Dan?"

He got up. "Let's walk." He wadded up his wrapper and headed to a trash can. I followed, still eating.

We walked the perimeter along the train rail and among the shoppers going about their business. A weekday. Didn't anyone work for a living anymore?

Dan finally spoke. "You know I can't tell you about it."

"Then what am I doing here?"

He stopped and gave me the mirrored-sunglasses routine. "But that's exactly what I want *you* to tell me. What the hell are you doing here?"

"We can play this stupid game all day. Or I show you mine, you show me yours."

He didn't smile. He just looked away, thinking about it, and after a moment nodded. "Okay, some of it, but not all of it."

I chuckled. "What, this about national security or some shit like that?"

He looked back at me, took his sunglasses off.

I said, "Ah, shit."

CHAPTER FORTY-TWO

I KNEW DAN Chulack to be a man of his word. Especially when talking business. At the next trash can, I tossed the remains of my pretzel and kept the soda. I'd lost my appetite. What the hell *had I* stuck my big nose into?

He didn't say anything and waited for me to tell it.

"They came for me," I said. "That's why I'm here."

He stopped. "Who did?"

"The Sons. They pulled one of our children out of his regular routine and wrote with indelible ink on his back. Wrote their phone number with two lightening bolt S's."

"Those sons of bitches." Dan Chulack never swore and he hated tyranny more than anyone I knew. "Why didn't you come to me?"

"What could you do? Legally, I mean. We're all the way down in Costa Rica. I'm wanted on federal fugitive warrants."

He said nothing. He knew about Costa Rica and the warrants.

I continued. "The Sons want to get even for what I did to their clubhouse and . . ." I didn't need to continue. He knew all about that, too. It had been his search warrant.

He'd been promoted out of the success of that bust that we . . . that he made. And he'd continue to ride that wave the rest of his career, known throughout the Bureau as the man who took down The Sons of Satan.

The Sons couldn't go after Dan and his FBI. They did the next best thing—they came after me and my family.

"I needed to come back here to the States," I said, "and make sure they got what they wanted, make sure they don't come after my family again."

"What are you going to do?" He lowered his tone, one of genuine concern.

"I don't have a solid plan. Drago over there"—Marie and Drago followed along thirty or forty feet behind us, trying to blend in and failing miserably. "Drago wants to start a little program he calls Crimes Against The Sons, until they yell 'uncle.'"

"Yes, with him along you might have a chance of making that work."

I nodded. I looked again, double-checked to make sure Marie wasn't sporting a new three-thousand-dollar purse on her arm.

We walked some more.

"Then what do you have to do with Bobby Ray and his group?" he asked.

"Independent of The Sons issue, Sonja called me, said she needed to see me, said it was real important."

"Sonja Kowalski?"

"That's right. Why? You working her?"

"How do you know her . . . Oh, you both worked Lynwood back in the day."

"That's right," I said. He'd ignored the question about working her as an informant.

He'd done his homework on Sonja. "You watchin' her, too?"

He didn't answer that question either but asked his own instead. "That thing with Jumbo, tell me about it."

"You have a tap on Bobby Ray's phone, that's how you got on to me, right?"

"Yes."

We stopped again. I said, "Bobby Ray's son, Bosco, got picked up on a gun charge by ATF."

Dan pulled out his phone and started typing, probably asking someone on his team to verify Bosco's arrest.

If Dan's team had been watching Bobby Ray's operation, then how come he didn't know Bosco had been picked up on a gun charge?

"This same agent who popped Bosco," I said, "approached Bobby Ray and told him he could make the case disappear for fifty K."

He stopped typing. "And that was this McCarty you were talking about with Bobby Ray just a little while ago?"

"That's right, but I think the name McCarty is just a ruse thrown out there to mislead the investigation. Bobby Ray and Sonja wanted me to make the drop with the fifty K and talk to the agent. I also think that they wanted me to make the agent disappear, but I wasn't going to do that. I just wanted to identify him, see what he was all about."

He nodded, his attention on a new text message that had just come back. "There is an ATF agent name McCarty, but he's not involved in this in any way."

I didn't know how he'd found that out so quickly. "Okay," I said, "now I guess it's time to trade the big stuff. You're just gonna have to trust me on this one."

"You have more?" he asked.

"One more thing."

I had the name Larry Gerber that Jumbo gave me, and I held it back to see what Dan would give me in return.

"Bruno."

"Did I steer you wrong last time? Tell me what you have, and I promise I'll give you what I got. And you know I won't tell a soul."

Dan looked around to see if anyone stood close enough to hear. I'd never seen him act like this. I sensed his fear, and it scared the living hell out of me.

"Two weeks ago, four Hellfire missiles were stolen from March Air Force Base."

He let me think about that for a minute. "That's not a big deal," I said. "If I remember from the briefings, those can't be fired without the weapons system and the software. The software's the only thing that can fire them. It's like a failsafe, right?"

He didn't say anything.

"Ah, man, you're kiddin' me."

"A month and a half ago, no, two months now, a fully outfitted tactical military drone was taken from a lowboy train car in Barstow on its way to March Air Force Base. We can't figure out how they did it." He lowered his voice almost to a whisper. "With that drone and its software, they could fly below most radar, fire on the White House, create havoc on Wall Street, blow Hoover Dam, the presidential motorcade, the list goes on and on. We could never prepare a defense for it, not if they're smart about it. We have to get it back."

My turn to look away as my mind raced.

Dan read my expression. "What? What?"

"And you don't have a clue who has the drone?"

"No. Bobby Ray has been selling arms across the border to the cartel. There's huge money in it. He's laundering his money through his custom motorcycle shop. We know that and haven't been able to nail him yet. He's too smart. We think Sonja's law enforcement experience, her cool head, is keeping him out of prison.

"We developed information that an Arab, going through the cartel, is about to pay four million for the drone and a million apiece for the Hellfire missiles. Word came through a third party that Bobby Ray Kilburn was going to be the middleman in the deal.

That's why we have a wire up on Bobby Ray. But like I said, he's smart. He hasn't tripped up yet, and we're coming down to the zero hour when they're going to make the deal. That's all of it, and my ass is now hung out a mile, so give. What do you have?"

"I know who has your drone."

Dan grabbed my arm and spun me around. I thought he might kiss me.

CHAPTER FORTY-THREE

"Bruno, you help get me the drone back and I promise you the FBI will join you in that little game of crimes against The Sons, and they will wish they'd never heard your name. Tell me."

"On the phone tap, you heard me mention Jumbo?"

"That's right, John Ahern. We did a quick work-up on him. He's into dope: coke and meth. Midlevel stuff, trying to break into the bigs, but he doesn't have the brainpower or the muscle to do it. We couldn't find any affiliation with Bobby Ray or any thefts in his background. None. Especially large, organized thefts like the one it took to grab a drone of that size, take it right off a moving train."

"Put a team on Jumbo, twenty-four-seven."

Dan went back to typing rapidly on his phone as he spoke. "Why? Talk to me."

"Two, almost three years ago, I did train heists for Jumbo. Several of them."

Dan looked up from his typing and whispered, "You're kidding me. That's good, real good."

I nodded.

Dan gave up on the typing and dialed. "Listen," he said as soon as someone answered, "I want to make this very clear. Pull Team Alpha and Baker off their targets and put them full-time on the target I just sent you in the text message. Tell the team leaders if they lose the target to go ahead and pack their bags, they'll be on a midnight transfer to North Dakota. That's right. Yes. Also, I want wiretaps on him with a pen register and a trap and trace. I'm on my way in with the probable cause for the wiretaps."

He looked at me when he hung up. "You're sure, Bruno?"

"Remember that train heist a few years ago, the entire train car loaded with computer chips?"

"That was this guy?"

I nodded. "He planned it, and I executed it for him."

"Beautiful. You're right, it's got to be him. Though I can't believe a pinhead like that has the brainpower."

"Wait, that's not all of it. That heist went down on the grade just outside of Barstow."

He shook his head in wonder. "Yes, yes, I agree with you, this has got to be our guy. But what does the ATF agent have to do with it? And if Jumbo took the drone for Bobby Ray, why was Jumbo making the pickup for the fifty-thousand-dollar payoff?"

I shrugged. "Jumbo told me that he got popped trading some guns for dope and was working the case off. That is, if he's tellin' the truth. But you're right, it doesn't make sense. I want to talk to Jumbo again."

"Not with McCarty," Dan said. "He's a straight shooter, and we checked into him. He's not involved." Dan glossed right over my comment about talking to Jumbo. I could get more out of Jumbo than Dan could. I didn't have to follow the Miranda decision and read him his rights or play nice.

"Try the name Larry Gerber," I said. "Put another couple of teams on an agent named Larry Gerber."

He typed some more notes into his phone as he said, "I've had the whole damn LA office working on this for the better part of two months and we get zip. You roll into town and in one day you—" He stopped abruptly and instead said, "Hey, I know it's asking a lot, but I need you to stay with this thing, get close to Bobby Ray."

He waited for me to agree to do it. I couldn't, not with a baby on the way. It would be irresponsible and unfair to Marie.

When I didn't say yes, he continued. "Bobby Ray's too savvy to tail. He does countersurveillance all the time, even on days we're not on him. And he's good at it. Once he makes one of us on his tail, he just shuts down for the day and tries again later."

Dan had just made another slip, a small one. How could he know Bobby Ray did countersurveillance even on days the FBI wasn't up on him unless he had someone on the inside of the Goths?

"You Lojack his car or bike?" I asked.

"Won't do any good, he never drives the same vehicle. He'll pull eight cars with tinted windows into that factory of his, close the doors, open them ten minutes later, and have them all leave at once. He really knows what he's doing. From the conversation I heard this morning, it sounds like you're in tight with him already, at least for right now anyway."

I again caught something in his tone. "What?" I asked. "What's goin' on?" My paranoia continued to eat away at me. Paranoia and guilt are not great bedfellows.

He didn't answer the question. He took a smartphone out of his pocket and said, "Here, use this to contact me anytime day or night."

I didn't take it. "I haven't said I'd do it yet. I can't, not now, not right now."

The *yet* part of me must've given him his true answer. He continued as if I'd already said yes. "This phone's all set up to look like a regular phone, with contacts, apps, previous calls, the whole thing. I can also track where you go. If you get in over your head, there's a panic button right here on the side." He pointed to it. "Press it down once, let off, then press it a second time and hold it for ten seconds. But only do it in dire circumstances, because I'll be rolling in hot with two teams to pull you out. We don't want to burn this op too soon, not unless we absolutely have to. I don't need to tell you how important this is."

"I guess it won't do any good to say it again, I don't wanna do it."

He didn't answer. He just gave me the Dan Chulack look that said you don't want to mess with the FBI.

CHAPTER FORTY-FOUR

"ALL RIGHT. ALL right," I said. "Marie's not gonna like this one damn bit. I'm gonna have to lay the whole thing off on you."

He smiled. "Go ahead." Then he grew serious again. "I'm sorry about this, Bruno, but this operation is too important. There's a lot at stake here."

Yeah, but I was the one with the most skin in the game, not him. I wanted to throw down the pregnancy card, but that wouldn't have been right.

"I said all right." I held up the phone he'd given me. "But this idea won't work at all. They're not dumb; they'll just pull the battery."

"Let them. In fact, do it yourself, show them so they won't take the phone from you. With this phone, there's a secondary GPS with an independent power supply. All you have to do is find out when the trade is going down—the money for the drone and the Hellfires—that's it. Then you get that info to me. We'll handle the rest."

"Really, that's it? That's all?" He didn't bite on my sarcasm.

My mind spun trying to figure a way out of this mess. What choice did I have?

None.

Right at that moment, all I wanted to do was lie down and go to sleep. Sleep for another two or three days with Marie snuggled up beside me.

The sun seemed brighter than I ever remember it being, and I had to continually focus to keep the contents of my stomach down, the pretzel and orange soda no longer my friends.

He didn't mention Disneyland, the largest soft target in the Western States. Everyone in law enforcement stepped easy around that one. If you didn't talk about it, maybe it wouldn't happen.

All those children visiting. The happiest place on earth.

What would four Hellfire missiles do to a crowded theme park? The symbolism—and worse, the exposure of America's vulnerability—would strike terror in every household for a generation. No, I truly didn't have any choice, not this time.

I started to walk away.

"Bruno?"

I stopped and turned, no more than five feet from him.

He lowered his tone as he closed the gap between us. "There's video of you."

"What are you talking about?"

"The CHP patrol unit shot video; a unit cam was running during the whole incident. The cop was wired with a microphone linked to the camera, got the whole thing."

My knees went weak. I swayed and might've fallen if Dan hadn't grabbed hold of my arm. "Steady, pal." I thought I had a little more time before the investigators processed the scene for trace evidence and the fingerprints I left behind.

My mouth hung open as I nodded. "Okay." I didn't know what else to say as I worked through the shock of it.

My dirty little secret wasn't a secret anymore. Dan knew and hadn't said anything right up front when we'd started our conversation. He knew exactly how this information would impact what I had to do—infiltrate the Visigoths. He held this card to throw right at the last, after I'd already agreed to do his little blackbag job. I'd been manipulated by a pro and didn't like it, not from someone who I thought of as honest and loyal, a friend. He had been all of those things, just not to me but to his job. I tried to think if I'd been that ruthless back when I worked with informants. I hadn't, not even close. What Dan did, the way he withheld vital information concerning the operation until he got what he wanted, mirrored exactly what Robby Wicks would've done. I liked Dan a little less for it.

I didn't have any argument left in me and resigned myself to just getting the thing done so we could go home.

"How's the cop doing?" I asked.

"She made it. She's going to be okay."

"Good, that's good." I swallowed hard. "What's her name?"

I didn't know why I had a need to know that. Maybe putting a name to her face would help a little with the guilt over the kid getting tossed out into traffic.

"Clevenger, Kris Clevenger. Her husband is a member of LA County Sheriff's prison gang task force."

I nodded, let that sink in a little. "Have I been identified yet, I mean by anybody but you?"

"No, but it's just a matter of time. Clevenger's husband has a lot of juice, and I can't imagine him being deterred too long. The CHP made copies and was going to send it around to every law enforcement agency in Southern California to try and identify you. They know you're an ex-cop by the way you handled yourself."

"Damn, why are they even looking? I didn't break any laws."

"You know why, for their investigation. They need a statement to wrap it up nice and tight. Come on, think about it, you shot and killed someone. So, of course, they'd need your statement."

"That shooting was absolutely justified."

He held up his hands. "No question about it." He hesitated, and then said, "There's something else."

"What? What else could there be?"

"They want to thank you."

"They'll wanna thank me, alright, until they find out who I am. Then they'll throw my sorry ass in prison for the rest of my life. I didn't get involved with that whole mess so someone could thank me."

The irony of the entire situation—standing next to an FBI agent while I had a load of warrants in the system, my wanted poster in every post office in the U.S., and me worrying about being outed—wasn't lost on me.

I thought about it for a second more and then said, "You know how that hangs me out on this thing, if any of the Visigoths see the video? They'll plant my ass in the desert. And you and I both know it's not a matter of if, it's a matter of when that video gets leaked."

"I know. And I know this is an understatement, but I'll say it anyway. You're going to have to be careful. And you're going to have to work fast."

"Understatement? You're sending me into the lion's cage without even a chair or a whip. Can you at least put a lid on this video by declaring it a matter of national security? Delay it a little, keep it from going public at least faster than it would normally? If it goes public, your op is blown, too."

"I did put a lid on it as best I could, but like you said, it is going to go public no matter how hard we try, so you have to push this exchange with Bobby Ray and the Arab, make it happen, and get out as soon as you can."

Another tick against him. He'd suppressed the video before he even asked me to help him. He knew me. He'd known up front that I'd do it. What kind of chump was I?

"I'll do what I can," I said.

"I know you will, Bruno."

I again turned to leave, more disheartened than before I met with him.

"Hey," he said, "that was a hell of a thing you did. I saw the tape. You stuck your neck out when you didn't have to, when you had everything in the world to lose."

CHAPTER FORTY-FIVE

I WATCHED DAN walk off. I let my mind chew on all the implications, the odds of success. They weren't good, not by a damn sight. I might've been able to pull it off had there not been the video. The video upped the chances of failure tenfold.

How many times had video leaked out in the past? The more concise question: How many times, if any, had a video of major media interest *not* leaked? Somebody in the know in the law enforcement circle, someone with a skewed moral compass, would eventually put it out, sell it to the highest bidder in the media. And if caught, they'd always have a fall-back excuse, the First Amendment, the public had a right to know. Of course they did. That same public also had the right to be blown to hell with drone missiles.

Marie came up behind me and took my hand—hers hot, mine cold. "You feelin' okay?" She leaned her head against me. We both watched Dan disappear into the parking garage.

"Come on," I said. "Let's get back to the room. I need a shower."

We walked back, my arm around her waist. I didn't know where the next twenty-four hours would find us, a fear of the unknown worse than most.

Drago stayed a few steps behind. I tried to work the problem out: how best to force the issue. To make the trade go down right away and at the same time keep my skin. That was my only chance, to make it happen now, not later. I didn't have all the pieces yet, who the players were, who was the middleman, who had the drone and where. The *where* being the big one. If I knew the *where*, we could all go home. I stopped. "Drago, let me use your phone." I didn't want to use the one Dan had given me. They'd for sure be up on that one, listening.

"Sure, bud." He handed me the phone.

I dialed Salvador's number in Costa Rica and continued walking back to the hotel.

He answered right away. "*Bueno, mi amigo.*"

"Salvador, how are things in your country?"

"Everything is fine here, *muy bueno*. It is a beautiful day. You need not worry about anything here. Take your time on your vacation, *señor.*"

"Thank you, my friend."

"I told you this was not going to be a problem at all."

"What about that little issue we had in town with those visitors?"

"There is no longer an issue. Those visitors will never visit this country again."

"Is that right?"

"Yes, they did not enjoy their stay here. They went out sport fishing on a boat."

"Too bad Jose Rivera doesn't have a passport. I could use his public relations talent right about now."

"I am sorry you have not yet resolved your problems there. But as I said, you do not have to worry about anything on this end."

"Thank you, Salvador, that means more to me than you know. Be safe. *Hasta la vista.*"

"*Vaya con Dios, amigo.*"

I hung up and handed the phone back to Drago. Marie heard my end of the conversation and squeezed my hand. I stopped in the shade of the building on the sidewalk along the side of the hotel.

Both Marie and Drago had a right to know the score and the seriousness of the problem.

"Here's the deal," I said. "Someone's stolen four Hellfire missiles and a military drone that fires them. There's going to be a meet and a trade, money for the arms. Dan wants me to find out when and where."

I watched Marie, expecting her to be stunned. She didn't show any emotion at all. I knew her well enough; she was doing a slow burn on the inside. She said, "And this has to do with the Visigoths' president, Bobby Ray?"

"Yes."

She waved her finger. "And this has nothing to do with the problem we came here for in the first place, The Sons of Satan, right?"

"Sort of. Kind of. We did come here to talk with Sonja—"

She turned angry and pointed her finger at me. "No, *you* came here to talk with Sonja. I told you we shouldn't have anything to do with her. That bitch. Anyone who'd dump a child off on the father and never look back doesn't deserve anything from us."

I didn't want to argue with her, especially when she held all the cards. I didn't know why it always happened that way, her holding all the aces, me a measly pair of deuces.

"I understand your anger," I said, "but I'm in this now, boxed in but good, and there just isn't any way I can back out and still be able to live with myself."

She just stared at me, fuming.

Drago, who stood off to the side, said, "You find these things, these hell missiles, and you're done, is that right?"

"That's right."

Oh, thank you, big man, for coming to the rescue.

He shrugged. "Shouldn't be a problem at all, not really. I'll go along and make sure he stays out of trouble. Okay, how's that?"

She flung her hand in the air. "What then, we start all over dealing with the problem with The Sons, the reason we came here to begin with?"

"Dan said, we help him with this, he'll make sure that our problem with The Sons goes away. We have his word."

Drago said again, "So we work out this one problem, then we're done."

She spun on him. "Don't you try and get Bruno out of the dog house. He's going to be there a long time. A very long time." She took off walking at a faster pace.

We caught up with her. No one spoke. We went through the lobby. The two off-duty cops talked among themselves, not looking at us. When we stepped into the elevator, Drago said, "What are we going to do first?"

"Sonja's son, Bosco, got hurt." I said. "He's in the hospital in grave condition." I used another term I'd learned from Marie, *grave*. I never realized until right at that moment the double meaning that the word carried.

Marie stuck her arm out and stopped the elevator doors from closing. "Ah, shit, why didn't you tell me that earlier, before I called Sonja a bitch? Come on, let's go."

"Where we goin'?" I asked.

"To see your ex-girlfriend Sonja at the hospital, you big oaf."

CHAPTER FORTY-SIX

LOMA LINDA UNIVERSITY Medical Center, in the city of Loma Linda, looked like a huge sprawling campus with multiple buildings scattered and intermingled among large trees and separated by vast parking lots loaded with a sea of cars. It took us a while to locate the wing that Bosco was in.

Down the long hall we walked by a closed door with a uniform from the Montclair Police Department sitting in a chair next to it, a rookie with a young face sitting guard duty on Bosco's room. A procedural move only, as there was no way Bosco could escape in his condition.

If Bosco survived, he'd be arrested for assault on a peace officer. And if the DA really wanted to get shitty, they'd file the felony murder rule. Someone had died during the commission of a felony: Ol' Hector, the guy I shot. Which opened up Bosco to a long stint, if not life in San Q as a murderer.

Sonja chased a toddler around a waiting area the size of a small living room at the end of that same long, starkly white hall. A television mounted up in the corner of the waiting area played the local news, the sound turned off. I made a conscious effort to pull my eyes from it.

Halfway down the hall, Sonja spotted us. She stopped, put her hand on her back like an old woman, and stood upright.

I didn't know what would happen when Marie and Sonja met. I'd never been in a similar situation and didn't know what to expect. They both possessed strong-willed personalities. I'd fretted about it the entire forty-minute drive from LA.

Sonja watched us approach as the toddler continued to paw Sonja's legs and whine, wanting to be picked up.

I held my breath as we closed on the last ten feet.

Marie went right up to Sonja and hugged her. Marie said, "I'm so sorry. Bruno told me what happened."

Except I hadn't. I hadn't told her anything about how Bosco came to be in the hospital, just that he'd been hurt. I looked at Drago to see if he was as stunned as I was at this form of greeting from these two women. What the hell?

Sonja nodded, her expression one of sorrow. Her face was lined with worry, making her look much older. "Thank you."

They looked at each other, eyes probing eyes for answers to questions I couldn't hear. And I really needed to. Women possess that eerie ability of nonverbal communication that drives men nuts.

Monster and Bobby Ray stood from their chairs and came over. Monster went right up to Drago and checked him out like some kind of dog sniffing another. Drago looked and acted like an outlaw biker. Neither spoke.

Sonja, without a word, picked up the toddler, with curly red hair and freckles, and handed him to me. The child belonged to Bosco and was Sonja's grandchild. Holding him inflamed my shame, increased my guilt tenfold.

Sonja took Marie by the arm and guided her to the chairs. They sat and spoke in quiet tones like a couple of long-lost sisters.

What had I been worried about with those two? I let out a sigh of relief and took a step closer, pricking my ears, and still couldn't hear what they said.

Bobby Ray stuck out his hands. "Here, let me take him. He's a real handful."

"No, it's cool, I got him."

The rambunctious child patted my head with one hand while he grabbed my nose with the other and pulled hard. Man, the little guy had a grip. He'd be a baseball player some day, a pitcher maybe.

He had hazel eyes like Sonja. I really couldn't see any traits passed on from Bobby Ray.

The kid could easily star in baby food commercials with his smile and cute little giggle. Or did they call it a gurgle?

Then the ugly thought weaseled in: What chance did this kid have growing up in an outlaw biker environment? Would he grow up and act just as Bosco had? Of course he would.

I looked up and checked the news again. I found myself doing it too often, waiting for that hammer to fall.

Bobby Ray said, "What are you doing here, Bruno?"

That same shame wouldn't let me meet his eyes, and I fought the urge to tell him the terrible secret I now kept suppressed, shoved down deep and festering in my gut, making me ill.

Or it could've been the concussion causing the nausea. Sure, that's what I wanted to believe.

"Just coming to pay my respects. Is he doing any better?"

Bobby Ray spoke through gritted teeth. "You know how the damn doctors are. They charge you out the ass in order to pay for their mansions and two-hundred-thousand-dollar sports cars. They don't give a damn about anything else as long as they get their money. They're the real cause of our health care crisis in this country, with their bullshit exorbitant wages. In countries where health care really works, doctors don't get paid like that."

I nodded as if I agreed with his off-the-wall rant. I didn't know what to say or do.

Outlaw bikers, as a rule, don't carry medical insurance, and Bosco's stay would cost Bobby Ray upwards of half a mil.

"Here," he said, "lemme have junior."

I didn't have time to answer before he took the kid from me. I loved kids, but an emotional weight lifted off me when Bobby Ray took this one out of my arms. He walked over and dropped him off in Sonja's lap. Sonja didn't even notice. She just accepted him and kept on talking to Marie.

What the hell did they have to talk about? I only caught my name tossed around here and there by the both of them, as they each occasionally looked my way. Man, I wanted to hear what they were saying.

Bobby Ray grabbed my arm and tugged me down the hall out of earshot of everyone.

Drago and Monster still had not said a word to each other, two yard dogs sizing each other up, deciding who'd be the alpha dog if it came to blows. Good thing I hadn't told Drago that Monster had been the one to whack me on the back of the head. Drago would've already ripped Monster's arms off his torso and beaten him with them.

"Now that you're here," Bobby Ray said, "maybe you would do me another favor?"

"Sure, whatever I can do to help."

I didn't need to stay in good with Bobby Ray as Special Agent Dan asked. Instead, for some insane reason, some crazy twist of fate, Bobby Ray wanted to stay in good with me.

"Can you get with this Jumbo asshole and find out what his game is? Why he's involved in this thing with that fed?"

"No problem. How do you know Jumbo? You done deals with him before?"

Bobby Ray's head moved back a little and his mouth went to a slit. "What's it to you?"

"Oh, hey, I was just askin' 'cause I know Jumbo. He isn't going to give me shit unless I put the hurt on him. And I didn't wanna do that if you got some kinda relationship with him, you know what I mean?"

"Yeah, right, I see what your sayin'. No, you can put the punk's nuts in a grinder for all I care. Just get that money into the right hands and get that fed off my back. I don't need to be worrying about Bosco getting thrown in the can, not for those guns, not when I got all this other heavy shit goin' down."

"I can do that."

"I'll owe you big. Thanks, pal."

If Bobby Ray did do the train job and took down the military drone with Jumbo, he didn't so much as twitch at the lie.

I swallowed hard and asked, "What about the cop outside his door? They going to file charges on Bosco for what happened out there on the freeway?"

"Nah, I'm not worried about that. The cops just went off on my people without any provocation at all. My guys were minding their own business. Some detective in plain clothes came up and started all the shit. When I find out who this guy is, I'm gonna pay him a visit, personal like.

"Dirk said this guy tossed my Bosco right out into traffic. You believe that shit? Right out in traffic like he was a piece of garbage or something. Cops got rules. They're not supposed to act that way. I'll fix him, you wait and see if I don't."

I again fought the urge to look back at the television. I started to sweat.

Bobby Ray didn't know about the video, the irrefutable physical evidence that would hang Bosco, send him to the Q for life. If he lived.

Someone tapped me on the shoulder. I turned around. Marie stood close, holding Little Bosco. She pointed over to Sonja, who was still seated. "She wants to talk to you. Alone."

"You sure? You sure you're good with this?"

"Yeah, I'm good with it. Go on, get over there, cowboy."

Bobby Ray stuck a thick finger into my chest. "Well, *I'm* not fucking good with it. You don't need to talk to my wife up close and personal like that, not without me there."

He now had a place to vent his anger over the detective who'd tossed his boy out into traffic. I didn't like getting poked, especially by him, and fought the urge to grab his hand and twist him up, take him to his knees.

Drago quick-stepped over, his fists clenched. Monster came on close at his heels, ready to do battle.

CHAPTER FORTY-SEVEN

I HELD UP both hands and said, "Hold it. Hold it."

Everyone stopped in a little circle, posturing for a fight, ready to dig in with fists and boots and secreted ball-peen hammers if anyone made the wrong move.

Sonja showed up, shoving her way into the middle. "This is a hospital. What in God's name is the matter with you bunch of thugs, acting like some punk kids on a schoolyard?" She shoved Bobby Ray. "And you, you horse's ass. I'll talk to Bruno if I damn well please. And you're not goin' to say a thing about it. You"—she pointed at Drago and Monster—"get your asses back over there and sit down. I'll tell you when it's time to do the ass kickin.'"

Everyone hesitated a long moment, not moving.

Sonja yelled, "Move!"

Monster slowly started to do as he was told. Drago looked to Marie first. Marie nodded. Drago went to the chair and sat down.

Bobby Ray still hadn't moved. Sonja went up on tiptoes and kissed his cheek. "Please, honey-bear?"

Bobby Ray didn't look at her. He stared me down and didn't immediately move. He tried to recover some of the mojo she'd stolen from him, giving him orders like that in front of men like Drago, Monster, and even me, all men who lived in a swirling world of violence.

She took his hand. "Please, honey."

He went. She watched him until he sat down in the chair, the one he sat in when we first walked up. Marie sat next to him, still holding the squirming toddler. I didn't like Marie anywhere near dangerous men, especially pregnant and vulnerable.

"Come on," Sonja said.

I followed her to the chairs and we sat.

She looked me in the eye and put her hand on my knee. "Bruno—" She glanced over at Bobby Ray and jerked her hand off my knee when Bobby Ray started to stand, his eyes lasers burning a hole through me.

He didn't have one thing to be jealous about.

In a crazy kind of way, I liked it that Bobby Ray cared so much about her.

She whispered as she smiled. "That big asshole. I hate him."

I couldn't read the smile, whether it was real or fake.

"Sonja, what's going on? Why are you doing this when it causes everyone involved so much heartache?"

By everyone involved I meant Bobby Ray.

She looked back from Bobby Ray to me. "You did good getting a woman like Marie. Don't you screw it up with her, you hear me?"

"I'm not trying to, but this world we live in has other ideas. I'm just a passenger on this bus."

She looked at me funny over that comment.

"What do you have to say, Sonja? I have some things I really need to get to."

"First, I don't want you to get involved with anything with Bobby Ray. Don't do anything else he asks you to do. You don't need that kind of trouble, especially with a baby on the way."

"Okay. That's easy. What's second?"

"No, I want you to promise me, Bruno."

"I promise."

She said, "Okay. Then I just wanted to clear up a few things about Bosco."

"It's okay, you don't have to."

"Please, just hear me out, okay?"

I nodded.

"I didn't want Bosco in this life. I didn't, not at all. I did everything I could to keep him out of it. I had him going to school, a technical school to learn how to weld. He liked it. I also told him I didn't want him riding with Ol' Hector, didn't want him anywhere around these assholes. Bobby Ray didn't like that edict, but he went along with it well enough. I made sure of it. At least I thought I did." Her voice caught. "The bastards, the sons of bitches. I told them, I ordered them, that Bosco was not to go on rides and not to wear the cuts.

"I didn't know, I swear I didn't know he was still riding behind my back. I respect you too much, Bruno. I didn't want you to think I wasn't paying attention to my own son."

She had her own guilt to deal with, which only served to pile it higher onto me. The shame of it. And still I couldn't tell her to relieve some of the pressure that continued to build.

"I believe you," I said. "You don't have to worry about that. He sounds like a great kid."

"He is. He doesn't deserve this, and when Bobby Ray finds out who did it, I'm going to be there when he gets his. You can bet your ass I will, I'll be there." She'd shifted just that quickly from sorrow to anger. Right at that moment I didn't know if I'd be able to defend myself once they found out and they came for me.

A lump rose in my throat. I couldn't sit there and take much more.

When I didn't respond, she continued. "Now this other thing, this last thing. I was talking with Marie and she said that you didn't understand what happened with Olivia, how I just *dropped her off in your lap* and walked away and never looked back. Now, after she brought it to my attention, maybe she's right. Maybe it would look that way." She'd changed her tone again with the *dropped her off in your lap* part, mimicking Marie.

I didn't like it and wanted to get up and leave. I didn't need that kind of crap, not added on top of everything else going on. Not Sonja disparaging Marie.

"Look," I said, "that's all old news. Olivia's gone now, so it doesn't matter anymore, does it?" Talking about Olivia made that lump rise in my throat and grow thick enough to choke and bring on the tears. I fought it.

"Don't you dare talk to me like that," she said. "Just listen to me for one damn minute, would you please? Let me say my piece and then you can go ahead and condemn me. Go ahead and blame me for all your life's chickenshit little problems. I won't care."

I didn't say anything and didn't move so much as an eyelash. No way did I blame her for everything in my life that went wrong; what a ludicrous idea.

I did blame her, though, for a chunk of what happened with Olivia.

Then, once I examined that blame a little closer, it didn't hold up. It was a cop-out. Those errors in judgment, my inability to raise Olivia, fell solidly on my shoulders and no one else's.

Now Sonja's eyes filled with tears.

Her tears made me feel like a heel. I said, "I'm sorry." I wanted to put my hand on hers but didn't, not under the circumstances.

"No, I'm the one who's sorry," she said. "You shouldn't have been left to raise our daughter alone, not like that, not in this world we live in. It takes two to watch out for a child these days. Lord knows Bobby Ray didn't help me out with Bosco."

I waited.

Olivia had fallen in with riff-raff, street people, and from there made the short leap into drugs. She'd overdosed and died, no small thanks to Derek Sams. So maybe in this case Sonja hit the nail on the head.

"You see," she said, "it's . . . it's just so damn hard to explain . . . to cop to such a failure. I buried all of that evil and ugliness years ago, and I really hate to dredge it up right now."

"Well, don't then. I'm not asking you to."

"Just shut up, Bruno, and listen, okay?"

I nodded.

She stared off to a place I couldn't see, even with the best telescope, and said, "I walked in and quit that night. I quit as soon as that asshole lieutenant Rodriquez told me Douglas Howard, the guy from Fruit Town, the guy I'd sapped too hard, that he didn't make it, that he died. I was sick about it, Bruno, sick up to here."

She held her hand up by her chin.

"First . . . no wait . . . I mean it really started with Maury Abrams, how those little bastards tried to rob Maury Abrams and forced him to shoot in self-defense. And then the Trey-Five-Sevens came back and burned them out. Killed them, fried that old couple right in their bed. The Abrams had bars on the doors and windows to keep the assholes out. Those same bars are what killed the Abrams.

"Then . . . then I went and shot at that two-eleven vehicle when I shouldn't have. I'd lost it, Bruno. I mean, I really lost it. Nothing seemed real anymore. I'm not making any excuses, I'm not. Really, I'm not. I just want you to understand what happened back then. I knew I was pregnant and with all of that shit going on and . . . and how could I bring a kid into this sewer of a world? Right? You understand what I'm saying here, right?"

"I've never been pregnant," I said, "but I could only imagine the pressure from all of that responsibility. I'm sorry you went through that."

A part of me wanted to argue that, if she'd told me she was pregnant and had not shoved me out of her life, we could've dealt with the pregnancy together.

Tears wet her face now. "You see—when the nurse told me I had a girl—I couldn't deal with a girl. Not when—"

I put my hand on her hand and that stopped her from what she was about to say. "I understand. I don't blame you. I don't."

"Are you sure, Bruno? Are you sure?"

I hugged her. Bobby Ray be damned.

CHAPTER FORTY-EIGHT

I STOOD UP, ready to go. I wanted in the worst way to get back to our children in Costa Rica. Under the circumstances, that goal looked a million miles away.

Marie and Drago got up and started walking from the room toward the long white hall we'd entered through, the one with the cop sitting in the chair halfway down. I nodded to Bobby Ray, who nodded back.

Marie still held little Bosco. "Hey," I said when I caught up to her, "come on, give him back. Are you kidding me? We can't take him with us."

Marie shook her head. "I told Sonja we'd take care of him until things calmed down."

"No, we can't. That absolutely will not work. That's just plain crazy."

"What are you talking about? You're the one acting crazy now. This little guy needs people who will love and care for him. His father's laid up in a hospital bed, and Sonja and Bobby Ray have too much going on to pay him the attention that he needs. Think about this child. We're doing this, Bruno, no arguments."

Oh, I had the argument that would trump her arguments, trump her decision in spades, only I didn't have the balls to tell her.

"Okay," I said, lowering my voice so Bobby Ray and Sonja had no chance of hearing me. "On one condition."

"No conditions, Bruno."

I took hold of her arm. We stopped. I looked her in the eye. "There will be this time."

I'd never talked to her that way.

Her mouth dropped open. "Okay, Bruno, whatever you say."

"I'm sorry, I shouldn't have talked to you like that." I put my arm around her and we continued down the long hallway.

Little Bosco reached up and patted my cheek.

"I think that knock to the head might've jarred something loose. I'm sorry."

"I understand. Maybe when we get back to the hotel you can trust me enough to tell me what's eating at you. Now what are these conditions?"

"Thank you for understanding. When we get back to the hotel, we're going to pack and immediately move to another hotel."

"Okay."

"And you are not to tell anyone where we're staying. Not even Sonja or Bobby Ray."

"Bruno, it's their grandson, they have the right to—"

I stopped in the hall and started to turn us around to take Bosco junior back.

She jerked out of my grasp and continued down the hall the way we'd been headed. "Okay, Bruno, have it your way, but you better have a good reason for all your bullshit."

"I do. I'm just worried about your safety, that's all."

"That's crazy. Sonja"—she looked back over her shoulder to see if they heard—"and Bobby Ray don't have any reason to harm us. You saw how they acted. They wouldn't have given us their grandson if they held any bad blood between us."

I didn't want to lie to her, so I didn't answer. We kept walking. She let it go. I'd catch the brunt of that penalty later. And deservedly so.

* * *

I sent Drago out to get a vehicle so we could move around without drawing attention to ourselves. He came back with a full-sized GMC truck with tinted windows and a red pinstripe that made the vehicle look like a black widow. I didn't ask him where it came from.

Out in front of the hotel, sitting in the big GMC with tinted windows, I phoned Special Agent Dan Chulack.

He picked right up. "Yeah?"

He was playing it professional. He didn't know if anyone was listening in next to my ear, like a Visigoth maybe, and said nothing extra until he knew the score.

"Where's our boy right now?" Meaning I wanted to know where to find Jumbo.

"Why? What's going down?" Dan sounded stunned that I'd even ask.

"I need you to back off your eye on him once I get up close. I wanna have a little talk with our big-eared friend."

Dan said nothing for a long moment as he thought it through.

I nudged him a little more. "Dan, it'll be plausible deniability for national security and all that shit. Come on, man, what's goin' on?"

"Can't do it, pal. It's not going to happen on my watch. What else you need?"

"You don't understand. I need—"

"No, you don't understand. I can't and won't do something like that. Stick to the plan and everything will be fine." He clicked off.

I looked at the phone in my hand. "What the hell just happened?"

Drago shrugged. "Fuckin' feds, what do you think happened? You can't live with 'em and you can't kill 'em. They just reeled you out there on a line as bait, and now your ass is left hangin' out blowin' in the wind. That's the FBI way. What now, boss, where to?"

"Drive. We'll just have to find Jumbo ourselves and deal with the FBI net around the little punk once we find him."

I couldn't get over what just happened. That wasn't like Dan.

Drago started up and took off, steering with one hand. His other went into his shorts pocket and pulled out his phone. He'd had it on vibrate. He flipped it open and said, "Yeah?"

He listened for a second and handed it to me. "It's for you. How'd those rat-bastards get my number?"

"Hello?"

"Bruno, it's me. Sorry about that earlier call. I couldn't talk on that phone."

"Ah, shit, no, that was my fault. I wasn't thinking. Of course you couldn't talk on that phone. I took a good chunk to the head and I haven't had a clear thought since. Sorry about that."

Dan gave a little chuckle. "No problem. Okay, since you've been away, Jumbo's bought himself an auto parts store. He's trying to go legit, or at least wash some more of his money. This new shop is on Crenshaw just north of MLK Boulevard, on the west side of Crenshaw in the Albertson's shopping center. And ah . . . Bruno, I'm going to have a hard time pulling my team off so you can have your little talk with him. Especially now, with that last phone call."

What he meant was that, if he pulled his team back now and something happened to Jumbo, it would make him look culpable.

"What happened to the old Dan? I want him back. I don't like this new and improved supervisor Dan, the Dan with the case of 'for reals.' But thanks anyway, I can take it from here and let you know what happens."

"I'm sorry, truly I—"

I hung up on him, more than a little angry. "Head up to Crenshaw and—"

"I got it," Drago said. He'd heard both sides of the conversation. "I gotta tell ya though, I don't think much of this. It isn't a good idea working with the feds. They don't play fair and they're not afraid of screwin' ya, once they get what they want."

"We don't have much of a choice, now do we? You want out?"

"Don't be an asshole."

I put the air conditioner on high, leaned back, and closed my eyes. The doctor might've been right about the rest my body needed. I continued to fight off sleep. The last thought that lingered in my mind before my brain shut down was this: Why did Sonja tell me not to do anything for Bobby Ray? She'd been so emphatic. Was it that she didn't want me to get wrapped up in his scandalous activity? Or was it that she just hated him right now and didn't want anyone to help her old man out?

CHAPTER FORTY-NINE

DRAGO SHOOK ME awake. The truck door on my side stood open. Drago stood in close. He held on to some long-haired hippy by the scruff of the neck. The guy squeaked a little like a mouse.

"Hey, man," Drago said, "you all right? You're droolin'. For a minute there I didn't think I'd be able to wake ya."

"Yeah, yeah, I'm good." I wiped my chin. He'd been right about the deep sleep. I'd dreamt I stood behind the cabana bar in Costa Rica, serving drinks to my regulars. This one seemed so much more real than other dreams, so much detail, right down to the scent of salt air. I'd never smelled anything in a dream before.

And I should've felt refreshed after a nap like that, but didn't. In fact, I just wanted to sleep some more. Sleep forever. Go back to that cabana, where life didn't have all the pressures.

The hippy didn't speak. He smelled of nicotine, and his facial skin reflected the damage of a longtime smoker, wrinkled and sallow. His hair needed washing, and he kept it held down with a sixties-style, beaded headband. He sported a raggedy blond goatee and wore a long-sleeve shirt open at the front with a chain and a peace sign medallion.

"Who's the dude?" I asked.

Drago dipped his shoulder down a little and nodded behind him. "He's agreed to let us borrow his truck for a few minutes. I told him if he kept his mouth shut, you'd give him a couple hundred bucks."

"His truck? What are you talking about?" I struggled up to see over his shoulder. We'd parked in a shopping center under a tree, away from all the other cars.

Next to our big GMC sat a smaller Ford Ranger painted all white with a blue business logo that said, "Big John Ahern's Auto Parts. Big parts without a Jumbo price."

What a cheesy advertisement. Jumbo had to have thought that one up himself. He had that kind of ego, one even bigger than his ears.

Drago, using his own initiative, had corralled the auto parts delivery guy in the parking lot and made the deal, all while I slept. I really needed to shake off the fatigue or we'd be in trouble.

Drago took hold of my arm and pulled me out of the truck. He shoved the hippy in. When the hippy shuffled by, his body odor all but gagged me and dispelled the final essence of salt air from my dream.

Drago pointed a meaty finger at the guy. "Don't fuck with the truck. Sit there and be good."

The hippy showed some balls. He held out a shaky hand and said, "How 'bout my duckets, amigo?"

Drago went to grab a handful of his throat. I put my hand on his shoulder and stopped him. "Here." I reached in my pocket and took out the roll of hundreds I had taken earlier from Bobby Ray's bag of money, a habit I didn't care to curb. I didn't like Bobby Ray much. I peeled off two hundreds. "You keep your mouth shut and stick to the story that we stole your truck and there'll be another two hundred in it for you when we get back."

He took the money and said, "Far out, man." He pulled a doobie out of his pocket and started to light it up.

Drago said, "Hey."

"It's cool, let him do it. Come on. I'll drive."

We got in the Ford Ranger, shoulder to shoulder, this truck much smaller than the GMC. I looked around to get oriented. I knew the area that Dan described but didn't recognize the shopping center we'd parked in. I started up. "Which way?"

"You sure you're okay to drive?"

"Which way?"

He pointed in a direction I would not have guessed. I headed that way and pulled out onto Martin Luther King Boulevard, which back in the day used to be called Santa Barbara. Now I recognized the area. Two or three years before, though it seemed liked decades ago now, I'd shared an apartment with a beautiful woman named Chantal. She'd given me a cover story for my parole officer, for my "residence of record." She gave me a place to lay my head while I capered, pulled train heists for Jumbo, and rescued abused children from toxic homes and stashed them with my father while Marie and I prepared to flee to Costa Rica.

Robby Wicks shot and killed Chantal, took my money, and tried to hang her murder on me.

Then, after I helped Dan Chulack take down The Sons of Satan clubhouse, he arranged for the FBI to adopt the Chantal murder investigation. Once he got control of the case, he closed it the way it should've been closed, with the killing attributed to the dead Robby Wicks.

The only thing Dan couldn't suppress were the kidnapping charges for the eight kids, one of which was Wally Kim, the son of a Korean diplomat. Those charges still hung over my head and always would until I was caught and punished.

I spotted Jumbo's Auto Parts right next to a Rite Aid and Ace Hardware. People walked all around the pharmacy and hardware store. No one came and went from the auto parts store. In the front, by the door, Jumbo employed one of those air machines that blew up and let sag an inflatable man to catch the shopper's eye. A bright purple man no one could miss.

Big posters on the windows obscured the view to the inside and advertised oil and oil filters on sale, 50 percent off, loss leaders to pull in suckers.

A red and white "closed" sign hung on the glass door, conspicuous and contrary to the posted business hours.

I drove around back without hesitating. I didn't see any of Dan's people set up to watch the place. He supervised a talented crew.

In the back, a deep loading dock led to the rear door. I backed in. We got out and went up the concrete steps to the landing.

I stopped at the door and held my finger up, pointing at Drago. I'd taken this move from Marie's playbook and didn't like it much when she did it to me, so I dropped it. I put my hand on his shoulder. "Listen, I don't want you goin' in here like some kinda Destructo-Man, you understand what I'm sayin'? Just follow my lead and back my play. No independent action. Got it?"

Drago shook his head and put his hand to his chest in mock surprise. "Me? I'm hurt that you'd think such thoughts when all I have is the milk of human kindness running through my veins."

I chuckled and socked him in the arm. "Come on, Dalai Lama."

I opened the door to the auto parts store.

Someone stuck a gun to my head and yanked me inside.

CHAPTER FIFTY

DRAGO SHOVED HIS way in right behind me. He didn't take any action, not with the gun to my head.

Just inside the door, the store opened up to a wider area where incoming deliveries sat before distribution to the rows of shelving. Four large men stood ready to fight. Jumbo stood among them, dwarfed by their size. He held his little chrome .25 auto down by his leg. He smiled, content with himself.

I stuck my hand in my pocket to the special cell phone Dan gave me, my hand on the panic button.

If I pushed it, the FBI would rush in and then we wouldn't have a chance at getting Jumbo to talk, not legally. And in all likelihood, with all the other agents watching, Dan would have to take me into custody for the kidnap warrants. I didn't push the button and knew that might well be my undoing.

The four men wore The Sons of Satan colors. Hard men, experienced men. Jumbo had set me up. Back in the weed-infested parking lot behind the Sears on Long Beach Avenue, he'd lied to me. He knew I'd come back on him for the lie and had called The Sons to take advantage of the twenty-thousand-dollar bounty they'd placed on my head. I could no longer believe anything Jumbo had told me in that parking lot. Not that it mattered at that moment.

The nausea rose up and made the polished concrete floor pitch like the deck of a ship. I put my hand to the side of my head to stop the world from rolling. The thug with the gun shoved it deeper into my temple. "Take your other hand outta your pocket real easy. That's right, now don't you move, asshole."

I turned as much as I could to look at him. He could've been forty or fifty with his black and gray hair down to his shoulders, unwashed and greasy. He wore a handlebar mustache and had a silver skull ring on the hand that held the Smith .45. The embroidered patch on his cut said he went by *Dead Dick*. The one next to him was taller and a little thinner, with a shaved dome. He went by the name *Dogman*. The way Dead Dick held me, I couldn't see the other two well enough, but they, too, would have weapons and know how to use them, none of them afraid of going to prison in the life they'd chosen.

Jumbo took a step back. "Holy shit, Batman. You know who this is? Do you know who this other asshole is who just come in here draggin' his knuckles with Bruno The Bad Boy Johnson?"

The biker with the shaved head said, "It's Dogman, and I'm not gonna tell you again. Next time I'll rip those elephant ears off ya and make ya eat 'em. You got it?"

Jumbo ignored him. He took another step back and, with a shaky hand, pointed the Raven .25 in our vicinity. "Jesus H, this is Blow Torch. Son of a bitch, and we just let him walk right in. Come on, man, you know this guy. Back in the day he used to be one of you guys. This here's Karl Drago. Shoot, man, shoot. Don't let him make any move at all. Shoot him."

Dead Dick let go of me, took a step back, and covered Drago as he, too, caught a little of Jumbo's panic and hysteria.

Dogman said, "There's five of us, you little dipshit, and we're armed and they're not, so cool your jets."

I rubbed my head where the gun put a little dent. "I wouldn't shoot my friend here; it'll only make him mad."

Drago looked at me and said, "Shut your piehole, meat."

Everyone looked surprised, including me.

Drago grabbed me in a headlock. "I'm not splittin' the reward with any of you swingin' dicks. I caught this nigger fair and square and brought him here for my money."

What the hell? "Drago?" I said. He squeezed a little tighter so I wouldn't blow it. I figured his game a second too late. Oh.

Drago didn't know his own strength, and he'd inadvertently started to choke me out. He held my head at an upward angle, though not on purpose, that's just how it worked out.

Jumbo's voice went up an octave or two. "Don't listen to his shit. Shoot, man, I'm tellin' ya, you better shoot this son of a bitch right now. It's probably already too late. He's gonna kill us all."

"Shut up, Dumbo," Dogman said. Then he looked at Drago. "How'd you know we were here and to bring this asshole to us?"

"I talked ta Clay on the phone, and he said you boys would be here and told me to go ahead and bring this prick and turn him over ta ya. Said you'd know what to do with him. You want I should get Warfield on the phone, let him tell ya himself?"

I tapped on Drago's arm. He eased off a little. I could breathe again.

Dogman let his gun drop down to his side. "No, we'll take it from here. Let his black ass go."

"Bullshit. Where's my twenty large?"

"Ah, man, I'm tellin' ya, don't do this," Jumbo said. "He's gonna take us all down and—"

Dogman spun, quick-stepped over, and booted Jumbo right in the nuts. Jumbo yelped and melted to the floor.

Dogman turned, reached into his denim cut, and pulled out a banded stack of hundreds. He tossed it on the floor in front of

Drago. From the look in Dogman's eyes, he didn't believe Drago's ruse, not entirely. "Now let him go."

Drago let me go and shoved me hard. I flew to the polished concrete floor and skidded along for several feet. Drago wanted me out of harm's way, out of the line of fire when he made his move. Drago took a step to the cash, bent over, and picked it up. He tore off the band and started to count.

Dogman and the other three Sons moved in closer to me, enough hate oozing from them to start another civil war, enough to take most of their attention off Drago.

Dead Dick put his boot on my chest. "What happened to Bone?"

"Who?"

"Bone and his girl. They went down to Costa Rica and haven't been heard from since."

"Oh them. I heard they went sport fishing."

Dead Dick grimaced. He pulled back and kicked me in the stomach. I lost it and threw up on his boot.

On the floor, not too far away, Jumbo said, "I asked for their best men and they send me Batman and Limp Dick. We're all fucked, I tell ya."

Dogman spun around and pulled back to kick Jumbo.

Drago made his move. He threw the bundle of hundreds at Dead Dick as he charged. He lowered his shoulders with his arms spread wide and roared like a lion. He hit all four Sons down low, driving hard with his legs, catching them by surprise.

One of them spun out of the trap. Drago drove the other three into a rack of auto parts. The shelving went over with a loud crash, taking two more shelves with it like dominoes. The three men, including Dogman, flailed, trying to get a piece of Drago. Drago took the hits without reaction, picked his targets, and slammed their faces with his huge fist, again and again.

The attack took only seconds.

The one Son left, Little Stick, recovered from the shock and raised his gun and fired at Drago. He missed and blasted a boxed air filter that popped and danced up in the air.

He took better aim this time.

Still on the floor, I pivoted on my hip, swung around, and kicked his leg just below the knee as hard as I could. Something snapped. He went down in an uncontrolled heap. The gun clattered to the floor.

One of the Sons got loose and pummeled Drago on the back with his fists. He got to his feet, pulled back, and kicked him. Nothing worked. The man grabbed a chromed tire rim and raised it high over his head to bash Drago's brains out.

I grabbed the gun Little Stick dropped and shot the man right between the shoulder blades.

CHAPTER FIFTY-ONE

HE FELL OVER onto the writhing pile. I struggled to my feet, moved over, and stuck the gun against the back of Dead Dick's leg and pulled the trigger twice. He screamed.

I shot Dogman in both feet.

That ended the fight.

But not for Drago.

Drago disengaged from the bodies, grabbed Dead Dick by the throat, and pounded his face with his fist.

"Okay," I said, "that's enough. They're done." Dead Dick lay unconscious and Dogman rocked in pain, cradling one foot.

Drago stood, a wild look in his eye. "Gimme the gun. Gimme it, I'll finish it. We gotta finish it or these four assholes will keep on comin'."

"No. It's over." I couldn't stomach mass murder. I'd shot one of them in the back, but that came out of self-preservation. Just like I had with Ol' Hector and . . . and Bosco.

Blood spread under and around the clutter of auto parts, black plastic pieces, black rubber belts, nuts and bolts, and the scattered mass of hundred-dollar bills. The green currency soaked up the blood. Turk, the one Son not shot, stayed frozen on top of the fallen shelving, his hands out and in plain sight. He knew he sat on the razor's edge of being gunned.

Drago held out his hand to me, wanting the .45. "Come on, man, don't be a pussy, let me finish this now. These guys are part of the cancer that messed with your boy."

I shook my head. If I had to become a serial killer to stop them, then it wasn't worth it. I didn't have it in me.

I turned around to deal with Jumbo. His back to me, he struggled, using his arms to climb up a counter. Once on his feet, he grabbed his balls and groaned. "I told them dumbasses," he said, still facing the cabinets. "Oow, shit. I told 'em, you heard me tell 'em, Bruno. I gave 'em fair warning. The dumbasses."

I couldn't see his hands. Guns didn't kill, the hands did. "Turn around, Jumbo."

He did, holding his little popgun. He wore that same ugly smile, like he owned the world.

I pointed my gun at him. "Come on, don't do this."

I really couldn't afford to shoot him. He knew too much about the drone and the missiles. We had to get him to talk.

Drago turned to face Jumbo.

"Don't," I said to Drago. "Let me handle this."

Drago still possessed pent-up anger from his inability to protect me by gunning The Sons. He took a long step around the men at his feet and the strewn and bloody auto parts.

"I'll shoot his ass. You better tell him to stop, Bruno. I swear to *God* I'll cap his sorry ass. Tell him, Bruno. Tell him."

"Drago, stop, don't."

Drago kept moving toward Jumbo.

Jumbo fired.

His gun didn't boom like the one in my hand had when I shot The Sons. It popped.

And popped again.

Drago didn't flinch as his bulk absorbed the two impacts, taking in the small lead pellets that had been fired at eight hundred and fifty feet per second, penetrating fat and muscle, tunneling deep. The contact slapped his body and sent a wave of fat in a concentric circle like a shock wave, easy to see even through his Raiders football jersey.

Drago grabbed the gun before it fired a third time. He socked Jumbo in the face. Jumbo's head snapped back. He wilted back to the floor, his eyes unfocused.

I rushed over. "Hey, hey, you okay, buddy? I'll get paramedics rolling." I took out the FBI phone.

Drago looked at me, still angry. "You need to sack up or you're not gonna survive this shit. I'm tellin' ya, man. And I'm fine. Get what you need from this little pinhead and let's get the hell outta here."

"How can I get what I need from him after you knocked the piss outta him?" I took a breath, stepped over to Drago, and put a hand on his shoulder. "I'm sorry, I shouldn't talk to you that way. Thank you for saving my life, again. I'm just worried about you. You've been shot twice. You need medical aid." I took the .25 auto from him and put it in my pocket.

Without looking over at the last biker with "Turk" embroderied on his Levi cut, who'd started to quietly pick his way off the shelves, Drago pointed at him with a beefy finger. "You make another move and you'll get exactly what your friends got." Drago shifted and kicked Dogman in the face, knocking him out. He shifted back and raised his black Raiders football jersey to show me. The two .25 cal bullets had hit him in the lower right abdomen, right in the tattooed breasts of a beautiful woman with long black hair. The beautiful, perfect breasts now had two red eyes.

Tattoos covered every square inch of his skin, all of them done in black ink. Jailhouse tattoos of Vikings, a large battle-ax, a Celtic cross, and several women.

Blood trickled out of both wounds and it looked like the breasts wept red.

"You're right," I said, "they don't look so bad on the outside, but you don't know what kinda damage they did inside."

Without the use of his hands and using his stomach muscles only, he rolled his immense belly. "Nope, don't feel like they hit nothin' important. Come on, let's get this shit goin' so we can blow this pop stand." He walked over to a stack of yellow gallon containers of antifreeze and picked up one. He reached into his pocket, took out a knife, and punctured a gaping wound in the container as he moved back to Jumbo.

"Hey—" I'd started to tell Drago that that stuff would kill Jumbo and realized Drago probably already knew.

Drago poured the luminescent green liquid right on Jumbo's face. The green contrasted with Jumbo's pale white skin. He coughed and choked, rolled to his side, and threw up. The act probably saved him from a torturous death by poison.

Drago continued to slowly pour the liquid, which Jumbo tried unsuccessfully to bat away, the green mixing with the blood and cash and black auto parts on the polished concrete floor.

Drago finished off the bottle and threw it down on Jumbo, who coughed and gagged. "Are you crazy? You're one crazy son of a bitch, that shit'll kill ya."

I moved over and, with my foot, shoved him back down. I put my shoe on his face and ground the sole in. "You're going to tell us all about the train heist with the military drone."

He tried to push my shoe off and couldn't. He spoke around it, his words muffled by my sole. "Don't know what you're talkin' about. Get the hell off me, Bruno."

I pushed harder.

"Aaahee—"

"Tell me."

"I can't tell you something I don't know."

"Drago, get another one of those bottles of antifreeze. We're gonna make sure Jumbo's radiator doesn't overheat this summer."

"No, man, no. Wait. Okay, okay, get off. I'll tell you."

"I don't have the time to dick around here, Jumbo. I let off, you better tell me or so help me—" I took a breath. "You get one chance, you understand? You shot my best friend, and I owe you for that."

"All right already, asshole. I said I'd give it up."

I let off and stepped back. Drago held a hand over his gut where the bullets had gone in. I said to him, "You're a bad liar, my friend, and you are going to the hospital." I looked back at Jumbo. "When's the meet for the exchange and where?"

"Tonight at nine at the steak house over in The Negro, off Hospitality Lane."

"The where?"

He tried to get up. I shoved him down into the viscous green and red.

"In San Bernarnegro, man, come on. San Bernardino. That's what they call it now 'cause all the blacks took over the whole city." He shoved my foot away. "Now let me up."

CHAPTER FIFTY-TWO

"You better be tellin' it straight, 'cause we're not letting you go until after the meet."

"Ah, come on, man, I got shit to do. I got my businesses ta deal with. I'm a businessman."

"Tough."

Drago, still holding his gut with one hand, reached down and grabbed a handful of Jumbo's shirt and yanked him to his feet. With the minor movement, Drago grunted a little. He said, "Where's your office?"

"Why, fat man? I told you what you wanted ta know, now leave me go."

Drago swung the full gallon jug of antifreeze he'd retrieved when I'd asked him to and knocked Jumbo in the air. He landed and slid seven or eight feet in the floor's hyper-slickness. He slid all the way over to the back door, leaving a snail path of green and red and balled-up cash in his wake.

Drago pulled back and threw the gallon jug. The yellow container struck Dogman with a thud. He yelped. Drago went over to Jumbo and grabbed him by the foot. "You gonna tell me where your office is or am I gonna have to tear this leg off at the root?"

"I'll show ya. Back off your dog, Bruno. I said I'd tell ya, just lemme up."

"Point to it."

He pointed.

Drago walked in that direction, pulling Jumbo along like a prone water-skier. "You—" He pointed at Turk, the uninjured biker. "You lead, keep your hands where I can see 'em."

Drago came by me and stopped. "What?"

I held my arms out wide. "Look at this place. What'd I tell ya just before we came in here? No Destructo-Man, remember?"

He grinned for the first time since we walked in. "Good thing I didn't listen to you about that and about that bullshit 'no self-initiated actions,' huh?"

"Hey, hey," Jumbo said, lying on his back with his foot held up by Drago. "You two wanna get a room or something? Jesus H."

Drago and I both laughed as we headed to the office, Drago dragging his charge.

It felt good to laugh.

In the office, Drago told Turk to sit on his ass in the corner. Then he put Jumbo in a chicken-wing wrestling hold and made him open the digital combination to his safe.

The tall double doors swung wide and revealed stacks of cash and guns. I looked at Drago. "We robbin' him, butch?"

"Nope. He owes you, remember? And I'm gonna tax the shit outta the big-eared runt for shootin' me, how's that?"

"Fine by me." From a stack next to the wall, I dumped out a box of Valvoline oilcans, the ones on sale out in the window. They clattered to the floor. I filled the box with cash.

"Hey, hey, I only owe you a hundred and twenty-five thousand. There's close to three hundert grand there."

Drago put his paw on Jumbo's face and shoved him. He bounced off the wall. Drago shoved him again when he rebounded back.

"Come on, knock it off," Jumbo yelled.

Drago stopped playing handball.

I stopped loading the box. "I'll make a deal with you. You tell me about Agent Larry Gerber of the ATF, and I'll only take what's owed me." I looked over at Drago. "You good with that?" I'd give him my whole one twenty-five. He deserved it.

He shrugged.

Jumbo looked over at Turk, who sat quietly taking it all in.

"Can't do it," Jumbo said.

"Drago, take that guy outta here, would ya please?"

Drago grabbed Turk by the shirt and jerked him to his feet. He escorted the biker out of the room.

"Don't hurt him," I said.

Outside the room, the wall shook. Drago must've knocked the guy out by banging his head against the drywall.

I looked back at Jumbo. "Now spill it."

"I told you all I know, back at the Sears. This Gerber's got a case on me hangin' over my head."

"No, he doesn't. You're lying. I don't know why I didn't see it the first time you fed that fat lie to me."

"Whatta ya talkin' about? I didn't lie, I'm tellin' ya true."

Drago came back into the room and said it for me. "'Cause you never touch any of the contraband or the money during your deals. You keep your hands clean. You have your intermediaries handle the deals."

I tossed the box of cash onto the desk and took a step closer to him.

He held up his hands to fend me off. "Okay, okay, what do you wanna know?"

"How'd you get that big drone off that lowboy train car without anyone seeing you?"

"Trade secret. I'll tell you anything else. You don't need to know that, anyway. I tell you, then the government will seal up that weak spot, and the way it's going, I'm not going to get a dime outta this shit caper. Even after all the time and money I put in it."

"Who has the drone?"

"That fatass Bobby Ray. He said we'd be partners, fifty-fifty. He fucked me like an altar boy. His guys did the heavy lifting, but it was my gig all the way. You know how that works. We did it on the computer chips, remember?"

He mentioned the computer chips deal as a way to remind me, a way to bring us together as compadres, so I couldn't so easily abuse him or kill him. Wrong on both counts.

"Where's the drone right now?" I knew the answer but had to try.

"Bobby Ray's got it and won't let me near it. Got it loaded up in some kinda truck so it's easy to move. Once he sees the money, he'll hand over the keys and tell the buyer where to find it."

I thought about it for a minute. "Who was in that van at Sears watchin' us?"

Jumbo squirmed a little. "Ah . . . ah alright. I already told you way too much anyway. I'm in this up to my nose now."

Drago said, "More like to those big floppy ears."

Jumbo scowled at Drago. He looked back at me and said, "Bobby Ray was in the van watchin.'"

"Bobby Ray? That doesn't make any sense. Why was he there?"

Jumbo shrugged. "Bobby Ray said the fed's are all over him. He's gonna do the deal tonight and wanted a test run to see who'd show up. A test to kinda see how much the feds knew exactly. Kinda a smart idea you ask me. Wish I woulda thought of it. You can bet I'll do something like that in the future."

"So the thing with Larry Gerber, the dirty ATF agent, is all a sham? He never arrested you and he doesn't have a case against you?"

"Never heard his name until Bobby Ray told it to me and said to feed it to you, but not until you'd put a little pressure on me."

I'd been played right from the start and never saw it. And I didn't like it one bit. I wanted to have a little talk with Bobby Ray, up close and personal, just like the way he'd said about the guy who'd tossed Bosco into the traffic—me.

Drago sat on the edge of the desk. "It might've been a test to see how many agencies were on his tail. Or maybe even to see if the cartel was on him ready to do a rip, get the drone without turning over the money. Smart, real smart. But he also had *you* handle the deal at the Sears. He wanted to see which way you'd jump. I know I'd smell a rat if you all of a sudden showed up wanting to talk to *my* wife, which happens to be your ex-girlfriend. Too convenient, you showin' up right outta the blue when this deal was set to go down."

"You really think," I said, "that Bobby Ray's that smart?"

"He's president of the Goths, ain't he?" Jumbo said.

I marveled at the beauty of it. "So he sent that fifty grand out as bait just to see what kind of predator would bite. Fifty grand he was willing to lose just to mark the players in his game." Then it hit me. "Oh, man."

"What?" Drago asked.

"If this little weasel's right, and Bobby Ray was in that van at Sears, then I really did misread him in a big way."

"How's that?"

"Because he should've been at the hospital with Bosco, not out testing the water for his future deal. Not out doing an integrity check on me. He's one cold son of a bitch."

Drago said, "Ah, shit."

"What?"

"Marie's all alone with his grandson."

CHAPTER FIFTY-THREE

I WANTED TO get back to Marie in a hurry. I dialed Dan's FBI phone. Dan picked up on the first ring. "What's going on in there? Is everything all right?"

"We're comin' out, meet us out front, two vehicles, make one of them your Suburban."

"Be there in thirty seconds."

I hung up. "Come on, let's get outta here." I picked up the Valvoline box of cash. I stuck the .45 Smith and Wesson in my back waistband and pulled my shirt over it.

Drago didn't have to, but he grabbed hold of Jumbo by the nape and shook him a little with each step as we walked through the store to the front door.

"Ouch, come on, man, leave go. I told you everything you wanted to know. And you got my money, for Christ's sake. Tell 'im, Bruno, tell 'im to leave me go."

"Jumbo, you shot him twice. Count yourself lucky you're still breathin.'"

We got to the front door.

Locked.

A ball of keys hung from the lock. I turned the keys to open the door but not fast enough for Drago. He banged Jumbo off the door like a sock puppet again and again until I got it open. Jumbo went a little limp, his eyes glazed over.

The sunlight seemed much brighter and the nausea returned.

From off to the left, the dark-blue Suburban slid up in front of us. The two doors on the passenger side opened. Dan stepped out with another agent, a new guy dressed in a blue suit and a white dress shirt. Drago handed him Jumbo, then took out his sunglasses, put them on, and climbed into the Suburban.

Dan watched all this, not saying anything. He turned to me. "What's going on, Bruno?"

"Keep Jumbo on ice, no phone calls, the same with what's left of those guys inside."

Dan nodded to the agent in the blue suit, who took Jumbo to the rear of the Suburban just as another Suburban pulled up. Two more agents jumped out. Blue Suit shoved Jumbo in. After a short discussion, the three agents drew their guns and ran into Jumbo's auto parts store.

Dan said, "Bruno?"

Dan had a wiretap on the phone, and I'd hung him out to dry with the phone call asking where to find Jumbo and then showing up in the middle of his surveillance to do a war crimes interrogation. Dan didn't bring up how I'd screwed him over. If he came away with the military drone, the Hellfire missiles, and the terrorist who wanted to buy it, nothing else would matter, especially the manner in which Dan pulled it off.

"The trade," I said, "the money for the drone is scheduled to go down tonight, nine o'clock at a steak house on Hospitality Lane in San Bernardino. Bobby Ray has the drone on a semitruck, keeping it mobile. He'll see the money, hand over the keys, and tell the buyer the location of the truck."

All the visible stress left Dan's body at the same time and he smiled. "Damn good work, Bruno."

I handed him the Valvoline box. "This is mine. Don't look in it. Just hold onto it for me and, if anything happens to me or Drago, get it to Marie, okay?"

"Sure, sure."

"Can you give us a ride back to our truck?"

"You bet, get in."

Blue Suit came out of the auto parts store, grabbed Dan by the arm, and pulled him aside. He whispered, urgently waving his hands, his expression one of confusion and fear.

I waited to get in, to see how Dan would react to the mess we had made inside.

Dan pulled away from Blue Suit and spoke loud enough for everyone to hear. "I don't care. Deal with it. Write it up as a gang fight and that they shot each other. This is national security we're talking about." With the Valvoline box under one arm, he pointed back to the auto parts store. "Tell me now, do you honestly think there are any victims in there, I mean, taxpayers?"

Blue Suit didn't answer.

I felt sorry for him. I'd written up many, many screwed-up crime scenes to justify legally wrong, but morally correct, things Robby Wicks pulled off. But nothing like the mess we'd left inside.

The agent didn't reply. Dan said, "I didn't think so. Deal with it. Keep me apprised." He turned to me and said, "Come on, Bruno, let's go."

We got in. The air conditioner cooled and soothed, dried the sweat instantly. I wanted to curl up and go to sleep. But I still had far too much to deal with.

I didn't tell the driver where to go. Drago and I had driven into their surveillance net. They probably watched Drago follow the hippy away in the parts truck, corral him, and carjack his ride, and the whole time they just looked on.

I put my head back on the seat, let the cool air work on my face, and closed my eyes. "There are guns and money in Jumbo's office. I told him he could keep it if he cooperated."

Dan said, "I understand."

"The deal with the ATF agent Larry Gerber was all bullshit, a fabrication to clean Bobby Ray's tail from any law enforcement surveillance."

"No, it's not, Bruno, it's real. At least part of it is."

I opened my eyes and looked at him. He sat in the front seat, looking back at us as we pulled to a stop next to the black GMC, with the hippy nowhere to be seen in the front, the windshield cloudy with a ganja fog.

"What are you talking about? What's happened?"

"Special Agent Larry Gerber has gone missing," Dan said. "He's been gone two days now."

CHAPTER FIFTY-FOUR

"Are you serious?" I asked.

"I need to know what was said about Gerber, Bruno, exactly what was said. We now have a missing federal agent."

"I told you that in the Sears parking lot Jumbo claimed Special Agent Larry Gerber was dirty and wanted a payoff." I pointed back to the store. "Well, not five minutes ago in the auto parts store, Jumbo retracted that statement and said that Bobby Ray told him to feed Gerber's name to me after I pressured him a little . . . ah, man, son of a bitch."

"What?" Dan asked. He hadn't caught on to what it all meant.

Drago, with his head back against the headrest, his sunglasses masking his eyes, answered in a less-than-vigorous voice. "This Bobby Ray asshole fed the name to Bruno, to lay the crime *off* on Bruno."

"What crime— Ah, damn." Dan, who just caught on, said, "The crime is that Gerber's dead. And once we locate the body and investigate, we'll find that Bruno has been throwin' Agent Gerber's name around, and we'll also find evidence that Bruno met with him, maybe even worse than that. And with—"

I finished it for Dan. "And with my record and outstanding warrants, I'm hung out for the murder."

I didn't want to say anything more in front of Dan; the frame already looked too tight. More from me on the topic could only force Dan into a corner, force him to take action against me.

What I found most difficult to believe was Bobby Ray. While in the hospital, in the waiting area, as his son lay in intensive care fighting for his life, Bobby Ray had asked me to take care of the problem with the dirty ATF agent. The one he had already murdered. Bobby Ray wound me up like some kind of toy soldier and sent me on my way to enmesh myself further into the frame he'd laid for me.

I intended to have a talk with Bobby Ray a lot sooner than later.

Then I remembered what Sonja had said: *Don't do anything Bobby Ray asks you to do.* She'd been trying to warn me about the Gerber murder frame.

"Do you have anything else on Gerber?" I asked, my head starting to pound with a headache.

"Yes, Gerber's supervisor told us that Gerber had flipped someone in the Visigoths' organization and was working a heavy deal."

"What deal? Not this same arms deal? Ah, man, it has to be. Did the supervisor say who he'd flipped?"

I could guess it had to be Bosco.

"Gerber wouldn't even tell his supervisor the name of the informant. Gerber feared for his informant's life. He said the Visigoths had 'too many ears in law enforcement.'"

"What office did Gerber work out of?"

"He's an older agent, close to retirement, working a desk job as a liaison in cold case investigations for both Los Angeles Police Department and Los Angeles County Sheriff's Department. He worked the *Drug/Fire* for them, shuffling their federal paperwork. His job was to submit all the ballistics, the bullets and guns from old cases, and have them analyzed with current technology. Between those two departments there are thousands of cases. They're scrambling to sift through them all now. To find which one he was working on."

Drug/Fire was a database that categorized each bullet, shell casing, and gun barrel—not unlike the AFIS fingerprint system.

"So Gerber," I said, "must've matched a gun or bullet to a motorcycle gang killing, linked it to a suspect, and didn't tell anyone about it?"

Dan nodded. "All this just happened within the last few days. The supervisor did say one thing, though."

"What?"

"Gerber wanted a tactical team on alert to respond at a moment's notice when the informant called him with a location."

"Let me guess: scheduled for tonight at nine."

Dan nodded again.

I looked over at Drago, his head lolled back. I grabbed off his sunglasses; his eyelids were mere slits showing all white. His mouth gaped open. A trickle of blood started and ran down the corner of his mouth.

"Drago! Drago!"

I slid over close to him, checked for a pulse in his neck.

Dan leaned over the front seat into the back. "What's the matter with him?"

"He's got a pulse; it's weak and thready. He's in a bad way."

"What's the matter with him?" Dan said again as he leaned way over the seat and lifted the now sodden part of Drago's Raiders jersey. On Drago's abdomen, all the tattoos below the two tattooed breasts looked tinted in red, awash in blood. Too much blood, the top of his shorts soaked with it.

"Are you kidding me?" Dan said. "He's gunshot." Dan turned to the FBI agent behind the wheel. "Get us to the closest hospital, now." The agent took off, the back tires screeched. The back end slewed to the right and then to the left on the smooth parking lot asphalt.

Dan opened his operational plan, checked for a number, and dialed his phone. Someone answered. Dan said, "This is FBI Special Agent Dan Chulack, we are rolling to your hospital with a GSW,

ETA seven minutes. Have a team waiting at the ER door." He clicked off his phone, reached under the dash, and flipped a toggle switch. The lights and siren came on. He looked forward out the front windshield.

He didn't turn around to scold me for not telling him sooner about my wounded partner. He didn't need to. I felt guilty enough. Vulnerable and a little ashamed, I needed to be doing something, anything.

The FBI agent whipped the large Suburban in and out of traffic, blowing through red signals.

I took off my shirt, folded it up, and pressed it gently but firmly against Drago's wounds. This would be the second time he'd gotten himself hurt because of me.

Time dragged on. Dan said the trip would take seven minutes. It'd been twenty or twenty-five already.

"Drago, hold on, we're almost there."

"I thought you said seven minutes!" I yelled at Dan over the siren.

Dan turned, looked at his watch. "It's only been three and a half. We're making good time, just hold on. Two more minutes, max."

"Hold on, Drago, you hear me, hold on," I yelled.

The driver finally made the last turn. The hospital came into view up ahead. He bounced the big Suburban into the driveway and skidded up to the rear door of the ER. Two men and a woman, all dressed in blue scrubs, waited with a gurney.

How the hell would we get him on the gurney?

Everyone tugged and pulled. A nurse ran into the hospital and came out with more help. We got him on the gurney. The doctor worked on Drago, yelling orders as they wheeled him in at a run.

I eased myself down and sat on the edge of the open door, naked from the waist up, my hands bloody, and tried to get my breathing under control.

I marveled at the horrible luck. What the hell.

Everyone who came around me ended up with a trip to the ER, critically injured, gunshot, or bludgeoned. How could that be? How was that even fair? How did I always come away unscathed?

I could hear Robby Wicks talking to me: "Quit feeling sorry for yourself, Bruno. You chase violence, it's going to turn on you and bite back. That's just the nature of the beast. All you can do is be ready for it. Now suck it up, you pussy. You live that life, be prepared to—"

"Shut up," I snapped. I put my hand to my head, which now ached something fierce. I didn't want to be friends with anyone anymore. Not if it meant hurting them.

Dan stood next to me, put his warm hand on my shoulder. "Hey, pal, you all right? You look a little pale."

"Huh, what? Oh, yeah."

He took off his suit coat. "Here, put this on. I don't want you going into shock."

I nodded and shrugged into the jacket. The midday sun made it at least eighty degrees out, yet the jacket felt warm and inviting. "Thank you."

He squatted down a little. "Bruno, I need you to do one more thing for me."

I held up my hand. "Don't. I'm done. I'm out. I know what you're gonna say, because in your place I'd be saying the same thing. I'm on the inside and this deal's too important. You want me to go back to Bobby Ray and try and get in on the deal tonight. Well, I'm sorry. It's not gonna happen."

"Bruno?"

"How could I possibly get back in? Can you hear what you're sayin'? We just now figured out that Bobby Ray's trying to set me up for the murder of a man I've never even met."

"We don't know that for sure."

"Ah, come on, Dan, take off those rose-colored glasses. No, I'm out. Here, take your coat."

"No, that's okay, keep it."

"Thanks." I got up and staggered a little, then righted my gait and moved off to make a phone call. Maybe Dan hit it right when he said I looked shocky—the headache, the concussion. That explained the way I walked, the hot sun, the chills. Maybe I should've stayed in bed.

I took out the FBI smartphone and dialed Marie.

"Bruno, is everything all right?"

I opened my mouth to tell her about Drago. I'd also kept the thing about Bosco bottled up too long. I needed to tell her about that as well. Maybe not on the phone; I should do that one in person. But I would do it, no more stalling. I'd do it just as soon as I got back to the hotel. "Marie, honey—"

Marie cut me off. "Sonja called."

"What?"

"Bruno, Bosco didn't make it."

CHAPTER FIFTY-FIVE

Bosco didn't make it?

Bosco died?

I'd done that. I'd killed him. All of a sudden I couldn't breathe.

"Bruno, Sonja wants to see you. She wants to meet with you. She said it's important she talk with you right away."

"Okay, okay. Just hold on a minute, okay, honey? Please." I took in several long breaths and then walked back to Dan, held the phone down to my chest, and said, "Can you keep an eye on Drago, call me if you hear anything?"

"Sure, where are you headed?"

"Sonja wants to see me."

He nodded and didn't say be careful. He didn't have to. He pulled his Glock from his shoulder holster and handed it to me. A major violation of FBI policy. A major law violation as well, giving an ex-felon a gun and aiding and abetting a felon. He wanted to step out on that limb with me, risk his career. I waved the gun off. "No, thanks, I'm good. But I need a car."

He pointed to the Suburban and yelled, "Mike, take him wherever he wants to go and back him with whatever he needs to do."

Mike got in the Suburban and closed the door, waiting for me.

I said to Dan, "Thanks."

"You call me," Dan said. "You understand? Keep in touch. We're going to be all over that steak house tonight. If you get in trouble, use that panic button on the phone."

"Huh?" No way did I intend to go to that deal. No way. What the hell was he thinking?

I tried to shift gears to the problems that lay ahead. The thoughts came a lot slower than normal. My mind had been working a problem, an issue my subconscious caught onto that I'd missed. It locked in now. "Ah, shit." I jumped in the Suburban and slammed the door. "Go, go. Head downtown, the Bonaventure Hotel."

I put the phone back to my ear. "Marie?"

"Bruno, what's going on? What's wrong with Drago? Where are you? What's happened?"

She'd heard my conversation with Dan. "Marie. Marie, listen to me. You said Sonja called *you*?"

"Yes, that's right. Tell me what happened to Drago."

"You didn't call her?"

"No, Bruno, I just told you she called me on the hotel phone."

"How did she know you were there?"

"I thought you'd changed your mind and called her, told her where we were staying so she could come be with her grandson."

I said to the driver, "Mike, hit it, put your foot in it, we have to get to the Bonaventure downtown right now."

Mike turned on the lights and siren.

"Marie, where's the baby?"

"Right here on my lap, why?"

"Check him over. Does he have a necklace, something attached to his clothes, anything like that?"

"Don't be silly, babies don't wear necklaces. They can strangle or choke on them. He's got a cute little bracelet, though."

"Take it off him and flush it down the toilet. Do it now."

"Bruno, you're talking crazy again."

"Marie."

"All right."

"Then get out of there. Don't panic. Stay calm and walk out of there right now. Don't take anything with you, just walk out the door right now."

"Bruno, what's going on?"

"Are you moving?"

"Yes, yes."

"I'm on my way there," I said. "I'll be there in ten minutes. Take a cab, get away from that hotel. You understand?"

"I got it, Bruno. You only have to explain things to me once. I tossed the bracelet in the toilet." The whoosh of the toilet sounded in the background.

"Don't grab anything, just get out."

"Don't worry about it, I'm walking out now. Oh . . . oh wait . . . I . . . Oh my God, Bruno."

"What? What is it? Is someone in your room?"

"No. The news, on the television."

"What news? The television?"

Oh no, not now. Not now.

I leaned back in the seat and closed my eyes as the whole world dropped down on top of me, tons of weight smothering me.

"My God, Bruno. You didn't tell me. Why didn't you tell me?"

I imagined her standing in front of the television watching the footage from the CHP unit cam.

Watching me fight the three Visigoths. The sickening violence of the event.

Watching me flip Bosco out into traffic, the horrified look on his face in the short flight to his doom a half second away.

Watching the Honda snatch Bosco out of the air and smash and mangle his body.

Every couple of seconds, she let out a little yelp, the kind a puppy makes. With each yelp I shrank a little smaller in the seat, shrank again and again until I no longer resembled a normal human being, until I no longer existed.

She came back on the phone, her breath fast. "Oh, Bruno, sweetie, I'm so sorry, are you okay? I mean—"

My voice came out barely a whisper. "Yes. Yes, everything's fine."

Only it wasn't.

"Marie, honey, we really need to talk about this later. You need to get out of there now."

"You . . . You. That's why you didn't want to take the baby. You're the one . . . Oh my God, Bruno, how awful. Are you sure you're okay? Where are you? I need to be with you."

All of a sudden I realized I needed to talk with Sonja and not Marie. I had to tell Sonja myself. Look her in the eye and tell her what I did to Bosco. I'd been a coward not telling her something so important. What the hell had I been thinking? I needed to fix it.

I swallowed hard to get the lump out of my throat and said to Marie, "Are you out of the room?"

"Yes, in the hall, moving to the elevator."

"Okay, grab a cab and find a place with lots of people around. Let me know where it is, and I'll have the FBI there in a few minutes."

I looked up to the rearview to Mike's eyes. He watched me and nodded, picked up his cell and dialed.

"Marie, where did Sonja say she wanted to meet?"

"Joey's. She said you'd know the place."

I pulled the phone down to my chest and said to Mike, "We're close to the GMC, drop me there and pick up my wife, and please take good care of her. I'll give you her cell."

Back into the phone I said, "Marie, I'm going to meet Sonja. I have to . . . I have to talk to her."

"I understand. I love you, Bruno."

"I love you, too." We stayed connected in the silence for a long moment.

Mike pulled into the shopping center and alongside the GMC. I said, "Gimme your cell." He handed it to me. I said into my phone, "I'm going to hang up and call you on another phone."

"Okay," she said. "I'm out front looking for a cab. It's going to be okay, Bruno, I promise."

How could she possibly know that? No way could it be okay, not after what happened, not after what I'd done.

"I know," I said. "I'll call you right back on the agent's phone."

I did. She picked up. "I'm handing you over to Mike. He's a good guy. Stay on the line with him until he picks you up. Love you, babe."

I handed the phone over. He took it. "This is Mike, Mrs. Johnson."

I got out of the Suburban. It took off, tires screeching, before I even closed the door.

I didn't want to go. I didn't want to face Sonja. This would be the most difficult conversation I'd ever had.

CHAPTER FIFTY-SIX

THE HIPPY IN the GMC truck slept prone across the front seat. I opened the door to the stale, sweet scent of marijuana smoke. "Come on, get up. Get out."

The FBI cell phone in my pocket rang. I didn't want to talk to anyone. I reached in and shook the guy. "Come on, get out."

The guy stirred, got up, and looked around with bloodshot eyes. "What the hell . . . what's goin' down?"

"Get out. Please get out now or I'll have to drag you out and I don't wanna do that."

"Keep your wigwam on, chief, I'm movin', I'm movin.'"

"I'm sorry. Look, here's the money I promised you." I handed him the two hundreds, moved him out of the way, and got in.

"Hey," he said. "You gonna gimme a ride over to the shop so I can get my wheels?"

I didn't have the time. I waved, got in, and took off. The forty or so miles to Chino might take an hour to an hour and a half with traffic on the freeways. I had to get there to get this extraordinary weight lifted off me.

The phone rang again. I answered it.

"Bruno, it's me, Dan."

"I know."

"It's out. The video, it's out."

"I know."

"Come on back, it's too dangerous now. You can't go."

"I have to tell Sonja in person. I have to tell her face-to-face."

"No you don't. You don't owe those people anything. Those men on the freeway were all adults. They made their choices, the wrong choices. You did exactly what I or any other cop would have done under the circumstances. Only we probably wouldn't have survived, not up against three of them like that. That was a hell of a thing to watch, Bruno. That cop, she wouldn't be alive if you hadn't interceded."

I whispered into the phone what Bobby Ray had said: "Cops would've played by the rules. No one else would've tossed Bosco out in traffic like that." I hung up the phone and drove on, my mind working my hands and foot, directing the truck while I wallowed in the dark emotion of it all. Back in the lizard part of my brain, I knew this move, going to see Sonja, to be idiotic. That video would be all over the media. In just minutes after it first hit, it would go worldwide. My God, now the whole world would know what I'd done.

Including all the Visigoths.

Including Bobby Ray.

And worse, far worse, Sonja would know. She'd also know that I'd known all along and had not told her.

She'd have already seen it on the news or on her computer or phone. She'd have already seen her son flipped out into traffic. Seen that horrible look on his face the moment before—the visual of her son . . .

* * *

The summer sun sat low in the sky by the time I turned onto Pipeline and then into the parking lot of Joey's Barbeque. The early dinner crowd already started to fill the parking lot. I recognized the large truck backed into the parking slot at the end of the building. The truck I first saw out in front of Bobby Ray's motorcycle shop, the truck that towed the trailer I rode in, unconscious on the floor, alongside Bobby Ray's motorcycle. The truck with the Good Sam Club sticker on the bumper.

Sonja sat behind the wheel of the rig minus the fifth wheel trailer. The mere sight of her made me sick with sorrow and bitter regret over Sebastian, the kid I'd tossed out into traffic.

I pulled up alongside in the black GMC and rolled down the automatic window on the passenger side. "Sonja, I'm so sorry about Sebastian and—"

"Not now, not here. Follow me." She took off before I could say anything more. I backed up and followed her out onto Pipeline, headed west the way I'd just come in, toward the general direction of LA.

She had looked haggard, her gray hair in disarray, dark half-moons under her eyes . . . and she looked older. She looked twenty years older. She'd somehow turned into an old crone, years before her time, and more so since I'd seen her last in the hospital.

I drove along behind her and tried to imagine how our conversation would go and couldn't envision it from any angle. Not those terrible words coming out of my mouth.

I needed to hear Marie's voice, hear her confident, soothing words. She'd know what to say and how to say it. I dialed the FBI phone. It went right to Marie's voice mail. I hung up, and before I could hit redial to try again, it rang.

I answered it.

"Bruno," Dan said, "where are you?"

I knew right then, based on nothing more than the tone of his voice.

"Marie? Where's Marie?" All the poor-me crap, all that sorrow bullshit, went right out the window. Anger rose up and cleared my head, made me think straight like I should've been thinking all along. Made me see the terrible mistakes I made in the heat of emotion.

Hot anger replaced all else.

"We don't know," Dan said.

I spoke through clenched teeth. "What happened?"

"We don't know. Special Agent Mike Donavan picked her and the child up and was headed to a safe house, and that's the last we heard from them. We've got everybody on, and I mean everybody. We'll find them, I promise you. Where are you? We're going to come to you."

I held the phone to my shoulder and took out the gun from my back waistband. I pulled the magazine; two rounds left. That's all I needed.

I said, "You know where I am. You're tracking this phone."

"Bruno, wait for us. I know you're angry, I can tell by your voice, and you have every right to be, but there's more at stake here. Think about this, please."

"There's no more time for talking or waiting. There's nothing more important than my Marie." I clicked off. Dan would have an airship headed our way along with a string of FBI vehicles. He wouldn't trust it to the locals, not something as important as this. I had maybe twenty minutes max. The FBI had a different agenda that they would push no matter what. They wanted the drone and the missiles, the military onboard software. I rolled the window down to toss the phone out just as Sonja turned off the main street onto a side road and into a light industrial area loaded with single-story manufacturing buildings. We'd driven somewhere deep into the west side of Pomona.

What I saw on that street changed the whole game.

CHAPTER FIFTY-SEVEN

BASED ON WHAT I saw, the way the scene developed, I didn't have any time at all to think it through, to put all the pieces together to see if they fit, before I had to act.

Not far down the curved street, headed right at me, a red Peterbilt semi pulling a forty-foot trailer chugged out of an empty parking lot. The trailer advertised for its company with a large painting on the side, in the style and creative motif of an old-time traveling circus, clearly by the same artist who'd done the airbrush painting on Bobby Ray's motorcycle.

The painting stopped me cold, made my mind run at full speed trying to catch up. It depicted a large gray elephant with big floppy ears, happy as he flew through a blue sky loaded with fluffy white clouds. The elephant wore a jaunty hat and a huge smile. Big red letters announced the logo, "Dumbo Auto Parts without a Jumbo price."

Nothing more than a ruse, a cover for what really lay inside.

Jumbo would never put up with being called Dumbo; he hated it. This reeked of Bobby Ray's morally bankrupt sense of humor—a cute, childlike character painted on a truck hauling a lethal payload.

Sonja pulled into the same driveway the truck came out of and disappeared from view around the back of that same truck as she drove deeper into the parking area.

I slowed, and at the last second cut in front of the Peterbilt, making the driver slam on his brakes. I got out, my hand in my pocket, pressing the panic button on the FBI phone. I held down the button and started counting as I waved and smiled at the driver.

One thousand one.

One thousand two

One thousand three.

I went up to the driver's window and looked up at a biker with a craggy face and dirty brown hair down to his shoulders. The small black tattoo of a cross in the corner of his right eye disappeared when he squinted.

"What the hell you think you're doin', asshole?" he said. "Get that piece of crap outta the way or I'll ram it outta the way."

One thousand six.

One thousand seven.

"Ho, hey, oh, sorry," I said, as the count continued in my head. "I just wanted to know if this was the warehouse for Jumbo Auto Parts."

"Hell, no. Now move it or lose it."

I waved again, took a step to the side, and tossed the phone on top of a folded-up blue tarp, the one strapped down with bungee cords in between the semi cab and the trailer. The phone wouldn't stay there long, a few miles anyway. But maybe long enough.

I'd just tossed away my safety net. I'd just tossed away Marie's safety net.

I got back in the GMC and went to find Sonja's truck.

She had parked right out in the open by a shorter, smaller side door next to a larger roll-up door. The faded, defunct sign above the small door read *Heavy Metal Extractors Inc.*

She stood next to her truck with her arms crossed, her eyes watching me park and get out.

"You bastard."

I thought in this situation that as soon as she spoke I'd slink away like the dirty, low-down dog that I was. I no longer felt that way, not with Marie's safety at stake.

"Where's my wife?"

Her expression of contempt turned to confusion. "What are you talking about?"

"Marie's gone."

She said, "What the . . . What about my grandbaby?" She didn't wait for an answer. She ran to the side door, yanked on the knob, and disappeared inside.

I drew the Smith .45, held it down by my leg, and followed her. Just before I went across the threshold, I looked up. A small closed-circuit TV camera, an older model under the high eave, watched all who entered. Bobby Ray knew I was coming. Nothing I could do about it.

We moved through a small office with a dusty and cluttered counter, right on to the pass-thru door and out into the warehouse.

The warehouse looked immaculate: stacked boxes, a big yellow forklift, shelving with more boxes. Lots of boxes marked *Lamboni Bros. Stereos, Big Steve's Appliances,* or *Dentco Inc.*

Shipping and receiving central for Bobby Ray's gun-smuggling operation.

And Sonja brought me right to it.

She didn't plan on letting me survive this little meeting.

In the open bay area sat the sleek new van from the meet with Jumbo at the Sears parking lot, the one Bobby Ray had looked out from.

He now sat at a desk in the center of the bay with his feet up. Monster stood right next to him, Bobby Ray's bulldog ready to be let loose. Neither overtly carried a gun.

I raised the Smith .45 just as Sonja yelled at Bobby Ray. "What the hell? What'd you do with my grandbaby? I told you not to mess with my grandchild, you son of a bitch."

"You need to settle the fuck down, woman." He stood and hooked his thumbs in his belt.

Monster started toward me.

Bobby Ray wore a black leather vest with *Visigoths* embroidered on the right chest. On the left side in smaller letters he had *President*. He wanted me to be sure what happened to me next came from the Goths' organization, the revenge for what had happened out on the freeway. He grinned and said to me, "So you—"

I shot Monster in the knee. He went down in a heap and rolled to his side, put both hands on his leg, his fingers instantly going red. The gunshot echoed off the boxes with a loud slap. A cloud of white gun smoke rose in the still air.

I pointed the .45 at Bobby Ray, who'd reached behind his back for his weapon. He'd gotten slow being president and not having to get his hands dirty.

"Don't," I said. "I'm not in a good mood. I only need one of you alive to tell me where my wife is. And the way things are going, I'd just as soon make it Monster. I don't like you very much, Bobby Ray." I spit his name out. "So do yourself a favor. Take it out slow and toss it on the floor."

He froze, his hand behind his back. He didn't lose his grin. "You think I didn't know you were coming, dickhead? You think I'd just let you waltz in here big as you please and throw down on me if I wasn't holdin' trump?"

Monster rolled and moaned, leaking on the clean floor.

I had one round left in the gun. That's all I needed for Bobby Ray.

Sonja stuck a gun to the side of my head. "Gimme the gun, Bruno."

CHAPTER FIFTY-EIGHT

WE'D BEEN PARTNERS, worked a patrol car together. That should've meant a lot. We were friends. We were lovers. All that didn't count for shit. I kept the gun pointed at Bobby Ray and said, "You want me to shoot your husband?"

She took her eyes off me and looked at him. She thought about it for a long moment and finally said, "Go ahead. Do what you gotta do, Bruno, 'cause if you pull that trigger it'll be your last conscious act."

I slowly nodded. "Just tell me if Marie's okay."

"Sure she is," Bobby Ray said. "She's in the van with the baby. She's a great nanny. Great ass on that, too, congrats." He waved his gun. "After all this is over, I think we'll keep her on."

Sonja stepped back, taking her gun out of range of my hands. She looked at Bobby Ray and said, "You brain-dead twit, what the hell's the matter with you, bringing a child into a thing like this?"

"Don't talk to me like that, Sonja. Don't you ever talk to me like that again. We're about to be multimillionaires, and if I don't want to, I never have to listen to you piss and moan at me ever again. So watch your mouth, woman."

I yelled, "Marie. Marie, come on out of the van."

On the other side of the van came the sound of the van door sliding open. Marie came around the back end. She wore black slacks and a red knit top and looked scared. I let out a long breath when I saw she was okay.

"They hurt you, baby?"

She didn't answer, just shook her head.

Sonja said, "Where's my grandchild?"

Marie pointed back at the van. "Inside asleep, but he won't be if you crazy bastards keep firing those guns. Think of the child. Bullets can go right though the side of that van."

"You mean like this?" Bobby Ray fired.

The round slammed into my hip. A searing pain spun me around like an out-of-control top. I went to the floor.

The cool concrete floor.

The .45 Smith left my hand and clattered out of my view. One round left in it.

"Bruno!"

Marie ran toward me. Bobby Ray caught her arm and slapped her across the face with his gun. She stopped clawing and kicking. He held her under her arm, slumped in his big hand. Her eyes rolled up, showing the whites under tented lids.

"Leave her alone." My words came out with only half the strength I intended. The intense pain snatched at the words on their way out.

Bobby Ray said, "Tape her to the chair. She can watch what we're going to do to her husband. Hurry, before he bleeds out. I hit him pretty hard, he's bleedin' good."

Sonja hesitated, then walked on wooded feet toward Marie, whom Bobby Ray held up like some sort of limp dishrag.

I didn't have any weapons left. Sonja had tossed me to the curb when she put the gun to my head. She'd made her choice. I now owed her nothing.

"Bobby Ray, you'd better think about that for a minute," I said. "Sonja here's flipped, she's working for the feds." I'd made it up on the fly. I had nothing left to use but words.

And as the words came out I realized maybe my mind had seen all the pieces as a whole and put them together without me.

Bobby Ray lost his grin. "Yeah, sure, you're right. Don't even. You're one mean son of a bitch, tryin' a simple shit game like that when your back's to the wall. It's gonna be a pleasure to take the knife and pliers to you pal, a real pleasure."

"That right? Well, ask her then. Go on, ask her."

Sonja stopped and turned, gave me a look of pure hate.

I'd somehow hit it just right. "That ATF agent," I said, "the one *she* told you was going after Bosco, that agent? He entered a couple of bullets into the *Drug/Fire* data bank and came up with her name . . . eh." I grunted. The pain started to spark and snap in my vision. Shock wouldn't be far behind. I said, "Sonja wanted Bosco outta the life anyway she could, so she flipped . . . eh, Jesus. She . . . she made a deal for herself and for her son. The price? That's right, it's you, fatass. She's tossed you to the wolves to save herself."

Bobby Ray shoved Marie down and came at me, his gun pointed right at my head. "You're a liar. You killed my son. You killed him and now you're makin' shit up to save your own skin."

"No. Ask her. Go on, ask her. Back when we worked a patrol car together, she shot at a robbery vehicle, an AMC Hornet station wagon with three suspects. Ain't that right, Sonja? That's where they got the first bullets, the ones Gerber entered into the *Drug/Fire* system. When was the second time? What other shooting did they hold over your head? Who did you shoot? Did you go after some of those Trey-Five-Sevens after you quit? The gang that torched Maury Abrams and his wife?"

From her expression of contempt, I could see I'd hit pretty close to home.

Bobby Ray saw the same thing I did.

"That right, Sonja?" Bobby Ray asked, turning angry at the prospect. "That what happened? You flip on me? You flip on the *president* of the Visigoths?"

She shoved her gun in the air like a pointer, not aiming, but in his general direction. "Don't be a dumbass. You're going to listen to this piece of shit, the man who tossed Bosco out into the traffic to be run over? Our Bosco? The same guy who, right after he did that, came to our place like nothing happened at all and pretended to be our friend?"

Bobby Ray looked from her to me, his brain working overtime to suss out the truth. Except that he didn't have the brainpower to do it. Sonja had been the woman behind the president, her hand up his back like he was some kind of puppet.

The pain reached up through my spine and now threatened to shut my lights off. I fought it. "Okay," I said to Bobby Ray. "You don't believe me, call your truck, the one with the flying elephant painted on the side, and talk to your driver. The FBI has that truck now, and your multimillionaire status has just been permanently revoked."

Bobby Ray, no more than three feet from me, pulled his phone out of his pocket and took his eyes off me to dial.

Sonja shot him in the chest.

CHAPTER FIFTY-NINE

BOBBY RAY THUMPED to the floor ten feet away from me. For a second he looked dumbfounded, like a dog kicked for the first time by his master, until the light went out in his eyes.

He'd landed not far from Marie, four of us on the floor now, Sonja the only one left standing.

I needed to get to Marie. I tried to crawl over to her. My hand on my numb hip brushed against something hard in my pocket. Jumbo's lady gun, the little .25 Raven, the same gun that had brought down the great and loyal Drago. I stopped and struggled to pull the little gun out.

Sonja walked over and stood right next me. A white curl of smoke came out of her gun. "Why'd you stick your nose into this, Bruno? Why?"

"What are you talking about? You called me, remember?"

She squatted down and grabbed onto my hand, pulled it out of my pocket. "What's that you got in there, Bruno?" She reached in and got the gun. Our last chance. Our last hope.

"I called you," she said, "because I wanted you to talk some sense into Bosco. He wouldn't listen to me anymore."

"He was a grown man of twenty-five," I said. "What could *I* say to him? That . . . wait, what? Why me? Why would you call me? I wouldn't have any sway over your son."

"You're an idiot," she said. "You had more than enough information to figure this whole thing out long before now. And you didn't. And you still don't know, do you? You want to know why you couldn't figure it out? Because you didn't want to know, that's why. You've always tried to live in that perfect world, that morally correct world, saving all those kids from abusive parents. What a big joke. That's irony, Bruno, the very definition of irony, and it makes me sick."

She stuck the Raven .25 up against the left side of my chest, her finger on the trigger, and spoke through clenched teeth. "That's right, Bruno, I can see it in your eyes that you've finally figured it out. And if I were really mean and wanted to milk every ounce of revenge outta what you've done, I'd let you live. That's right, let you live with what you've done. But I'm not like that. I live for the moment, always have. You know that. And I want my pound of flesh now, right now."

I wasn't afraid of dying. But I wanted her to shoot before she said the words I knew were coming. I did know all along. I didn't want to hear the words that would bring the truth out into the light of day. I turned my head away from her, brought my bloody hands up to my ears, and closed my eyes tight.

"That won't help, Bruno. You can still hear me." She raised her voice. "So here it is. I had twins, and I named them Sebastian and Olivia. Twins run in families, I know you know that. You should've realized it long ago. That was the big clue, Bruno. Olivia had twins, remember? Alonzo and poor little Albert, remember?

"I tried to tell you in the hospital, but you cut me off, and I didn't push it, remember? Go on, think back on that conversation, I was going to tell you then. What I did tell you was that I couldn't imagine raising a girl, not in this crazy, screwed-up world. So I gave Olivia to you to raise and I kept the boy. Our boy. And you screwed that up, too, didn't you, Bruno? What do they call it? I remember from my patrol days. *Failure to supervise*. That's what happened with Olivia. Ain't that right, Bruno? But that wasn't good enough, you killing our little girl, was it, Bruno? You had to go and take my son, Bosco, away from me, too, didn't you?"

I shifted around to look at her, awed at her intense hate, awed at her ugly words.

She drove the gun into my ribs and gritted her teeth even more. "You tossed *your own son* out into traffic, Bruno. You killed *your own son*. That's what I wanted to tell you when I called and asked you to meet me here tonight. I wanted to look you in the eye and tell you that you'd killed your own son, just before I dropped the hammer on you."

She took a deep breath and said it again, said it for the last time. "You killed our son, Bruno."

She pulled the trigger.

The round parted skin and muscle and burrowed past the cartilage between the ribs. The small lead round, fired point blank, entered my chest cavity with a pain like nothing I'd ever felt before. I welcomed it as the darkness slammed down on me one final time.

CHAPTER SIXTY

Robby Wicks sat on the tailgate of a truck and tilted back a beer at ten o'clock in the morning in the parking lot of the Safeway, a short two miles from where we'd taken down Myron Hobbs, the hard way.

Robby and I had been on Myron's trail for forty straight hours with no letup. At eleven thirty the night before, we'd tracked him to an apartment in Cerritos. We'd only been set up on the apartment for an hour when Robby wanted to go kick in the door, see if our information was correct, see if Myron Hobbs was in there. I'd talked him out of it, told him that if Hobbs wasn't there and the apartment was empty then we'd have burned our last lead and wasted the last forty hours. It was better to wait, far more logical. Robby wasn't good at waiting, or at going with the logic of it. He always acted like a shark—if he quit moving, he'd drown. I'd no sooner talked him down when he said, "I'm goin' in, check it out." He got out and walked in the street in the shadows under the overhanging trees.

Fatigue hung in my bones like some kind of incurable disease that would never go away. I hesitated, not more than sixty seconds, and then got out to back him in his folly.

Down the street, a dark shadow came out of the apartment we'd been watching. Robby kept walking, not missing a step, not going to cover as any sane cop would. He slung back his brown suit coat with an elbow and drew his Colt Combat Commander from a pancake holster on his hip. He held it down by his leg.

The shadow must've seen Robby, saw his move, ready to go to guns. The shadow moved out to the street anyway.

"Robby!" I drew my gun and ran.

The shadow came out under the streetlight.

Myron Hobbs, the man wanted for the brutal double murder of his wife and mother-in-law. He'd used two feet of chain as a mace.

Neither Robby nor Hobbs said a thing. They threw down and fired. The guns lit up the night. They banged away at each other, the instant violence sharp enough to taste, wet and metallic on the tongue.

Hobbs spun as a bullet took him high in the chest. His gun arm swung wild toward the ground and continued to fire into the asphalt. Robby hesitated for a millisecond, took aim, and fired. The round took Hobbs in the neck and ended it.

In our time together, that had been the third incident when Robby had gone head-to-head with a violent predator. And it took three times for me to realize that's what Robby lived for, that moment out on the edge. He only used the law to facilitate his insatiable need.

In that parking lot, sitting on a truck that belonged to some random guy who'd gone into the grocery to buy food, Robby tilted his beer and finished it. He tossed the bottle in the back of the truck. He wore a Band-Aid on his left ear where the lobe had been shot off by Myron Hobbs. "What's the matter with you, skillet?"

That's when I knew this had to be a drug-induced dream, Robby never called me *skillet*, not to my face. Johnny Mack had been the one to tell me that Robby called me *skillet* behind my back.

"I don't like the violence anymore," I said. "I want out. I gotta get out or go insane."

Robby opened another beer. "You need to man up, skillet, and quit being such a pussy." He took another long chug of the beer, held up the can, burped. "Too bad, skillet. Once you join the club, you can never get out. Once a BMF, always a BMF." He chuckled. "Remember . . .

Remember? I remember when you signed up. You remember?" He always talked giddy like this right after a violent confrontation.

I shook my head.

"It was that nigger cowboy you tracked down, remember now? That guy hit that little girl so hard with his big ol' Cadillac it ruptured the radiator. You tracked his radiator water for two miles on foot on a hot summer night, running your ass off before the water dried up. You tracked him right to his house. By the time I caught up to you, you'd damn near kicked a lung outta that asshole."

"I killed my own son, Robby."

"Oh, shit, you're not bemoaning that old saw again, are ya? I'm gettin' tired as hell of hearin' about it. You're killin' my buzz here, skillet. Okay, okay, this kid, he might've been sired from your loins, but he was still one of them, he was an asshole, am I right or am I right?"

The man who owned the truck came out of the store with a few bags in his hand. "Ah, excuse me, but you're sitting on my truck."

Robby gave him that predator stare, the eyes of a hunter fresh from a kill. The guy moved off, back toward the store.

"I don't need your macho bullshit right now," I said to Robby. "You have no idea how I feel, what it feels like to—"

He threw the second, half-empty bottle into the back of the truck, trailing a stream of foam. "How the hell do you know that, skillet? You only know me from the time we've worked together. You don't know me for shit. You don't know my past." He slid off the tailgate and got right up in my face, his breath hot on my chin. "Son, here's what I do know: if you don't pull your head outta your ass soon and quit cryin' in your Cheerios, they're gonna put you away for good. Slam your black ass into a concrete room and lock the door. Now get up off your dead ass, skillet, and get movin'. I'm ashamed of you, lyin' there like some kinda Democrat. Get up off your ass and do something. You're BMF, remember that. Always remember that."

CHAPTER SIXTY-ONE

THREE WEEKS AFTER I woke for the first time in the county jail ward, Dan Chulack came as like he always did on his lunch break, sat and read over FBI reports from his agents submitted from a multitude of different cases, and waited for me to break my silence.

Which I had no intention of doing.

He looked up, saw my eyes open, and put down his papers. "How you feelin' today, Bruno?"

I said nothing, just like all the other days when he'd tried to talk to me.

"I knew you'd break down and talk to me eventually, but we're out of time now. It's today or not at all. Come on, talk to me. Please?"

I said nothing.

Every other time after he attempted to talk to me and I didn't engage with him, he'd simply put his readers back on his nose and go back to his reports. This time he moved over to the bed and took my hand, secured with a soft restraint to the bed rail. Both my hands stayed restrained due to my "unstable mental state." Even though I'd not given them any overt cause to think otherwise. I'd sunk into a depression so deep and dark I'd never rise up again to see the sunlight.

Dan had never touched me before. This act of pure friendship pinged at my emotionally barren body.

Physically, I'd healed quickly, the docs and nurses had said. They always talked without any reply from me at all. The .25 cal bullet missed my heart and lodged in a lung, now removed. The 9mm in my hip caused them more problems. An infection had set in after surgery, and after five days of me in a delirium, the docs got it under control with intravenous antibiotics. Five days of out-of-control nightmares where I relived old cases with Robby Wicks—all those violent confrontations, nightmares that always ended with a shift to Bosco's expression, inches from my face, and ended with his plea for his life: *"Don't. Don't."*

And every time in the dream I did it anyway. I tossed him out into traffic and the Honda snatched him out of the air.

Last week, detectives came in to interview me about the children I'd kidnapped—rescued really—from abusive parents and foster care. The same children who now lived a happy and safe life down in Costa Rica.

I told the detectives nothing, not so much as a word. They left after they said I'd be arraigned as soon as the docs cleared me—arraigned on eight counts of kidnapping. They told me they had me cold on eight and didn't mention anything about the other two children. They told me I'd go away to the big house for a stay that would last a couple years past the other side of forever. Dan couldn't do anything to help. Not with the county attorney, who had a big ax to grind. He'd petitioned for intervention from the Attorney General, who declined to enter the dispute—not with someone with my past.

Dan said, "I came today to say good-bye."

I stared straight ahead. I didn't feel sorry for myself. I couldn't, because I didn't feel anything at all.

"Bruno, Drago's going to be okay. He's out of danger and doing great." Dan hesitated and then said, "Marie went back to Costa Rica.

She had to, to take care of the children. She'd been away from them too long. She said she'd be back for the trial though, said for you not to worry, she'd be back."

I said nothing.

I'd not heard anything about what happened after I was shot in Bobby Ray's warehouse. Or maybe I had and I either tuned it out or erased it from my memory, or the fever and drugs kept it from sticking. Or I just plain didn't want to know. This was the first I'd heard that Marie walked away from it safely. For the first time in three weeks, I thought about Marie. I let her image, her smile, her warm kisses play in my memory. The thought of her finally broke through. Skin on my legs and back tingled. I did feel some emotion after all.

Dan looked back over his shoulder, then back at me. He lowered his voice. "I gave her the Valvoline box and . . . and, Bruno, she took your grandchild with her. He's safe."

Bosco's son, my grandson.

A lump rose in my throat and tears blurred my vision. Dan saw them and gripped my hand tighter. "That's good, Bruno, that's real good. You're getting better. So let me tell you again. I need to explain what happened—how you ended up in custody. I feel real bad the way it went down."

I didn't answer. His conscience bothered him.

He said, "We got to the warehouse too late. Marie had already called paramedics. You were critical; she had to make the call. The Pomona police were on scene, and they'd already transported you to County."

I turned my head to look at him.

Dan said, "Pomona identified you and had you in custody. They took your prints and ran them. Your real name popped with the warrants."

He waited for a response.

I didn't give him one.

"We got the truck, Bruno, the one with the drone and the missiles, thanks to you. That was a neat little trick with the phone." He squeezed my hand. "We missed the Arab connection. We'll backtrack him, though. We still might get him."

He glanced away, then looked back at me and squeezed my hand again. "Bruno, you're being transported tonight to the hospital ward at MCJ. Today's Friday. You'll be arraigned on Monday. I'm sorry, but I have to go now. I just wanted to say good-bye."

I nodded.

Dan turned, scooped up his reports, and headed for the door.

I tried to speak. Only a croak came out. Dan rushed back to my bed and said, "Yes, go ahead, what?"

I swallowed hard, my words came out in a rasp. "What . . . what happened?"

"With what, Bruno?"

"Sonja?"

Dan shook his head. "When I came on scene, she was DOA, gunshot nine times. Last I checked, the investigators had not determined who gunned her. I was able to get Marie and Sonja's kid out of there on the pretense of being a material witness in a matter concerning national security."

"Who shot Sonja?"

"I don't know."

I knew, and Dan did, too.

"Bruno? One more thing." He wanted to change the subject away from Marie. "Your nephew, Noble's son, he's missing. I'm working on it though. You don't need to worry about that, I'm on it."

I said nothing. Not my nephew. What could I do about it? Nothing.

Dan waited a moment more and then said, "Take care of yourself, Bruno, and let me know where you end up. Drop me a line, okay?"

I nodded.

CHAPTER SIXTY-TWO

THAT SAME NIGHT, four deputies in perfect uniforms and polished leather, along with a hospital orderly, escorted the gurney with me strapped to it with soft restraints. They trundled me out of my room, down the long hall, and over to the elevator. The deputies weren't young jail deputies like they should've been for a routine transport. The epaulets on their shoulders said that these four deputies came from SEB, the Sheriff's Special Enforcement Bureau, the SWAT team. Stout young men, experienced and street hardened. They made a big show of it, one of the FBI's ten most wanted, on the run for three years, finally captured.

Right, real dangerous.

No one said anything in the elevator.

I knew the routine. I'd been involved in transports as a jail deputy. They'd take me down to the prisoner entrance of the county hospital, to a secured area in the back, and load me up in a sheriff's transport van. Then they'd drive me the short distance to MCJ—Men's Central Jail—where I'd be transitioned through IRC, the Inmate Reception Center, classified, and sent up to the hospital ward on 3300.

The elevator opened. The SEB sergeant in charge of the detail said to the orderly, "We'll take it from here."

Without waiting for the orderly to reply, they took control of the gurney and two deputies now wheeled me the rest of the way, the other two following along. It was all about control. They didn't know the orderly and didn't want to worry about him.

They pushed the gurney through the swinging double doors to the loading dock outside. Backed in at the loading dock sat a red and white ambulance. Next to the two open doors stood a deputy who wore jeans and cowboy boots with a green Sheriff's raid jacket. My escort wheeled me up to the deputy in the raid jacket.

The deputy in the jacket extended his hand. I couldn't shake if I wanted to, my hands restrained. The deputy looked at the escort and didn't need to say anything. The sergeant reached into his boot and came out with a dirk. He cut off the leather restraints. The guy in the raid jacket again offered me his hand. "My name's Roy Clevenger, Mr. Johnson, and I'm here to tell you thank you."

"What?" The name rang a bell, and my mind spun trying to catch up to all that was happening. "I'm sorry, who are you?"

He smiled hugely. "My wife is Kris Clevenger. She works for the Highway Patrol."

"Oh—" was all that would come out.

Roy said, "You didn't have to stop that day, and I'm damn glad that you did. There's no way you're going to jail today. You get a free pass courtesy of Los Angeles County Sheriff's Department."

For days I'd felt no emotion. At that moment the emotions overwhelmed me. "Thank you. Thank you." I wanted to say more, something eloquent, but couldn't.

They wheeled me into the back of the ambulance. On the bench inside sat my lovely Marie.

AUTHOR'S NOTE

IN MY NOVELS, I try to take the reader into my world of law enforcement. I want them to feel what it's like to work in a patrol car, what goes through the mind of a detective chasing dangerous felons, the emotions involved, the good and the bad, the pain and the pride.

The Vanquished, although a work of fiction, was inspired by one of those incidents that occurred one hot summer night when I was on the job. That night I responded Code-Three—red lights and siren—to a residential robbery. I found Maury Abrams just as I described—that wasn't his real name of course—with his head split open and bleeding. He tried to tell me in his own way what happened, unable to get the words out, the ordeal still too fresh in his mind. And he might have succeeded had I sat down with him, calmed his jagged nerves. But I was young and anxious and full of the thrill for adventure.

So when the second call went out, *"shots fired, man down,"* I left Maury Abrams to respond to the call, fully intending to return. When I arrived at that second call and saw the gang member shot in the back, smelled the blood, I realized my mistake. I immediately returned to the Abrams' home and sat on the edge of Mr. Abram's bed as he told me the story. How the two thugs tricked him into opening his reinforced door. How he shot them both in the defense of his wife who lay in that same bed with the covers up to her nose, still too terrified over the recent event to say a word.

I did refer the incident to the gang unit and tried to impress upon them the vulnerability of this elderly couple, trapped in their own home, in a dangerous neighborhood. I was worried about retribution, gang retaliation.

A week later, a detective in OSS—Operation Safe Streets— stopped me in the parking lot in back of the station to tell me the Abrams' home had been firebombed. I remember standing there a long time overcome with emotions. Despite our best efforts, we couldn't save the Abrams; we couldn't keep the street from eating them.